FAITH IS FEARLESS

Normal is Overrated

D. PICHARDO-JOHANSSON

ACKNOWLEDGMENT

Special thanks to Shannon Purchis, Ryan Walsh, John Sullivan, and Pat Reilly—my consultants on Irish culture—for guiding my humble attempts to capture the essence of being Irish.

To all children with special needs—especially the real-life success stories who inspired some of the characters in this book—and to the heroic special education teachers and therapists who never give up on them.

DEDICATION

To my children, especially my daughter Liliana, an undercover angel disguised as a child with special needs.

To the wives, husbands, and lovers of physicians everywhere: yes, it's not an easy life, but hang in there. You're the unsung heroes who create the healing love-energy we then carry to our patients.

ABOUT THIS BOOK

This stand-alone novel is the third book in the *Sunshine Series*. Each book can be enjoyed on its own, but I strongly recommend reading Book 2, (*Just for Joy: Beyond Achievement*) first to maximize excitement and avoid spoilers for that story's mystery arc.

If you haven't yet read *Just for Joy*, you can sign up for my newsletter and download it here for free: [Insert link]

Book 1 (*Hope for Harmony: Baby Makers vs. Peter Pans*) is a separate story with some intersecting characters and can be read in any order.

FE'S LIFE RULES

1- Never trust a man who owns a Chihuahua.

2- If the dress or the shoes don't take your breath away, they're not worth the closet space. Everything you own must make your heart skip.

3- Never complain; no matter how bad you think you have it, someone else wishes they had your problems.

4- Treat special needs kids like a treasure. They're angels sent to Earth to keep us in perspective.

5- Life is a baseball pitcher throwing fastballs—and when a ball knocks you down, you get to walk to first base. Good luck is nothing but bad luck plus stubbornness.

6- Never date a Latin man who still calls his mother "*Mami*"—you'll never win that contest. Never date a lawyer—you'll never win an argument. But most importantly, never date *a doctor*.

7- Worth repeating: Never, *never*, EVER date *a doctor*.

SHAWN'S LIFE RULES

1- Always expect the worst and prepare for it.

2- Critically ill patients are often kept alive by the sheer mental power of their physicians. If I stop fretting about them for just one minute, they might die.

3- No matter how good you are at your job, how much you've accomplished, or how much money you have, there will always be someone who does it better, achieves more, and makes more money—and that sucks.

4- Life is harsh, and the world's a hard place. Seize any moment of happiness. And never forget we're here to lighten each other's burdens.

5- If you're going to do something, do it right. Splurge on quality. Go the extra mile. Doing things with passion takes barely more effort than doing them half-heartedly—and the results are far better.

6- Even when doing something wrong, *do it right*. Breaking a diet? Drinking too much? Making out with the wrong person? Don't hold anything back. You'll feel guilty afterward, anyway; make it a big slip, worth the guilt!

7- We all slip and fall. The day after a fall, pick up your sorry arse and your self-beating whip and start over.

FAITH IS FEARLESS

CHAPTER 1

EVEN THE PSYCHO CHIHUAHUA WORKED FOR GOOD IN THE END! Early Saturday morning, as Fe Hernandez ran through the park, her thoughts went to Taco. That nippy, yapping Chihuahua had chased her relentlessly around the neighborhood for months. Taco's owner was moving to Colorado, and Fe might almost miss the little beast. Her friends had seen the dog as evidence of Fe's chronic bad luck, but she disagreed.

Fe stopped for a break at the convenience store near the park. There, she bought her usual water bottle, a bagel sandwich, and apple juice for the homeless man sitting on the bench outside.

A whiff of urine reached her from his ragged, soiled clothes. Used to work in the hospital, it didn't bother her.

"Hi, José. Where's Jenny?" she asked, as she handed him the paper bag.

"She went to the pharmacy," he replied, scratching his underarm and peeking in the bag. "I wish this were donuts and beer instead, but thank you, miss." He twisted the cap open and took a sip of juice, then rubbed his graying beard. "Yeah, Jenny has some health issue now, on top of everything. She's the only person in the world with worse luck than me." He released a long sigh. "Why is it that some people have all the luck in the world, while others have such terrible luck?"

Fe wished she had an answer.

She held on to the back of the bench as she stretched her right hamstring. "José, did I ever mention my name means *faith* in Spanish? Actually, some people call me Faith."

Frowning, José deadpanned, "Only like a billion times."

"Having faith that everything happens for good is the trick to changing your attitude," Fe continued, ignoring the sarcasm in his voice. "And *everything* is about attitude. You can see anything as bad luck or as good luck wrapped in clues you just have to puzzle out."

She switched to stretch the other leg. "Take this week, for example." She flourished a hand to emphasize her words. "On Tuesday, an elderly patient chased me through the hospital, threatening to hit me with her oxygen tank. My coworkers assumed I had bad luck—but it worked out! Thanks to that scare, my boss gave me the next day off, and I went for a wonderful bike ride."

She touched her toes to stretch her calves. "On that ride, my bike broke, and I fell into a creek and got stranded miles away from home with a dead cell—but that worked out for good too!" She bent sideways to stretch her waist. "I caught a ride in a live poultry truck. The driver took me through a different part of town, and guess what? I discovered an awesome consignment store and bought the cutest dress!" She held up a hand in triumph. "And I rescued my cell with a hair dryer and a bag of rice!"

She pulled the cell out of her fanny pack and nearly shoved it in his face.

He stared at the phone blankly. "Miss, a quarter of the screen is black."

"Yes! And the other three-quarters are okay! Isn't that great?" Beaming, she stowed the phone away. "But now I need to lose a few pounds to fit into that new dress." She lifted a finger. "Yes, the price was too good to pass up, even if it was a little tight. I'll see you later, José!"

She took off again.

As she re-entered the jogging path, Fe impressed herself with her improved endurance. Even her joints seemed more flexible.

And she owed it all to Taco, the psycho Chihuahua! If she hadn't spent months running from him, she'd never have trained this hard.

See? Even senseless bad luck brings something good in the long run.

Fe's good mood felt unshakable—until circus music burst from her fanny pack.

Her heart plummeted. It was her ex's ringtone.

A cold knot tightened in her stomach; her palms turned clammy. *No, please, not him again! Not today.*

Not ever!

She stopped running. Anxiety made her fingers fumble as she dug for the phone and shut it off.

Seconds later, it rang again.

And again.

Caramba!

After rejecting the call a third time, she sent a FaceTime request to her friend Joy.

A few rings later, Joy answered, a quarter of her face blackened by Fe's busted screen. Behind Joy, half a dozen children played at the beach. "Good morning, sweetie! Are you on your way—"

"He's calling me again!" Fe blurted.

Joy blinked. "Who?"

"Him. Bozo the Clown." Even three years after their divorce, Fe couldn't say his name easily.

A disapproving grunt came from just off-camera. Hope, Joy's sister, entered the broken screen. "Just don't answer."

"I have to answer eventually, he's the father of my kids," Fe mumbled. "He deserves some respect for that, doesn't he?"

"No!" Hope snapped. "That idiot has earned no one's respect. He's lucky you haven't put him in jail for the money he owes you."

Fe paced down the road with slow, heavy steps. "You know he'll catch up with his child support payments sooner or later. He's just doing this to scare me—*again.*" With a groan, she dropped onto the next park bench. "Why did he have to call? I was in such a good mood! This is such a beautiful morning, and my run was going so well!"

"Then turn off your phone! Block him!" Hope replied. "Never answer, and he'll get the message!"

"You know how it works," Joy added. "Every relationship is a dance. If you change the steps, the other person will either pick up the pace or stop dancing." The psychiatrist and thinker of the group, Joy always had some pearl of wisdom to share.

Fe picked an oleander flower from a nearby bush. "I feel sorry for him," she confessed, fiddling with the flower. "His ego never recovered after I left him."

"You dumped him for good reasons," Hope said. "So stop feeling sorry for him and send him to hell. Let him keep his stupid child support. No money is worth the stress he puts you through."

Unless your credit cards are about to explode.

Fe wished she could shove Bozo's money down any of his body holes. But even with two jobs and her mother's occasional babysitting gigs, she struggled to support their five-person household. Especially when *Abuela* insisted on feeding half the neighborhood.

She resumed pacing. "It's all my fault. I should've never married him."

Fe stopped walking and palmed herself on the forehead. "What am I saying? Of course, it all ended up being for good! If I hadn't married him, I wouldn't have Diego and Gabriela!"

On the screen, pity flickered on her friends' faces before they gathered themselves to cover it.

Oh yes, they think Gabriela isn't an asset, but a burden. If they only knew.

Joy recovered first. "Fe, stop blaming yourself for marrying him. It's not your fault the man is a narcissist."

Fe swallowed a knot in her throat. "He wasn't always like that, you know. Medicine changed him. He saw too many patients die and stopped caring about anything but himself. All doctors are a mess like that." Fe winced in apology and forced a smile at the screen. "*Except for you, Joy,* of course." She cleared her throat. "Anyway, everything will be better when my new business venture goes through. Once I take over Rainbows Child Services, I'll make more money, and Bozo won't be able to control me anymore."

Unmistakable worry flashed on her friends' faces.

The girls didn't trust her skills as a businesswoman, but she couldn't blame them. *I don't exactly have a sparkling record of good decision-making.*

Joy tucked a long, brunette lock behind her ear. "Sweetie, forget about Bozo and go enjoy the rest of your run. You need a break."

The practical solution finder of the group, Hope added, "We'll send a taxi to pick up your kids, your mom, and grandma, so you don't have to drive them. Then, join us here at the beach house whenever you're done. That a-hole doesn't deserve to ruin your morning."

"Yes!" added Joy. "Super-Dad Tom is here—also Ella and Ray. We have plenty of hands to babysit Diego and Gabriela. It will even be a break for your mom and *Abuela.*"

Moved and full of gratitude, Fe muttered, "Thank you, girls. You're the best."

After ending the call, Fe closed her eyes and pressed the phone to her chest. She felt blessed—so many wonderful women in her life. *Abuela, Mami,* Joy, Hope, her boss Marla … even their new friend, Allison-the-man-hater. She had all the love and support a woman could need.

The circus music played again, and the words *"El Desgraciado"*— Despicable Wretch—lit the caller ID. Fe sighed.

Feeling much stronger after her chat with the girls, she declined the call once more and texted, *"Email only, please."*

Then, she searched for the number in her contacts and selected Block Number. After briefly hovering over the option to confirm, she pressed Yes.

A surge of euphoria rose in her chest, stronger than she expected. Returning the phone to her fanny pack, she picked up the pace and took off again. Ecstatic, she savored the cool morning breeze in her face and the sight of the cloudless sky. She pumped her arms in the air and let out a hoot. Life was beautiful.

An urge to climb something in celebration overtook her. She jogged toward the causeway over the Indian River.

Maybe Taco's owner moving away was another sign. A new era had begun! Her luck *was* changing for the better. Everything would be okay!

Someone yelling yanked her out of her thoughts.

"WATCH OUT! MOVE!"

Her body kept jogging, but her mind froze as a green blur came straight at her—a bicycle speeding down the pedestrian path, the rider seemingly out of control.

She jumped left to dodge him.

But he swerved the same way.

The biker tried to correct his course, veering into a large rock instead.

Then, in slow motion, he launched into the air—hurtling straight at her.

Oh, shoot.

CHAPTER 2

Thirty minutes earlier.

Y EARS OF WORKING IN THE INTENSIVE CARE UNIT—WHERE the sickest of the sick fought for their lives—had taught Dr. Shawn McDevitt to always expect the worst. But that lesson started long before med school.

Shawn's first taste of bad luck came just hours after birth, when a well-meaning nurse misspelled his name on his birth certificate: S-H-A-W-N instead of S-E-A-N. For the thirty-five years since, he'd been the running joke in his traditional Irish family. Yet no one ever bothered to fix it. Being Irish-Catholic meant accepting some pain as part of normal life.

Yes, beneath his lighthearted façade, Shawn was convinced he was born unlucky. He rarely experienced pure, unfiltered bliss—the kind of moment that made him feel fortunate.

And today was one of those rare days, as he rode his bike.

Why don't I do this more often? Shawn asked himself for the hundredth time as he pedaled along the tree-lined trail. Spanish moss draped from the branches, giving the path a nostalgic feel. As he sprinted, the morning wind cooled the burn on his face from the effort.

Ultra-light carbon-fiber road bike. Black helmet. Wraparound glasses. Kelly-green jersey. Black bike shorts. Fingerless gloves. Expensive cleats … Yes, the initial investment had been hefty—Shawn believed in doing things right. But now, with the sticker-shock long gone, few pleasures came as cheap and accessible as riding.

Right now, he didn't mind that his day had started with an anonymous hate letter in his mailbox, and a threatening voicemail from FirstHealth's lawyer.

Shawn stopped his bike at the beach path—the meeting point. His friend Jay, a stronger rider in far better shape, had already arrived. Knowing Jay, he'd probably pedaled to Key Largo and back in the time it took Shawn to circle the park's trail.

Shawn grabbed the water bottle from his bike holder, took a long sip, then splashed the rest on his face.

"Bike riding is so therapeutic!" He tossed the empty bottle in the trash. "Why do I always find a reason not to do it?" Shawn signaled Jay to follow him into the convenience store.

Dragging his bike behind him, Jay snorted. "Tell me about it! I practically have to twist your arm every time!" He used a mocking tone. "I have to start rounds early. I have records to complete."

As Shawn secured his bike with the U-lock, a guilt-tinged excuse popped into his head: *I have to find paternal feelings for Aidan.*

Reflected in the store window, six foot five, muscular Jay made five foot ten Shawn feel small.

"Seriously. How can you look half-decent, let alone good, when you haven't been in a gym in ages?" Jay asked, handing Shawn a cold bottle from the fridge.

"It's all diet control. Whipping myself with discipline comes naturally, thanks to my father and medical school." Shawn headed for the protein bars.

Jay gave him a look. "Says the man who had both the cheesecake and the key-lime pie last night."

Shawn flashed his most charming smile. "Letting the pendulum swing now and then is part of a balanced program of neurotic discipline."

As they exited the store, two homeless people—a man and a woman—loitered on a nearby bench. Shawn's eyes landed on the thin, middle-aged lady with brittle blond hair and sallow skin. Her hands trembled as she reached for a cigarette. Protruding eyes and a bulge on her neck gave Shawn pause.

"Excuse me, miss." Shawn approached her. "Have you been having palpitations, weight loss, insomnia … jitters?"

The woman whipped her head to gape at him, her leathery forehead crinkling in surprise.

Her companion glared. "Hey, rich boy. If you're not handing out cash, beat it."

"Wait, José." She shushed him and then turned to Shawn. "Yes! How do you know?"

"I'm a doctor." He reached for the money belt under his jersey, grabbed a hand sanitizer wipe, and cleaned his hands. "Mind if I check something on your neck?"

The woman nodded. He gently palpated the area, then took her wrist to feel her pulse.

"I suspect you have Graves' disease, an overactive thyroid." He fished out a pen and a Post-it. "Do you have a primary care doctor?"

Raising her eyebrows, the woman tilted her head. "Hottie, do I look like someone with health insurance?"

"Then just write your name, date of birth, and a pharmacy here." He handed her the pen and paper. "I'll call in a med to slow your heart rate. It's an old generic; it shouldn't cost much."

She narrowed her eyes. "Do I look like I've got extra spending money?"

Shawn dug into his belt and handed her a bill. "Here, this should cover it." Then, grabbing a second Post-it, he scribbled a note. "Call my office Monday, and ask for my office manager, Crystal. Tell her I want you to have these tests; it's on me. I'm not an endocrinologist, but I can run it by a friend who is."

She hesitated at first, mistrust shading her expression. But as they exchanged papers, her features relaxed. "Thank you. I'm Jenny."

The man next to her had been eyeing Shawn warily. Now, he took a step forward, scratching under his arm. "So … you're a rich doctor. How about giving an old man some money too?"

The Hispanic man's graying beard and shaggy hair didn't trick Shawn—the guy was barely older than him.

He smiled. "You seem pretty strong and healthy. How about I give you a job instead?"

The man stared as if he'd just said a cussword. Mumbling unintelligible words, he clasped the woman's arm and led her away.

As Shawn returned to his bike, he called in the prescription to the woman's pharmacy.

"I'm torn," Jay said, unlocking his bike. "A part of me wants to kiss you—"

"I'll punch you." Shawn cut him off. "Don't you ever dare to kiss me—again.

You have plenty of women around, eager to oblige."

"Then I'll go for option two and slap you instead." Throwing his hands up, Jay huffed. "For goodness' sake, Shawn. Can you stop diagnosing people for *one hour*?"

Shawn shook his head. "I can't. Diagnoses find me. It's my blessing and my curse."

They dragged their bikes toward the parking lot. "Man, you've gone through a lot this past year," Jay said. "You need to start unwinding."

"I can't. Not until the police solve the mystery of Tara's death and I clear my name."

Never one to dwell on anything serious, Jay ignored the comment. "Do you want to go out this weekend before I head back to Atlanta? We should get you a new rebound woman to get you over the last one."

"Please don't remind me of Gina." Shawn winced. "I still avoid the hospital lab, afraid I'll run into her and she'll make another scene."

Jay tapped a finger on Shawn's forehead. "Earth to Shawn. Never get involved with a woman where you work."

Lesson learned. He pushed away Jay's hand. "Single women are scarce in this retirement town. And Dr. Jones has scared me off on-line dating. He says those websites are full of gold diggers. He met his last ex-wife there."

An epidemic of divorces seemed to have swept the medical staff. Every other physician in the hospital currently talked about nothing but lawyers, custody sharing, and child support.

Not Shawn. When Tara died, she'd spared him that destiny.

They arrived at the parking lot. Jay said goodbye with a fist bump and jumped back on his bike to keep riding—the man was unstoppable.

Shawn started stowing his own bike in his SUV, but hesitated. He could head home and shower before meeting his friend Richard. But the moment he arrived, Betty would jump on him with a list of complaints about Aidan. The nanny was going crazy, locked in the house with a three-year-old.

He needed to stretch this relaxation. He jumped back on his bike and pedaled away.

• • •

Shawn zoomed down the park's bougainvillea-lined path, his racing thoughts keeping pace. That was why he loved biking. While sprinting, his brain sharpened, and his problems unraveled from new angles.

Fort Sunshine, Florida's flat terrain posed no challenge. The closest thing to a hill to climb was the causeway over the Indian River. At its base, he shifted to low gear.

He pedaled fast, muscles burning, yet the incline dragged on just like the last few months of his life. So much effort, so little progress.

The pieces of his life stretched out before him: his sickest patients, his legal battle with FirstHealth while launching a solo pulmonary practice, his second job as an ICU doctor...

And then, the personal mess. The haunting task of reconnecting with three-year-old Aidan—a miniature portrait of himself, hell-bent on punishing him for their separation. Tara's murder investigation. The lingering drama with Gina. Two months post-breakup, and his body ached from the sex deprivation.

Yup, this ride is the closest I've come to panting, heart-racing action in a while.

Heat built with every uphill push. Just when he thought he couldn't take another stroke, he reached the peak.

Breathless, he stopped at the top and turned east, taking in the majestic view. Beyond the peaceful Indian River, shimmered the first hint of ocean. He soaked it in, catching his breath.

Then, he tightened his helmet, adjusted his gloves, and shifted to high gear. He placed his foot on the pedal.

And let go.

He smiled as the bike cruised down the causeway, wind sweeping across his face. It felt like flying—no effort, no struggle. The closest he'd ever come to freedom. To happiness.

Until the old man appeared.

An elderly man off the pedestrian lane, pushing his walker down the bike path.

Only in Fort Sunshine.

Adrenaline surged. He squeezed the hand brakes until they squeaked, but gravity prevailed. A truck approached on his left, so he veered right onto the pedestrian lane, narrowly avoiding the crash.

But the path wasn't clear.

Blinded by the sun, he squinted at the blurry, fast approaching figure of a jogger.

"Watch out! Move!" he shouted.

He swerved right. At the same moment, the jogger stepped left—straight into his path.

Collision: inevitable.

The world switched to slow motion. In a flash, his brain devised a plan to minimize injuries. Crash into something. Jump off the bike. Fall to the right and let the grass cushion the blow.

He aimed for a rock and launched himself, but it was too late. He flew forward, tackling the jogger into the hedge.

Their tangled bodies tumbled out of the bushes and rolled down the grassy slope before coming to a stop.

CHAPTER 3

His racing heart reassured Shawn he wasn't dead, but he considered it possible. How else to explain that he wasn't in pain after such a fall? At least not yet. The woman he'd tackled must've broken his fall with her body and taken the worst of the hit.

If bodies could get knotted, theirs had. Their legs were tangled, their necks hooked, and his arms wrapped around her. At least he hadn't killed her. Through the thin fabric of his jersey, he felt her chest rising and falling quickly—and two soft breasts pressing against him. The awareness of her feminine body made his own react automatically. Something weighed heavier in his bike shorts.

Damn sex deprivation.

"You're crushing me," a muffled voice said beneath him.

He scrambled to lift his weight, planking with one arm. The other stayed trapped—gripping a buttock that felt unsettlingly perfect: soft, round, and firm.

He must've still been paralyzed with shock. A part of him—the responsible gentleman—barked orders to get up and help her. Another part—the touch-starved man—wanted to savor the moment a little longer.

"Are you okay?" he asked the tangle of hair on his face.

"I'm not sure," she said, hoarse. "I heard something crack. And now my chest hurts when I breathe."

Terror slammed through him, and the physician sprang into action.

Oh, shite! Broken ribs? A pneumothorax?

Janey Mack!

It was regression. In moments of panic, his Irish grandma's expressions always popped back into his head.

And of course, he hadn't brought a stethoscope.

He untangled his limbs and rose to his knees. Placing his open hands on her ribs, thumbs touching, he said, "Breathe in and out deeply."

As she inhaled, his thumbs moved apart in perfect symmetry. Relief flooded him. The bushes might've saved her from real harm. "You don't have a collapsed lung. And if a rib was broken, you wouldn't breathe that deeply. Is your back hurting? Can you move your legs?"

She wiggled her hands and feet. "My back and legs feel fine."

"Good. It's unlikely you hurt your spine, but we should—"

The next words caught in his throat, as his brain finally registered the woman beneath him.

His gaze dropped from her striking face to two shapely breasts stretching her purple T-shirt—breasts he was still touching. The fact that he was kneeling over her, legs straddling hers, snapped into awareness.

He shot to his feet, aware his bike shorts clung in all the wrong places for a moment like this.

"Would you help me up?"

He'd been so distracted staring at her that her voice startled him. "No, wait! You can't move until we've X-rayed your back. I'm calling an ambulance."

"A what?" She rolled to her side, pushed to her knees, and stumbled to her feet. "I'm *not* going to the ER! ER docs are maniacs!"

She tried to walk off, unsteady on her feet. He caught her arm and steered her toward a bench.

Holding her head, she drew in a deep breath. "Great, now I'm lightheaded. I got up too fast." She yanked the ponytail holder loose and combed her fingers through a cascade of honey-blond waves that fell to her mid-back.

An image flickered: his hands threading through that hair, his lips feasting on hers.

He shuddered and shoved it away. "I insist. Let me take you to the ER."

She rubbed her shoulder. "ER docs spin a little roulette wheel to decide your fate. Either they give you Tylenol and boot you out while your appendix is bursting, or they CT-scan you from head to toe when all you wanted was help with a fingernail."

He chuckled, surprising himself. He'd thought he was still too shaken to laugh. But the woman had a point and a warped kind of wisdom.

He studied her. No wedding ring. Honey-colored eyes, same shade as her hair. Skin with a sun-kissed glow and features with a hint of the exotic—maybe Italian? Hispanic? Middle Eastern?

"I'm really sorry I crashed into you," he said.

She waved him off with a grin. "I'll be a little sore tonight and find some black and blues tomorrow. I know the drill—I'm accident-prone." She brushed off her clothes while talking fast. "On Wednesday, my bike broke and I landed in a creek. I hitchhiked my way back in a live poultry truck. Three days and two shampoos later, I'm still finding feathers in my hair."

It took him a second to grasp her words. He'd braced for a scold and couldn't understand why she kept smiling.

And what a smile! It felt like clouds had cleared and the sun came out.

She retraced their steps to pick up her sunglasses. His gaze followed her.

She has the most beautiful smile.

His eyes dropped to her curvy behind, highlighted by spandex shorts. A little devil in him whispered, *And also the most beautiful butt.*

Reprimanding himself, he took off his sunglasses and helmet and ran his fingers through his auburn hair.

As she turned back to him, a spark lit up her face. "Wait! I've seen you before. You work at Holloway Hospital!"

Me and my bad luck. Did she work there too?

She kept going. "I've seen you in the ICU, adjusting ventilators. You're a respiratory therapist, right?"

He hesitated. Did he want to reveal he was a deep-pocketed doctor to someone who could still sue him?

Before he could answer, she added, "You wear those teal scrubs that match your eyes and make them pop. You must be the only person alive who looks hot in scrubs."

She slapped a hand over her mouth.

Wait, was she flirting with him?

Before she knew he was a doctor?

"Sorry," she said with a wince. "I wasn't supposed to say that aloud …" She pointed at herself. "… Or be dressed like this. I swear, I usually look much better. Please erase this image from your mind, would you?" She sent him one last dazzling twinkle, then walked away.

Seeing her limp away unsettled him—almost caused him pain.

Leaving his bike behind on the ground, he caught up with her. "Wait! Can I at least drive you home? I'm worried about you."

She picked up her pace, and he had to jog to keep up. "My car's not that far, thank you."

He intercepted her, so she had to stop walking. "Can I at least have your name?"

Reluctantly, she offered her hand. "I'm Fe Hernandez." They exchanged a handshake. "But now I have to go beat myself for looking like a battered parrot the one day you crashed into me."

He held on to her soft, warm hand to stop her from leaving. "Nice to meet you, Fe. I'm Shawn. Now that we've been formally introduced, may I ask you to join me for coffee?"

She blinked in surprise. Caution flickered across her face, then faded. "Well …" she tittered. "In my Dominican family, turning down coffee is practically an insult."

• • •

At times, in med school, Shawn had been convinced he suffered from whatever disease he was studying. That touch of hypochondria still relapsed from time to time and, today, he self-diagnosed with split personality disorder. His usual self was having a blast. Yet, next to him, sat the imaginary man he'd named "Dr. McDevil," drooling over Fe and plotting how to seduce her.

They sank into brown leather armchairs in a corner of a Starbucks, sipping coffees and chatting. She'd made him howl with laughter, re-enacting the vivid horror movies that had crossed her mind when he tackled her to the ground.

God, she's so much fun! his usual self said. *I really want to date this woman!*

She sipped her second latte and licked the foam from her lips. His eyes locked on her mouth.

Change of plans, McDevil whispered. *First, I want to* kiss *this woman. Then I'll date her.*

Talking with someone who didn't know he was a doctor felt refreshing. But he didn't want to deceive her. He still looked for the right moment to correct her about his occupation. Yet every time he thought he'd found it, someone interrupted to greet Fe—she seemed to know half the town.

She nibbled a muffin, explaining how she'd become a speech therapist. "I was born and raised in New York, but spent most summers with my grandma in the Dominican Republic. When I was seven, my father needed a kidney transplant, and my mother had to care for him. So, Abuela kept my brothers and me for an entire year—even enrolled us in school there. When I returned home, I had *an accent*!" Giggling, she pressed a hand to her forehead. "My classmates in New York teased me like crazy."

The lack of bitterness impressed him. "That must've been tough."

She shook her head, still smiling. "I had enough personality to brush it off, but I was surprised to learn people judged others and assumed they were less smart, just for sounding different. That gave me compassion for kids around me who had a lisp or a stutter. I wanted to help them fit in, make sure their speech didn't distract from their good qualities."

Dang it. She was good-hearted too.

"You must be great at your job. The last lady who stopped to say hi raved about you. Didn't she also say you saved her marriage?"

Fe waved off the praise. "My grandma and I babysat her son some nights so she and her husband could have time alone." She scrunched her face in apology. "My friends say I have 'issues with professional boundaries' because I help my clients' parents too, but they don't get it. Working with children is tricky. If their parents are stressed and miserable, the kids can't make progress."

Dang it, she's amazing. Why does she have to work for—

Hopeful, he straightened. "Wait, I thought you worked at Holloway Hospital."

"I do. I work with stroke survivors in the mornings. I give speech therapy to kids in the afternoons."

His brain registered the facts. Two jobs. Hard worker. Less likely to be a gold digger. She was getting better by the minute. "Do you like your job?"

"I love it! My favorite part is working with speech-delayed children—especially autism."

He raised his eyebrows. "How come?"

"I love to see them blossom." She sipped her coffee. "Every new word they learn empowers them. Now they can ask for water. Now they can tell you something hurts. Today, they learn the word 'butterfly,' and tomorrow, they see butterflies everywhere. Language is power, and words are magic spells."

He lowered his cup, stunned. "I love that!"

Encouraged, she tucked her feet into the armchair and leaned closer. "Yes. Words are magic. And their spells work the other way too. When we refuse to acknowledge what's bothering us—don't say it aloud—we can shrink it in our minds. But that can backfire. We can't control a problem until we name it. Naming it makes it concrete."

His jaw dropped. He hadn't expected such depth from the same woman who'd just rambled about feathers in her hair.

She picked at the crumbs of her muffin. "The phrase I use most with kids is 'use your words' instead of throwing a tantrum. Once they can name what's upsetting them, they're halfway to solving it. I think it's true for adults too."

Beautiful. Hard-working. Brilliant. And with a heart of gold. He didn't just want to date her; he already imagined introducing her to his parents.

But after how complicated things got with Gina, he knew better than to get involved with another hospital employee.

It was so disappointing.

"I can't believe I've never seen you at the hospital!"

She wrinkled her nose. "I keep a low profile there, wear my ugliest, baggiest scrubs, try to turn invisible."

He wondered if that was code for *doctors hit on me too often.*

"But I'm hoping to leave Holloway for good soon," she added. "Working with children is my real calling. My boss at the speech-therapy center is retiring. I plan to buy her place and make that my full-time business."

Impressive. She was ambitious, hard-working—definitely not a gold digger.

And she's leaving the hospital. Yes!

His pulse picked up. This was too good to be true. Was his bad luck finally changing?

He'd always been a practical man, committed to logical thinking. Yet now he struggled to contain his enthusiasm. He had a very, *very* good feeling about this.

He forced himself to slow down. First, he needed to confirm she was single.

"Fe, you mentioned picking up your daughter later, but I don't see a ring on your finger."

She averted her eyes, suddenly shy. "I'm divorced. I have an eight-year-old boy and a five-year-old girl."

She must've had them very young.

He smiled. "I have a three-year-old boy. I'm kind of divorced too."

Her grin vanished. "*Kind of* divorced? Not again!" She stood abruptly. "Let me guess. You're not 'technically' divorced. You've been separated 'forever,' but she refuses to sign the divorce papers." She grabbed her things. "Sorry, but I don't hang out with married men."

His heart kicked faster. He hated sharing this so soon, but he couldn't let her walk away.

He rested his hand on her wrist to stop her. "Not exactly. I can't officially say I'm divorced because she never got to sign the papers. She died."

She froze, then turned to him, eyes searching. Slowly, she eased back into her chair.

"So, I guess I'm 'technically' a widower," he said. "But I don't like to use that term. I hate it when people give me pitying looks."

"Ouch." She bit her lip. "I should say 'I'm sorry.' But since we've established you hate commiseration, I'll ask instead, how's your son doing with it?"

Tense, he played with the coffee stirrer. "It's been an adjustment for both of us. He used to live with her. We're kind of … getting to know each other all over again."

He kept to himself the part where Aidan had been taken from him for a year. Or how shattering it was to finally find him—only to realize the boy didn't remember him at all.

"How are *you* doing with all of this?" she asked with caution.

He didn't want to go into it. Not the nightmare of being falsely accused, not the whispers that still followed him around the hospital. What worried him most wasn't the damage to his name—it was Aidan.

She kept looking at him, like she was silently inviting him to talk. Something inside him quivered.

"This single parenthood thing isn't easy," he said finally. "And my son is … acting out a lot."

"Acting out?"

"He's throwing terrible tantrums. Hitting other kids at preschool …"

He left out the part that haunted him most—that Aidan might've witnessed his mother's death. That his acting out and refusal to speak weren't just grief, but trauma.

"I don't blame the little guy," she said. "Maybe that's his way of telling you he misses his mom."

He ran a hand through his hair. "I never realized how exhausting it is to take care of a kid. I feel like the worst father in the world for saying this, but …" He hesitated. "Today's bike ride? It was kind of an excuse. I needed to get away from him for a while."

He braced for judgment—disgust. But she didn't flinch.

Instead, she placed a small hand on his knee. The simple gesture soothed him more than he expected.

"I know exactly how you feel," she said. "Hang in there, it gets better, I promise." She flourished her free hand as if searching for the right words. "You know how kids are. They beat us up with all they've got ninety-five percent of the time." She chuckled. "And then they do one tiny thing that makes our heart burst with love, and somehow, it makes the rest worth it."

Relief surged through him. Her words filled him with unfamiliar peace.

Gee! he thought. *I don't just want to date this woman. I want to marry her!*

His heart jolted.

And just like that, half in excitement, half in terror, he realized the truth beyond any doubt.

She's The One.

This is the woman I want to spend the rest of my life with.

Janey Mack!

CHAPTER 4

FE COULDN'T BELIEVE HER GOOD LUCK. THE GUY WHO'D LANDED on her turned out to be the eye-candy who'd caught her attention in the hospital. How mind-blowing was that?

Yet something impressed her even more—he wasn't just handsome. He was fun, smart, and a gentleman. It was adorable how he'd cleaned her hands with sanitizer wipes before they ate at the coffee shop.

But the more she liked him, the deeper in trouble she got. Like every time she got excited, she couldn't stop talking.

As they wandered through a shell souvenir store, she rambled, "So, if I hadn't found that consignment store and bought the too-small dress, I wouldn't have gone exercising today. And if my bike hadn't been broken, I would've been riding it instead of jogging. And if Taco hadn't chased me all over town, I would've been out of practice and too tired to keep running today."

Callate mujer, por amor de Dios! she scolded herself. *Stop talking before you scare him away forever!*

He lifted his gaze to hers and summed it up. "So, if it hadn't been for the old lady chasing you with her oxygen tank, a broken bike, and a Chihuahua, you wouldn't be here."

She gawked at him, then nodded. *Oh my God! He not only heard my whole rant—he got it!*

"And we wouldn't have met today." He beamed, and his gorgeous teal eyes seemed to sparkle. "Now I want to find that lady, the old guy in my bike lane, and that Chihuahua, and kiss them."

Her knees buckled. *How about we save some time and you kiss me instead?*

With a shudder, she looked away.

He rummaged through a pile of sea stars. "You're lucky to have a big family in town. Like you, I grew up with so many cousins I had trouble keeping track—yet we rarely see each other." He picked up a sand dollar. "Back then, we lived in Newton, near Boston. Our house was always packed with kids. Those are the best memories of my life."

"Yes, big families are great." She sighed. "Always loving and supporting each other ... *almost* makes up for all the feuding."

"Yes!" He chuckled. "And someone always keeping tabs on everyone else."

"And," she added, "someone always getting drunk at the party and dragging out a twenty-year-old grudge."

He stopped in his tracks and turned to her, eyes wide. "My goodness, Fe! Are you Irish too?"

She giggled. "No. But I'm sensing an eerie similarity between your family and mine. Replace the fiddle with an accordion and the potatoes with rice and beans, and your Irish *Mamó* could be a twin of my *abuela*. Full of personality, a nurturing force of nature, passionately Catholic ..."

"Does your grandma light a candle every Christmas?"

She popped a hip and wagged a sassy finger. "She lights a candle *every day*. She's got an honorary Ph.D. in which saint handles which request."

The sound of his laughter gave her goose bumps. She'd never heard a clearer, more beautiful laugh.

"Wow," he said, shoulders relaxing. "It took me until now to realize what a rare privilege it was to grow up near family." A flicker of melancholy crossed his eyes. "My parents live only an hour away, in Pineapple Beach, yet we rarely get together. You're lucky to have a good relationship with your family."

He seemed sad, and she felt like hugging him. "You can have my family anytime," she said. "My grandma didn't stop at six children and twenty-plus grandchildren, she keeps adopting everyone she meets."

His smile returned, and it took her breath away. She didn't want to get her hopes up, but something felt promising.

I have a very good feeling about this.

• • •

Shawn's car was nearby, and he'd offered Fe a ride to hers, parked a few blocks away. As they strolled to the parking lot, chatting, he pushed his bike beside him, helmet hanging from one handle.

He loved how she touched his arm when talking, emphasizing her words. He found excuses to touch her too—poking her arm with his finger, elbowing her, nudging her with his shoulder … He felt like a teenage boy with his first crush.

She's amazing. I really *want to date her.*

A voice inside him whispered, *And then, ask her to go to Paris with me. Then ask her to marry me and honeymoon in Venice.*

What was happening to him?

It took every ounce of his physician's logic to reel in the mad man springing to life in his head.

He had to slow down. First things first—date her.

They reached his blue Mercedes SUV. Forcing a cool expression, he opened his mouth to ask her out when she spoke.

"Oh no!" She pointed at the parking sticker on his car's back window. "One of the Holloway doctors must be nearby."

Dazzled for a moment, he stopped. He'd forgotten she still thought he was a respiratory therapist. "Why say it like that? Don't you like doctors?"

"Who likes doctors?" She made a face. "They're the most boring people in the world. And they're all neurotic."

He blinked in surprise. "Not *all* of them."

Her crystalline laughter filled the air. "Oh yes, honey. Except for my friend Joy, they're all compulsive workaholics, with zero spontaneity and no clue how to enjoy life."

Suppressing a smirk, he narrowed his eyes. "How about if I prove you wrong?"

"And how do you plan to do that?" She raised her eyebrows, mirroring his playful tone.

"Well, I happen to know the owner of this car." He pointed at his SUV. "Wouldn't you say we had a great time together today, and I might be a good judge of who's fun?"

Pressing her lips together, she nodded.

"So," he tapped the hospital-parking sticker in the back, "if I found the car's owner right now, introduced him to you, and proved he's a cool, fun guy, that would disprove your theory, right?"

She crossed her arms, tapping a foot on the ground. "I seriously doubt it, but go ahead."

He pulled his keys from his money belt. Locking eyes with her, he made the car beep and flash its lights.

The pretty blush on her cheeks drained away.

They stared at each other for what felt like an eternity. Her stunned expression nearly cracked him up.

Yes, it was awkward, but he wasn't worried. The time they'd spent together had been too perfect for one small blunder to ruin it. Someday, they'd laugh about this.

Smiling, he held his hand out. "I should re-introduce myself more accurately. I'm not a respiratory therapist. I'm Dr. Shawn McDevitt. Pulmonary and ICU specialist."

Bewilderment filled her expression. After a long pause, she finally spoke. "You … you're Dr. McDevitt? The ICU doctor?"

He'd heard it before—he looked too young to be a specialist in anything. Since she still hadn't moved, he reached for her hand.

"Sorry I didn't correct you earlier. I was having too much fun getting to know you. How about we continue tonight over dinner?"

Her expression shifted, and his heart dropped.

Oh God! He knew that face! He hadn't seen it in years—maybe since high school—but he recognized it instantly.

She's about to reject me!

"I'm so sorry!" she finally said. "If I'd known you were a doctor, I wouldn't have wasted your time. I can't go out with a physician. Please forgive me."

Before he could react, she took off, sprinting.

He stood frozen. It felt like she'd pushed him off a mountain peak. He was still falling, so nothing hurt yet. But in seconds, he'd crash to the ground and fracture every bone.

As her shape shrank in the distance, he snapped out of it. He couldn't let her go.

He'd never catch her on foot now. He leaped onto his bike and chased after her.

Dang it, she's fast!

The grass slowed his tires. No chance of catching up this way. Hadn't she said she parked at the Riverside lot? He veered onto the road and picked up speed.

Just as he predicted, he reached the parking lot right before she arrived. He brought his bike to a halt in front of her, forcing her to stop.

Startled, she stumbled back, eyes darting as if deciding where to run.

He jumped off his bike and grabbed her arm before she could get away.

"Wait, Fe, stop! What's this about?"

Breathing hard, she raised both hands. "Listen, Shawn, you know when people break up and say, 'Don't take it personal,' but everyone knows it *is* personal? Well, this is the opposite of that."

She pointed between them. "We just met. I don't know enough about you to dislike you. See? There's no way this can be personal. It's just a matter of principle. I don't date physicians."

She spoke so fast he struggled to keep up. Her expression was apologetic, her words rushed.

"And I'm sorry I said doctors are boring and workaholics. I didn't mean to hurt your feelings. It's not your fault! You guys spend so many years studying and training that by the time you graduate, you don't even remember how to live."

Unable to process her words, he gaped at her.

Slowing down, she added, "It must suck to finally make decent money and never enjoy it, because you never have time and forgot how to relax."

He stood speechless. None of it was news, but hearing it laid out like that felt like a slap in the face.

She patted his arm. "We good?"

The ground beneath him seemed to shift. A million dreams he'd glimpsed that day crumbled to dust. Trips together, bringing her to family gatherings, honeymooning in Venice, a mix of Hispanic and Irish names for their future kids.

Every bruise from his earlier fall started to ache at once.

What shitty luck.

The first woman to truly move him in *years*—let's face it, Gina was just a rebound—and she was rejecting him with *this* ridiculous excuse?

What a way for the universe to laugh in his face.

"Use your words." Fe's voice pulled him back. He'd been staring at her in silence.

"Excuse me?"

She sighed. "You're having the adult equivalent of a tantrum. You're shutting down and giving me the silent treatment. I know you're upset, just say it. I can take it. Use your words."

The numbness gave way to soul-deep disappointment and then to fury. "Fine! I'll use my words!" he snapped. "No! We're *not* good! You're rejecting me without even giving me a chance to show who I really am. You're being closed-minded and judgmental."

He hadn't meant to sound so harsh, but the anger burst out.

To his surprise, she beamed. "See? Everything turns out for the best! Isn't it great you found out now instead of after we'd been dating for a while?"

He frowned. "No. It's *not* great! And you're *not* talking me into feeling glad this happened. You're basing your assumptions on a stereotype. You're discriminating against me! It's not fair and it's not right!"

After a pause, she said, "So, if I'm wrong—and you're not a workaholic—tell me. You said bike riding is your favorite hobby. How often have you gone lately?"

Clearing his throat, he looked away. "Three times."

She stepped in front of him, meeting his eyes. "Three times this week, this month, or this year?"

He groaned. "This year."

"And when was the last time you took a break?"

"Well." He perked up. "I just came back from a month-long leave of absence. I took it to be there for my son when his mother died."

She gave him a slow once-over. "So basically, it took a tragedy for you to even consider taking time off. How about before that? When was the last time you took a real vacation?"

For a moment, he couldn't recall the answer.

Her voice turned gentle, almost sad. "Pal, I'll give you that one. You seem like a wonderful father, determined to be there for your son. That deserves my full respect and applause, but you just proved my point."

Change of plans. He didn't want to date this woman. He wanted to *spank* her. Maybe he wouldn't even pinch her butt afterward.

"Trust me, you don't want to date me," she said, grinning. "I talk too loudly. I invade personal space. I'm way too jealous and hate it when my man's out of reach. I'm the exact opposite of what a physician needs."

He studied her face. The answer struck him with the clarity of a diagnosis. "A physician broke your heart, is that it?"

Her blinding smile faltered, then vanished. A subtle quiver in her lips answered for her.

His voice softened. "I'll take that as a yes. And on behalf of my entire profession, I'm sorry." He stepped closer. "I just met you, and I already know you're amazing. Whoever the jerk was who hurt you, he deserves to rot in hell."

Her eyes turned suspiciously shiny, but she forced a smile and flicked her wrist. "It's not a big deal. But thank you."

She plodded toward an old light-blue Honda, pulled keys from her belt bag, and unlocked it. Then, she turned to face him with the same apologetic look that was starting to get on his nerves.

"Listen, Shawn, I don't want things to be awkward if I run into you at the hospital. How about you look at it like this: Right now, you probably want to push me to the ground and beat me up, right?" She beamed. "Guess what? *You already did!* Tonight I'll be just as sore as if you'd punched me in the ribs. It just happens to be that you did it *before* I offended you. And now we're even." Her grin widened. "Hey! You even got to grope me when we rolled on the grass!"

Damn it. She'd almost made him laugh.

She offered her hand, looking up at him from under her eyelashes. "Are we good?"

He scowled. She deserved for him to walk away, to leave her standing there with her hand in the air. But dang it, he was a gentleman. He shook her hand.

McDevil whispered, *But being a gentleman didn't get you anywhere today. Maybe it's time to prove to her and to yourself that you can be spontaneous.*

He tugged her toward him and kissed her.

He expected her to push him away, but when that didn't happen, he cradled her head, his other hand settling on the small of her back. He'd just meant to startle her, but then desire rose, and he couldn't stop. Her lips were amazingly soft and plump. Tasting them alone would've been enough of a treat.

Then she parted them and kissed him back.

He nearly fainted.

Oh My.

Cripes.

Jaysus.

Bejabbers!

She was kissing him back. Her divine mouth was sucking on his too, her tongue playfully entangling with his. Her hands wrapped around him, bringing him closer. She rubbed against his body.

Janey Mack!

He walked her back until she leaned against the rear door of her car. The thin layers of spandex between them felt like torture, deepening the longing to feel her skin to skin.

Change of plans. I don't want to spank this woman.

I want to bring her home with me. Then I'll figure out the rest.

Shawn lost track of time. He'd completely forgotten they were in a public place until a sound snapped him out of it—distant snickering.

A passing biker shouted, "Get a room!"

It was Jay. Only a maniac like him would still be riding this long.

Shawn pulled back, gazing down at Fe, still pinned between his body and the car door. They both were breathing hard.

Getting a room was exactly what he had in mind.

She slid sideways, slow and cautious, slipping free from under the weight of his body. He stepped back.

She looked as stunned as he felt. Straightening her hair and her clothes, she wiped her mouth with the back of her hand.

Her voice came out hoarse. "I guess we're even now. Goodbye."

Before he could process the words, she climbed into her car. Her shaky hands fumbled to start the engine.

When she finally backed out of the parking space, he had to step aside to avoid being run over.

Their eyes met for a heartbeat.

Then she hit the gas and peeled away.

CHAPTER 5

S ITTING WITH HOPE AND ALLISON AT THEIR FAVORITE MARINA-
front restaurant, Fe forced a grin. "Everything happens for the
best. I learned a great lesson about keeping my mouth shut and
my opinions to myself. Can we please get back to my new business
instead of the most embarrassing day of my life?"

As Hope stirred her margarita, the shine on her giant engagement
ring could've blinded a pilot. She looked effortlessly classy in her little
black dress, making Fe feel self-conscious about her bright red lipstick.

"But you still haven't answered my question," Hope said. "It's been
two months. When do you plan to face Dr. McDevitt?"

"Face him?" Fe straightened her gold lamé batwing top. "Today I
saw him coming and threw myself under a nurse's station to hide. My
knees are all bruised."

"Did he see you?"

"No, thank God." Fe shuddered, jingling her golden chandelier earrings. "Unfortunately, I did see *him*. He looked stunning in those blue-
green scrubs—the ones that make his eyes pop." She sighed. "Those
gorgeous eyes are probably why I didn't realize he was a doctor. Usually,
I can spot them by the proud way they walk."

She reached into her golden tote, pulled out her makeup kit, and
plugged her curling iron into a nearby outlet.

Hope rolled her eyes. "Fe, you're not doing my hair again. Stop
avoiding the subject!"

Fe studied her friend. Hope looked flawless—nude lips and smoky eyelids that made her dark eyes even bigger. Allison, on the other hand, could use a little help.

Rising from her chair, she lifted her makeup kit and gave Allison a pleading look. "Please?"

In her signature flat tone, Allison replied, "It's bad enough that you give people unsolicited back rubs, Fe. But unsolicited makeovers crosses the line."

Fe batted her eyelashes. "But you're a therapist. And there's nothing more therapeutic for me than making beautiful people even more beautiful!"

Allison glowered without moving a muscle. "I'm in favor of Botox and anything rejuvenating. But makeup is just one more way society objectifies women."

Feminist bestselling author Allison Connors still intimidated Fe a little. But the canvas of her porcelain skin was too tempting to resist.

"In fact, I consider makeup a feminist statement," Fe said. "Cleopatra was a pioneer of makeup. And she was a kick-ass pharaoh, bossing around all the male Egyptians."

Allison considered it for a moment. "Okay, then."

"Thank you!" Fe dabbed blush onto Allison's cheeks.

Hope twirled a caramel-highlighted strand of her dark brown hair. "Fe, this is the first time I've seen you this impressed by a man. You should go for Dr. McDevitt."

"Sorry, Hope! I seriously can't stomach doctors." Fe moved on to the eyeshadow. "If you've ever had food poisoning from, say, eating bad sushi, you're not exactly eager to try sushi again."

"It sounds like you're craving that sushi roll." Hope chuckled. "I'd say, shove it down!" She paused. "Wait! Did I just invent a new penis euphemism? *The sushi roll?*"

Fe groaned and focused on Allison's eyelashes.

Hope narrowed her eyes like she did when analyzing a failing business. "Fe, listen to yourself. You won't date doctors. You won't date men who can't dance. Or men who remind you of your brothers …"

"And don't forget, men who own Chihuahuas," Allison chimed in.

Fe used the lip gloss to silence Allison.

"Jeez!" said Hope. "Bottom line? You *don't date*. Period."

Fe dropped into her chair and crossed her arms.

"I'm in shock," Allison said, staring into the mirror, though her monotone and deadpan expression betrayed no emotion. "I actually like your speed makeover, Fe."

Fe beamed. "The shadow makes your eyes look bluer!" From her seat, she used the curling iron to add volume to Allison's golden hair.

"But I'm also in shock," Allison continued, "because, for the first time in my life, I agree with Hope." She set the mirror down. "Fe, I think you're looking for excuses to shut men down because you have unfinished business from the past."

Fe rolled her eyes, annoyed that Allison was analyzing her again. "I don't push men away because of unfinished business."

"Yes, you do," Allison insisted. "You're doing the right thing for the wrong reasons. If you're going to push men out of your life, do it for the right reason—because they're intellectually inferior, sex-obsessed, hairy, smelly creatures who'll never be at our level of maturity."

Fe held back a chuckle.

"No," Hope countered. "Men are a delicacy crafted by the Creator for our enjoyment."

Allison's tone stayed flat. "And thank God, Tom domesticated you, or you'd be tasting them all."

Trying to reel her friends back in, Fe slid the binder across the table and set it in front of Hope. "Okeydokey. Let's get back to why we're here. I need financial advice, not romantic advice. What's the verdict, Hope?"

Hope scanned the financial reports. "Let me get this straight, Fe. You know nothing about finances—you practically have a phobia of numbers. You have zero business experience. You have no savings as a cash cushion ..."

"Yes?" Fe replied.

Hope drummed her fingers on her chin. "… And yet you plan to use every penny of your father's inheritance as a down payment to buy your boss' business?"

Fe stared at her blankly. "And your point is?"

"Don't you think this is a little risky? How did you even qualify for that loan if you can't afford the down payment?"

"Marla's getting someone to cosign with me. And I do have the bank account to show I can afford it—except that half that money's technically my mother's." She sighed. She was desperate to regain financial independence from her ex. "Hope, this is a once-in-a-lifetime opportunity. Please, just translate these reports for me."

"T.J. says it's a self-supporting business," Hope explained, referring to her fiancé, Tom, an accountant. "The rent the other providers pay covers the mortgage. Their membership fees cover the utilities, overhead, and most of your loan. And by cutting out the middleman, you'll keep a bigger portion of your income."

Fe blinked rapidly. "Can you say that in English?"

"It means you'll be making more money than you are now, and owning the place instead of renting." Hope closed the book. "It's a solid deal. But still, you shouldn't go around without an emergency fund. If it hadn't been for that savings account, you wouldn't have made it through all the times your ex withheld child support."

"That's not what worries me. I'd rather not touch Mami's money. It's already not much, since Dad's inheritance got split five ways between us and my three brothers." Fe found it ironic that her father had worked himself to death in his convenience store—literally. Yet four years after his passing, his life's work was quickly evaporating. "I'd rather use Mom's money to start a business she can run herself. Something to ensure her future."

"You can't afford both. Either you buy Rainbows, or you buy Doña Carmen her business. Unless you find another way to cover half the down payment," Hope said. "And remember, all of T.J.'s calculations assume you keep Rainbows' numbers up. To afford that loan, you'll have to stay busy."

Fe slumped in her chair, stirring her frozen daiquiri. "I already know we'll be losing clients. Once it's official that Marla's retiring, they'll go somewhere else."

"No way. All your cases adore you."

"And I adore them. But let's face it, I'm a nobody compared to Marla Desmonds."

Hope's phone buzzed with a text, and she cheered. "Great! Joy's pulling into the parking lot!"

Allison huffed and rolled her eyes. "Oh! So *His Majesty* Agent Fields is granting us the privilege of Joy's company for an hour today?"

Fe wasn't sure why Allison disliked Joy's boyfriend—an FBI agent—so much.

"Allison, drop it," Hope warned, shooting her a look. "We're not giving Joy a hard time just because she's in the honeymoon phase. Understood?"

Allison gave a sarcastic military salute. "Yes, ma'am!"

"And," Hope rubbed her hands together, "I can't wait to hear what her hospital gossip sources said about Shawn McDevitt!"

Fe's hands turned to ice. Her mouth went dry. "I don't know about this, Hope. This feels like spying."

"No. It's called *research*!" Hope tapped her hand on the table. "We need intel on this guy."

Joy approached, spotting Allison first and greeting her with a hug. "Allison! Look at you, wearing makeup. You look terrific!"

Tense, Allison accepted the hug without returning it. Even that was a privilege—everyone knew she hated hugs. "Look who's talking, Joy. You're glowing!"

Allison wasn't just being polite; Joy actually looked a decade younger than she had a few months ago.

"You know what I always say!" Hope grinned and stood to hug her sister. "The best skincare routine is frequent orgasms."

Joy blushed deep red.

Giggling, Fe tried to help her friend out of the moment. "It's the inner peace, Hope. Joy and Richard spend a lot of time meditating."

Clearing her throat, Hope widened her eyes. "Of course! T.J. and I also love to …" She used air quotes "…'meditate' every day—sometimes twice a day. In fact, after I leave here, I fully intend to 'clean his chakras' and ask him to 'open my third eye.'"

Fe chuckled, getting up to hug her friend.

Supermom, super doctor, and the sweetest person in the world, Joy was Fe's hero. The secret to her success as a psychiatrist? She made everybody feel good about themselves.

The four friends placed their dinner orders. Then, without wasting time, Hope turned to Joy. "Okay. Spill it."

Slouching, Joy sank in her chair. "Ugh, girls. That wasn't fun. You know I'm pathologically distracted and never follow gossip or current events. I worked with Shawn on the Hospital Ethics Committee for years, but I never learned anything about his personal life."

"Well, have you remedied the issue?" Hope snapped her fingers.

"I asked a few colleagues. But now I'm feeling guilty because what I found out is … a little disturbing."

Fe's pulse sped up. The women pulled their chairs closer, fixing their attention on Joy.

"What is it, woman? Cut the suspense!" Hope begged.

Fidgeting, Joy cleared her throat and looked away. "So the rumor running around the hospital"—she stirred the ice in her glass with her straw—"is that he killed his wife."

CHAPTER 6

A SHARED GASP RESOUNDED AROUND THE TABLE. FE'S INSIDES twisted.

Joy began her story. "Shawn moved to town from Miami five years ago, fresh out of a fellowship program. He was going through a crazy phase, catching up on all the partying he'd missed during medical training.

"About four years ago, in the club scene, he met the daughter of a local primary care physician. They got involved, she got pregnant, and coming from a conservative Irish-Catholic family, Shawn felt obligated to marry her. But he soon discovered the poor young woman was an aimless soul and a psychological mess."

"You mean a typical doctor's kid?" Allison asked, flat as ever.

"Worse," Joy said. "She was on drugs. Even injected opiates." She shifted in her chair and leaned forward. "Shawn had to keep her practically hostage during the pregnancy to make sure she wouldn't drink or use. Apparently, she got clean for a while. Motherhood calmed her down, and Shawn tried to make the marriage work. He even bought that huge house he lives in now, hoping they'd have more kids someday.

"But she never moved into the new house. He found out she was back on drugs and filed for divorce, asking for full custody of the kid. Then one day she vanished—with the child. When there was no sign of her for a whole year, rumors started that Shawn had her killed for refusing to give him the divorce."

Fe blinked. "*A year?* All that time, he had no idea where his son was?"

Joy sucked in a breath through her teeth. "I know. Poor Shawn must've been devastated."

"So, what happened?" Allison asked.

Joy lowered her voice. "They found her body a few months ago in an extended stay motel in Gainesville, Georgia. Reportedly, she'd died of a heroin overdose."

Bracing herself, Fe asked, "And where did the rumor come from that he had her killed?"

"They found marks on her arms that suggested she'd been re-strained. But Richard says Shawn passed all the interrogations and had plenty of alibis. The police found the kid a couple of blocks away from the mother, and he was untouched."

Fe tried to process the information.

Joy slapped her sister's arm. "Hope, why did you make me dig all this up? I feel terrible for Shawn now! I wonder if there's anything Richard can do to help clear his name."

Allison growled at the mere mention of Joy's boyfriend.

Groaning, Fe added, "I feel awful, too. This poor guy's having a horrible year, and not only did I mop the floor with him, now we're snooping into his life."

"I'm warning you." Joy jabbed Fe's arm. "If he asks me for gossip about you, I'm telling him everything—just to make it up to him."

"Be my guest! I deserve it!"

Like that's ever going to happen.

• • •

Saturday morning, Shawn sat outside the oceanside restaurant, waiting for Agent Fields to finish surfing. The cloudless sky gave the crashing waves the deep aqua hue of a summer day. He regretted not wearing swim trunks under his striped button-down and jeans.

Still angry at himself, Shawn cringed at the memory of that morning with Fe, two months ago now. Usually a coolheaded physician, he hardly recognized the delusional idiot he'd become, fantasizing about Paris and grandkids with a perfect stranger.

Her rejection added to his mounting stress. But it hadn't ended there. Just last week, Dr. Luqman, a lifeless developmental pediatrician, had scared him stiff with a list of possible diagnoses to explain Aidan's speech delay.

Yup. I must be the man with the worst luck on the planet.

Still, maybe today will bring a shift. Out of the blue, Joy Clayton had called, checking on him and Aidan. She'd asked if there was anything she or her boyfriend could do to help with the investigation. He'd been so grateful, he hadn't even minded that the only time they were all free was quite early on a Saturday morning.

Wearing a wet suit and carrying a surfboard under his arm, tall, athletic Richard Fields approached them. His wet brown hair was slicked back, and his hazel eyes—fixed on Joy—sparkled with approval.

Joy's face lit up. She jumped off her seat and kissed him as fervently as if she hadn't seen him in years—though they'd arrived together.

Shawn felt a pang of envy as their kiss lingered longer than what seemed proper for public display. He cleared his throat. "Would you two please stop eating bread in front of the hungry?"

Reluctantly, Richard let go of Joy and extended a hearty handshake.

"Sonova Beach, you're still alive?" Shawn teased. "I must've done a good job gluing your pieces back together in the ICU, *Agent Fields.*"

Richard smirked. "Drop the formalities, Shawn. Don't expect me to call you *Dr. McDevitt* just because you ripped me off death's grip a couple times. I've seen you shit-faced enough to lose all professional respect."

A former party companion, Richard's good mood surprised Shawn—as did how much younger he looked since the last time he'd seen him.

Getting laid regularly is really flattering. Am I the only man in the world not getting any nowadays?

Richard's blend of contradictions intrigued Shawn. A no-nonsense, hard-ass federal cop, he was also a surfer and regular meditator. He was trying to become a vegetarian, so as not to hurt animals—yet had no trouble shooting a human.

Richard kissed Joy on the cheek. "Give me a minute to shower. I'll be right back."

He leaned his board against the table, grabbed a bag from the floor, and disappeared inside.

Joy stared after him, dazed.

Shawn waved his hand in front of her face.

"Sorry. What were we talking about?" she asked.

He'd seen Joy and Fe talk in the hospital and figured they were friends. He debated asking—then gave in. "What's the deal with your friend Fe?"

Joy shot him a cautious look. "Can you be more specific?"

He held her gaze while rubbing sanitizer into his hands. "I asked her out and she turned me down—said, 'I don't date physicians.' Now, she avoids me like I've got smallpox. Why does she hate doctors so much?"

"It's against the Sisterhood Code of Honor to serve as an informant for a guy." Despite her words, her brown eyes seemed to invite persuasion.

"Let me guess." He narrowed his eyes. "Some doctor impressed her with his money, promised her the world, used her for a while, then left her heartbroken. Am I close?"

Joy slanted him a look. "Not exactly. Try a medical student impressed her with his charm, married her, gave her the worst years of her life, then was crushed when *she* left *him*."

"She was married to a physician? Are you saying her kids' father is a doctor?"

Joy bowed her head in confirmation.

Fe had told him she was raising her family on her own, so he'd assumed the father was some unemployed deadbeat.

"So, that's the story. Her ex was a doctor. She hates all of us now. And I'm doomed."

"It's not that simple." Joy fidgeted in her chair, clearly torn. "Look, it's a small town, you'll hear the rumors sooner or later. Better you hear the real story from me."

Shawn leaned in.

"Fe is too stubborn and cheerful to admit it, but her claims of not liking physicians might be a cover for something deeper." Joy lowered her voice. "She's afraid of being punished by her ex's family if she draws attention in the medical community."

"Punished?" Shawn's curiosity sharpened.

"Her ex is a surgeon at Riverview Hospital, in Pineapple Beach," Joy said.

Shawn didn't round at that hospital, thirty minutes away, but he knew it well. His father had worked there before retiring.

Joy fiddled with the halter straps of her multicolored sundress. "He never forgave Fe for the humiliation of leaving him. He tortured her in the divorce, and still haunts her."

"What do you mean?"

"For starters, he left her with nothing. After years supporting his training, all she walked away with was the clothes she'd packed the day she grabbed the kids and left. If her mother hadn't just relocated here from New York, Fe would've been homeless, and then he even stopped subsidizing her mom's mortgage."

"That's low!" Shawn said, appalled. "But he must be paying child support."

With a huff, Joy flicked her hand. "His lawyers found all kinds of tricks to minimize it. And even then, he's failed to pay regularly."

Shawn shook his head, stunned. That man's behavior was so disgraceful that he felt embarrassed on behalf of all physicians. Heck, of all men.

Joy added sugar to her coffee. "But the worst part is, she's always afraid he'll sabotage her work. He's done it before."

"He sabotaged her work?"

"You know how most speech therapy referrals come from physicians? Well, he and his wealthy family blacklisted her at Riverview and badmouthed her to their friends. It's taken her years to rebuild her reputation."

Now it made sense. Fe wasn't just avoiding him—she was protecting herself. Even if Riverview was across town, many doctors at Holloway held privileges there too.

"The divorce papers don't allow Fe to move without giving up custody of the children," Joy added. "So she's trapped, forced to play by this powerful family's rules."

"And you're saying her ex does all this to punish her?"

"My theory? He's never gotten over her. He does it all to force her to keep talking to him—which is pathetic, because he's remarried." She rolled her quartz bracelet. "And if he's outraged with her, his family's even worse. They were never happy about him marrying a humble Latina from Washington Heights. They thought they were being generous just for 'accepting her despite that.' So, when she left him, they took it as a personal insult."

Shawn scoffed, "Those in-laws sound like pricks. No wonder she left him."

"Trust me, he earned it without his parents' help. The man was a hopeless workaholic—never home. He wasn't even there when his daughter was born. He was in the OR! You have to know how family-centered Fe is to understand how much that hurt her." With a half shrug, she tilted her head. "Bottom line: Don't take it personally. I think Fe's scared of outraging those people if she dates a physician."

Staring into his coffee mug, Shawn processed the information. "So not only do all physicians remind her of her jerk ex, but also, if she dates one, she risks provoking her ex-family's wrath. I'm not only doomed, I'm double-doomed."

Joy placed her small-boned hand on his shoulder. "Sweetie, I'm afraid you are more like triple-doomed."

Shawn shot her a look. "There's more?"

Averting her gaze, Joy stirred her coffee. "There's another reason why Fe avoids dating in general." Holding her mug with both hands, she took a long sip. "But it's a more sensitive issue. And I think she should be the one to tell you, if and when she's ready."

Shawn opened his mouth to protest, but Richard's return cut him off. He'd changed into cargo shorts and an olive-green T-shirt that brought out the green flecks in his hazel eyes.

"Okay, Shawn." Richard pulled out a chair and sat. "Let's talk business. How can I help you?"

CHAPTER 7

JOY EXCUSED HERSELF FOR A BEACH WALK, GIVING THE MEN SOME privacy.

Shawn opened, "You probably know my estranged wife's body was found across the state border, in Georgia. So the state police handed the case over to the FBI."

"I know," Richard said. "Since we're friends, I can't work on your case officially, but I've stayed in the loop. The last person to see Tara was a friend of yours?"

"My friend Jay. He came to visit me at my old house and saw her leave in a white pickup truck with a man who looked 'Indian or Middle Eastern.' My cleaning lady overheard Tara saying she was running away 'with the lawn guy.' But I never had one who matched that description. She'd been gone a year when they found her body, so we don't know if she was still with him."

"And the only person who might've seen her killer is your son. A three-year-old."

Shawn leaned back in his chair. For months, he'd been haunted by what Aidan might've witnessed—or suffered—during that year. "We don't think he saw the murder. He didn't seem scared when they found him, a few blocks from her motel. We assume they'd sent him away."

"But it's possible he saw the killer." Richard placed a steady hand on Shawn's arm. "I know this is hard for you, but Aidan could help us identify him."

"It's not that simple." Shawn shifted in his seat and swallowed hard. "Aidan has … a speech delay. He's being evaluated right now." He stopped short, unwilling to say more.

"Has he started speech therapy yet? Ideally, we'd want to work with him soon—before any memories fade."

Shawn avoided his eyes, drumming his fingers on the table. "I'd rather leave Aidan out of this."

Richard gave a single nod. "Then how can I help you?"

Shawn lifted his laptop case onto the table. "It's important to me to solve this—to clear the rumors that I was involved. My case agent is hard to reach, and I've been hesitant to call him directly. But I've noticed something else lately… and I'm starting to wonder if it might be related."

"What is it?"

Shawn pulled out a folder and slid it across the table. "A couple years ago, I started getting hate letters. After a year of silence, they picked up again a few weeks ago."

"What do they say?"

"They don't make much sense. Random accusations that I'm evil, followed by death wishes. When they first started, I went to the police, hired private security, even paid a private investigator … Waste of time. They found nothing, and no one ever tried to hurt me."

His brows knitted, Richard read the typed letters one by one. "Has anything changed lately—something that made you take them seriously?"

Shawn searched for a sheet at the bottom of the pile. "This one says, 'Losing your wife was only the beginning of your punishment.' That's when I started wondering if they could be connected to Tara's death."

Richard went quiet. After a moment, Shawn asked, "What do you think?"

"Walk me through it." Richard rubbed his clean-shaven jaw. "Anyone who might hate you enough to want to scare you, maybe even hurt you? A business rival? Angry patients? A resentful ex?"

Shawn gave a sour chuckle. "Try all of the above!"

Richard studied him. "Start from the beginning. Business competitor?"

Leaning back, Shawn sipped his coffee. "I'm in the middle of a nasty split with FirstHealth, the medical group I worked with for the last five years—I was their medical director for a while."

"From what I know, they pretty much monopolize Fort Sunshine's healthcare. Don't they own both the hospital and the biggest insurance company in town?"

Shawn nodded. "They're a moneymaking machine with little regard for their doctors. But it's hard to compete with them solo, which is why they get away with it. Two years ago, when the letters started, I was trying to leave them and open my own practice. They threatened to sue me, claiming I'd be competing with their doctors."

"And who's 'they' exactly?"

"Dr. Lee Stewarts, cardiothoracic surgeon at Holloway and president of FirstHealth. We've never gotten along."

Richard jotted the name down. "So he may've wanted to scare you into moving away. Anyone else who didn't want you opening your practice?"

"The only solo pulmonologist in town is Dr. Mark Jones. I asked him to partner with me back then, and he practically laughed in my face. Now that I'm on my own, I'm his main competition for referrals."

"So he might've had a motive too."

"I doubt he'd stoop that low. And our relationship's a weird mix of rivalry and respect—almost love/hate. I even took care of him in the ICU a few months ago."

"I'm putting him on the list anyway. Next, patients or their families?"

Shawn shrugged. "Too many to count. Most people don't leave the ICU alive. It's not unusual for grief-stricken relatives to associate me with their loss."

With narrowed eyes, Richard considered it. "Can you pull a list of cases where someone blamed you for a bad outcome?"

"I can get a partial one from my risk management advisor."

"Okay. Anyone else?"

Shawn hesitated, uneasy. "My ex-girlfriend Gina didn't take the breakup well. And I've learned she has some … untreated mental health issues that make her unstable."

"What do you mean?" Richard's eyebrows lifted.

"When we started dating, she said she was bipolar. That didn't bother me. But later, when her mood swings continued despite taking the meds, I started to suspect something else. Then it clicked—her paranoid outbursts, self-harming episodes, the intense, unstable relationships in her past … I believe she has borderline personality disorder."

Richard let out a breath. "Thank God for Joy curing me! You and I both had a thing for women with a touch of crazy."

Shawn winced. His mother, a non-practicing trained therapist, believed he'd spent his life conforming to rules and now kept gravitating to women who broke them. "Don't call her that. I feel awful that I wasted a year of her life. I never meant for it to last—she was a rebound when my divorce started. But then Tara and Aidan disappeared, and I didn't have the energy to end it."

He reached for his pocket-sized hand sanitizer. "Anyway, I doubt she's behind the letters. They started before we even got together."

Richard scanned the dates Shawn had written on the photocopied pages. "Still, we'll need to compare tone and wording—whoever's sending them now might not be the original sender. I'll put Gina on the list."

Shawn's phone buzzed. He glanced at the screen, surprised to see a call from Dr. Luqman, Aidan's developmental pediatrician. As a professional courtesy, the doctor had given him a direct number.

"Excuse me a minute," he said, stepping away. "Hello, Dr. Luqman?"

"Hello, Shawn. Sorry to call on a Saturday. The clinic was hectic yesterday, and I didn't want to rush this call. I just received the report from Aidan's second-opinion evaluation at the Smith Center."

Shawn straightened. "What's going on?"

The pause that followed made Shawn's chest tighten.

"The evaluation confirmed my original conclusion," Dr. Luqman said. "Your son is on the autism spectrum."

CHAPTER 8

THE NEXT WEEK BLURRED IN SHAWN'S MEMORY. UNTIL THAT second opinion, he'd been in denial about Aidan's speech delay. Then came the anger phase—he decided he hated Dr. Luqman. He skipped bargaining altogether and plunged straight to depression.

No one in medical school had warned him that the grief cycle never followed the right order.

It'd been a frantic case of "hurry up and wait." All the experts said he'd wasted too much time—that therapy should've started before age three. But the Smith Center, the top autism facility in the state, had a six-month waitlist. Marla Desmonds, Dr. Luqman's top recommendation for speech therapy in town, had stopped accepting new cases. After disappointing interviews with two other providers, Shawn brought Aidan to see her anyway, hoping to change her mind.

The frail woman cleared her throat for the tenth time, her voice ragged from effort. "I wish I could help you, Dr. McDevitt," she rasped. "But I can't work with cases anymore. Even if I could push through the hoarseness, I'm physically unable to take on an intense program like this."

Who would've thought Aidan's best hope in town was about to retire early due to health issues? Marla had just completed treatment for a vocal cord tumor. Chemo-radiation had put her in remission, but cost her forty pounds and her voice.

Before Shawn could speak, his father cut in. "I'm sure we can make you an offer you can't resist. We'll pay you double your usual rate."

Marla gave Seamus McDevitt an impatient look. Shawn flinched. *Of course, throwing money at it always fixes everything.*

Shawn's mother had offered to join the appointment for support. Then, she'd backed out at the last minute, sending her husband alone. It was probably her way of forcing father-son interaction, like she'd tried and failed to do all of Shawn's childhood. Or maybe she just wanted a few hours without him. According to her, Seamus had become insufferable since retiring from cardiothoracic surgery a year ago.

Shawn dared to look at Aidan, an auburn-haired miniature copy of himself. The boy sat on the office carpet, spinning his toy car wheels over and over, making no effort to engage in pretend play. His blue eyes—bluer than Shawn's own teal—darted away at once, as if his father's gaze burned him.

Shawn's soul cracked.

"Ms. Desmonds, is there anyone else you can recommend?" he asked.

"There's someone I trained myself. She's worked with me for years and has a gift for kids on the spectrum." Marla rested her hand on Aidan's thick evaluations file. "I have no doubt she can review and carry out the Smith Center's recommendations."

After so many frustrating interviews and re-evaluations, Marla's conviction filled Shawn with hope.

She pushed through her hoarseness. "When I heard what this meeting was about, I asked this speech therapist to join us today. But there's a potential issue. She'll be quite busy with administrative tasks over the next few months. She's buying the practice from me now that I am retiring."

Something stirred in Shawn—a quiet dread.

Please, God, no. Not her.

As if summoned by the thought, the office door swung open and an upbeat voice rang out behind him. "Sorry I'm late, Marla. You'll never believe this! The psycho Chihuahua jumped off the moving truck and chased me one last time! It was so sweet!"

He recognized that voice even before he turned and faced the shock in her honey-colored eyes. She'd traded the scrubs for a white knee-length, A-line dress that hugged her hourglass figure. Perfectly made up, she looked like a model straight out of *Summer Living* magazine.

Of course, Marla's star therapist had to be Fe Hernandez.

• • •

As he watched the evaluation from behind the one-way glass, Shawn regretted wasting his time. For two months now, he'd been dodging her in the hospital—turning around at the nurse stations, storming into restrooms, even supply closets—to avoid running into her.

"She's way too young! We came here for your experience, Marla," Seamus said. "How about you name the price and we start from there?"

Shawn resisted the urge to roll his eyes. Mom's plan had already backfired. He didn't need to parade Aidan's struggles in front of his father to prove, once again, that he couldn't get anything right. Not even make a normal kid.

As if another evaluation weren't punishment enough. It hurt to watch his son fail over and over, unable to answer simple questions, refusing to interact.

Aidan went straight to his favorite routine, gathering toys scattered around the room and dropping them into a big toy bin. Then he'd dump them out and start again. He ignored Fe's every effort to engage him. Shawn braced for the tantrum he knew would follow—Aidan's usual refusal to cooperate.

Unable to watch, he turned to Marla. "Is Ms. Hernandez our only other option?"

Marla's ashy forehead creased as she faced him. "Just keep watching. Trust me; this woman's a natural."

Shawn turned back toward the one-way glass and the sounds coming through the speakers. As he predicted, Aidan flung himself to the floor and screamed. And just like that, the last bubble of hope burst.

But then Fe flopped down facedown beside him—kicking her legs, banging her head on the carpet, mimicking him with perfect flair.

Shawn stared, stunned.

Aidan seemed startled too. Then he stood and smacked her on the back.

Shawn shot up from his seat, ready to scold him, but Marla held his arm.

"Just watch. It started. He just closed his first circle of communication with her."

"Circle of communication?" Shawn blinked, confused.

Marla nodded. "Slapping her may not be ideal, but it's progress. He just acknowledged her existence."

He watched Fe work for the next half hour. Quiet and patient, she sat on the floor, passing toys to Aidan to load into the bin. He took them from her hand without making eye contact. Then she began hiding the toys behind her back, forcing him to touch her hand to retrieve them.

Every time he protested with a tantrum, she'd drop to the floor and fake one alongside him. Then the cycle of slapping, making up, and playing would begin again.

The fifth time they shared a tantrum, a miracle happened: Aidan giggled.

Shawn gasped.

"I told you she's good," Marla said, grinning. "That's the Floortime Approach. She's targeting his preferred activity. Every time he engages with her, he closes a circle of communication, and the more circles he closes, the closer we get to wanting to connect. It's like rehab for the brain—training it for verbal exchange."

Shawn's father, clearly having missed the moment, asked, "When does the evaluation start? All she's doing is playing with him. Isn't she supposed to ask him questions or take notes?"

Shawn didn't answer. He was watching Fe hide a toy behind her back while flexing her fingers, teaching Aidan the "give me" sign.

The timer bell rang, signaling the end of the evaluation. Shawn knew it: this had been their most successful office visit yet.

• • •

After thirty minutes of fake tantrums, Fe's body ached—but she was satisfied with Aidan's progress.

"Great job, honey!" She lifted him to help wash his hands in the playroom sink. Putting away leaky art supplies had left his hands and shirt smeared with watercolors.

As she dried his fingers, Marla stepped into the playroom, followed by Shawn and his father. Fe's hands trembled. It had taken every ounce of professionalism to stay composed through Marla's introductions and Shawn's polite handshake.

Aidan returned to loading and unloading toy bins. Then, out of nowhere, a middle-aged, heavy-set blonde appeared. She wore a baggy football jersey that read "Redneck and Proud of It."

Shawn addressed her. "Betty, would you please drive Aidan home? I'll be there as soon as I can."

"Yeah, right," the woman mumbled, peering over her red cat-eye glasses. She glanced at the boy. "What have you done to your shirt, you little devil? Lucky I brought clean clothes."

Aidan whimpered in protest as she picked him up and carried him out.

A mix of doubt and admiration crossed Shawn's face as he turned to Fe. "That … that was amazing. Marla was right. I need you to take over Aidan's case."

Fe shifted her weight, tense. No matter how badly she needed new clients, she couldn't handle the discomfort of seeing Shawn every day. "Dr. McDevitt, I really wish I could help. But I can't take this case." She tried to send him a message with her eyes.

With a soft cough, Marla elbowed her. "Uh, Miss Faith is obviously confused. Of course she can." She widened her eyes, tilting her head toward Shawn and his father. "They'll be hiring several of our providers—occupational, behavioral, and especially speech therapy. They'll be using *many* hours of your time. And they're offering to pay above our usual fee."

Shawn's father cut in. "Cash. No insurance involved. Money's not an issue."

Fe swallowed. *Please stop tempting me.* She gathered the strength to meet Shawn's eyes and found him scowling. Darn it. He clearly wasn't used to people telling him no.

His words were slow and deliberate. "Fe, we both know there are a few elephants we need to get out of the room. Please, let's find a place where we can talk in private."

She couldn't believe he'd said that in front of other people.

Marla cleared her throat. "Well, we should let you two come to an agreement." She motioned for Shawn's father to follow her out, then threw one last suspicious look over her shoulder before she left them alone.

Shawn stood in the middle of the playroom, shoulders squared, meeting her gaze. "Where can we sit?"

Heart pounding, she signaled him to follow her into her office. She would've preferred to sit behind her desk—to put some distance between them—but she'd been packing to move to Marla's office, and boxes now crowded the space. Instead, they sat across from each other on two chairs.

Shawn drew in a breath. "Fe, let's get this out of the way. If I offended you the day I kissed you, I apologize."

That caught her off guard. She'd been a glad recipient of the kiss—and full participant in it.

"I'm a proud man," he continued, "and I don't forgive rejection easily. You can rest assured, I'll *never* approach you again."

That's supposed to be good. Isn't it?

"Now that we've clarified that," he said, "let's start all over. Would you be willing to take this case?"

Fe sighed. "Dr. McDevitt, I assure you, Liza, one of our other therapists, can manage Aidan's case just fine."

He shook his head. "You already connected with him. In record time. What if this other therapist doesn't?"

Darn it! Why doesn't he get it?

"Sorry," she said. "I can't work with *you*."

"I knew it!" He slapped the desk, making her jump. "This *is* personal! Your bias against doctors is getting in the way of my son's care."

She stood, arms folded. Her voice rose to meet his. "No, it's not. The problem is that you're so used to getting special treatment, you can't handle someone telling you no."

He rose with a growl, eyes lifting to the ceiling. "Can you show some compassion? Do you even remember why I'm here? I just got some of the worst news of my life about my son. And it hurts!"

She didn't answer. His pain filled the room, like second-hand smoke, impossible to ignore.

"Shawn," she said, switching to his first name, "let's drop the act. We both know we can't work together." She stopped.

How could she explain that a magnetic force pulled her toward him—something she couldn't resist for long? That they were doomed. That if they spent time together, it was only a matter of time before something happened.

Words may be magic spells, but sometimes they're just not enough.

Instead, she stepped closer. "And you say you're absolutely sure I'm no temptation to you."

"Yes." He straightened his back.

"Then let's prove it." She closed the gap between them. "I'm going to kiss you, and I dare you not to kiss me back."

CHAPTER 9

SO MUCH FOR BEING A PROUD MAN.

Shawn's pulse raced. Fe now stood so close, her soft scent reached him. Her gaze slid from his eyes to his mouth, and she licked her lips. Heat surged through his body.

She leaned in. In her high heels, she only needed to lift her chin a bit—her lips were nearly at his. Her warm, minty breath brushed his skin.

Her voice dropped to a whisper. "Here I come, I'm going to kiss you."

Oh shite.

He imagined yanking her to him, kissing her hard. The memory of her mouth was so vivid, he could conjure every curve, every texture. He saw himself deepening the kiss, felt her lips part under his, his hands sliding over her body. He'd swipe the desk clean and lean her on it.

Frozen, he waited for her to close the last inch between them—but she didn't move. As if drawn by a magnet, he leaned forward.

His lips had almost touched hers when she stepped back.

It felt like someone had ripped away his oxygen tank underwater. His hands flung out in protest, reaching for her, but she slipped away.

Damn it. She'd made her point.

If she hadn't pulled back, he would've pounced on her. He gripped the back of a chair to keep from doing it now.

She seemed a little unsteady as she walked away. Then, she cleared her throat and turned to face him. "I'm going to be brutally honest. I always tell my clients to 'use their words,' so I'll use mine." She returned to her chair and motioned for him to take a seat.

His gut twisted as he sat.

"My point is ..." she paused. "You're extremely hot"—she gestured between them—"and we have a dangerous amount of chemistry going on."

His usually sharp, analytical mind had turned to fog after their almost-kiss. "Why are you saying that like it's a bad thing?"

Her honey-colored eyes darted away, then returned to his. "That day at the park, if we would've kept kissing ... we would've reached a point where we couldn't stop."

He knew exactly what she meant. Swallowing hard, he nodded.

"We have two options," she continued. "Option one, the only way I'd consider taking Aidan's case is that we pretend that morning never happened and swear to never kiss again."

Blinking, he crossed his arms. "What's option two?"

She straightened her spine, like a soldier marching into battle. "Option two, we get it out of our systems. We kiss right now, sleep together, feel awful about it tomorrow, then never see each other again."

Her dead-serious expression told him she wasn't bluffing.

"What's option three?" he asked.

"There's no option three."

Yes, there is, he wanted to say. *I ask you to be Aidan's stepmother instead of his therapist.*

He scolded himself. *Idiot.*

"What I mean," she said, "is that if we ended up in bed, it would be knowing nothing real will ever come from it."

A long silence fell.

He offered, "And you're so sure about that because ..."

She braced herself, eyes avoiding his. "Because I can't. I just can't be a *doctor's woman* again."

His heart sank.

"Fe, I'll admit I've done some digging. I've heard how badly your ex treated you. But have you considered maybe *he* was the problem, not all doctors?"

Tense, she rose and walked to the window, her back to him.

"Don't believe my friends' biased versions. For a marriage to fail, two people make mistakes. And I carry at least half the blame." She faced him and tapped her chest. "*I* failed. I'm not the kind of woman a physician needs."

She paced the office.

"It takes a special person to be a doctor's wife. A woman willing to share him with his patients. A woman who can give without expecting anything back. I couldn't do that. I've never been someone who comes second. I don't do well without consistent affection—I'm a clinger."

She kept her eyes on the boxes stacked on her desk. "I didn't handle it well when he left for the hospital in the middle of the night. I took it personally when he chose to check on patients over the weekend— even when he wasn't on call. And of course, that was unreasonable." She gave a mirthless chuckle. "What kind of selfish witch complains because her man is out *saving lives*?"

Her eyes shimmered with a hint of tears, but she held steady.

Meeting his gaze, she added. "So, in summary, Shawn. If anything happened between us, it would have to be … call it any name you want—a hookup, a fling, a one, or two, or three-night stand. But it could never become serious."

A long time went by before he answered. "I appreciate your honesty," he finally said. "I've complained more than once when a woman wasn't upfront at the start of a relationship." He hesitated. "And as tempting as it is to take what I can now, and figure out the rest later, I can tell *you* don't want just a hookup." He paused, struggling. "So, option two is out."

Those words were harder to say than he'd expected.

"But after some thought, I agree. We shouldn't work together." He stood and shook her hand. "Thanks for your time, Ms. Hernandez. I'll look for a different speech therapist."

As he turned to leave, his phone rang—Betty. The moment he picked up, Aidan's piercing wail burst through the line.

"Everything okay, Betty?"

"Your son is not a kid—he's a wild animal!" she shrilled. "He's been screaming nonstop since we left Rainbows. He unbuckled himself in the middle of the highway, and when I tried to fix it, he scratched me and bit me! I turned around. We're back in the parking lot. Come get him, Doctor. I quit!"

• • •

With the phone still to his ear, Shawn rushed toward the parking lot. "I'm sorry, Betty. I—"

"I'm done, Dr. McDevitt. I can't take this anymore!" Her voice shook, barely holding back tears.

He exited the building and followed the sound of Aidan's shrieking. His son lay on the floor beside the van, kicking and screaming.

Dread tightened Shawn's gut. *Not again, please!*

The last time Aidan had spiraled like this, nothing had worked. He'd screamed for what felt like hours, and only stopped after crying himself to sleep.

How could someone so small fight so hard? Shawn tried to pick him up, but Aidan turned into dead weight, arms locked tight against his body, legs thrashing.

Shawn's patience snapped. "Aidan! Stop it—now!"

He knelt to lift him, but one of the boy's kicks smashed into his face.

Pain exploded. Shawn staggered back, nearly blacking out. He sat on the ground, clutching his nose, tasting blood in the back of his throat. A hot pulse warned him that swelling had already begun.

He was done.

He couldn't do this anymore.

But, unlike Betty, he didn't have the option to quit. Despair filled his soul.

When he opened his eyes, still pressing his nose, Fe knelt beside Aidan, with a juice box in hand.

"Here, honey. Let's get that blood sugar up. Are you thirsty?"

Aidan resisted, but she managed to squirt some into his mouth. After a few seconds, he accepted the straw.

The sudden quiet felt like a miracle.

Then the crying resumed—softer now, broken by pauses to sip juice.

Fe turned to the babysitter. "Did anything scare him? Any loud noises?"

Shaking and drenched in sweat, Betty shook her head, her graying blond bob bouncing.

Fe sounded confident—like a physician taking charge. "When was the last time he ate? Could his blood sugar be crashing?"

Betty frowned, confused. "He had some cheese crackers not long ago."

Aidan let go of the straw and started crying again.

"What was he doing when the tantrum started?" Fe asked.

"I don't know …" Betty's voice quivered. "He started fussing as soon as I changed his clothes."

Fe's eyes lit up. "Is that a new shirt?"

Betty didn't answer, so Shawn did. "Yes. Why?"

Instead of replying, Fe slipped her hand inside the back of Aidan's shirt and tore something. She dropped a price tag to the ground, then repeated the motion. Soon she'd ripped out a second tag, a plastic fastener, and the laundry label.

She gently scratched the back of his neck with one hand while showing him the tags with the other. "All gone! All gone!"

Shawn watched in disbelief as Aidan stopped screaming and shifted to quiet sobs.

Fe kept her voice soft. "Itchy tag—all gone. Poor Aidan was itchy."

The boy's eyes met hers. Shawn froze, stunned, as Aidan held her gaze.

Then, between sniffles, the boy spoke.

"Itchy."

Shawn's breath caught.

Smiling, Fe nodded. "Itchy."

She lifted Aidan and settled him in the car seat. He didn't fight her.

Without looking at Shawn, she buckled the seat straps. "You'll want to check his shirts—cut off any tags and labels. They can really upset a child with sensory issues, especially one who can't tell you what's wrong. And always carry juice. Even if something else triggers the meltdown, low blood sugar or dehydration can make it worse."

Still dazed, Shawn brushed off his scrubs. "Thank you, Fe." He stared at her. "How did you figure out what was bothering him?"

"I saw him get upset when the paint smeared his fingers. That can mean he's hypersensitive to touch." She held the juice box to Aidan's mouth, encouraging another sip.

Shawn shook his head, still in awe. "But how did you teach him a new word in minutes? We've tried for months."

She shrugged. "When we care about something, we learn fast. And he *really* cared about that itchy tag. That's how I work. Step one is finding out what matters to the child—then use it."

Betty mumbled a shaky string of thanks.

Fe turned suddenly shy. She grabbed her purse from the ground, gave a small wave, and hurried to her car a few lanes down.

Shawn caught up and held her arm. "Wait!"

She stopped but didn't turn around, so he softly tugged her elbow until she faced him.

"Fe …" He hesitated. "Maybe we should start all over."

Tense, she straightened. "Shawn, you're not going to change my mind about taking this case. I'm a very stubborn woman."

He gave her his most disarming smile. "I bet I'm worse."

CHAPTER 10

F E WISHED THE EARTH WOULD OPEN AND SWALLOW HER WHOLE. On her back porch, Joy, Hope, and Allison were drilling her about Shawn.

"Wait. You'll be working with this guy for months—twice a day, including weekends?" Hope clapped. "Oh, you're *so* eating that sushi roll!"

Allison shot her a glare. "How on earth did he make you cave?"

"I made the mistake of listening to his offer," Fe said, panic stirring. "Then I tried to scare him off. I quoted him a ridiculous price, said we'd need to work weekends and holidays, and he'd have to pay double on those days. Not only did he agree without blinking, but he also insisted on adding a monthly fee for the right to call me during tantrums. He said Aidan would be my *concierge patient.*"

She took a large gulp of Hope's homemade sangria. "Then, he started chatting about me buying Rainbows. He got me talking about the down payment money I still need—and guess what he did!"

Allison's tone stayed flat as ever. "Fe, dogs all over town are howling to the shrill of your voice. Get to the point."

"He offered me an advance to cover the down payment!" She shuddered. "He said it's a no-interest loan. We'll deduct it from his sessions, and I'll reimburse him the difference—if any—when our contract ends." She dropped her head on the table. "Please give me a break, girls. Saying no was impossible. Forget the money, Shawn's boy is the cutest thing alive! And he has so much potential! Passing on Aidan's case would've been like … DaVinci turning down the perfect canvas!"

She wasn't kidding. She'd stayed up late, poring over Aidan's evaluations, dreaming about everything she could do for him.

The smell of frying pickled onions hit her. "Uh-oh!" She bit her lip. "Abuela's making *mangú.*"

"Yes!" Joy and Hope clapped.

"No!" Allison flinched. "She puts enough butter in that stuff to give me five pounds and a coronary—but I can't stop eating it!"

Fe slashed the air with her hand. "Add don't forget the fried salami and cheese she serves with it. As if my butt needed help expanding. Spanx can only do so much."

Stout, mocha-skinned Abuela emerged from the house, in her eternal gray dress and tight hair-bun. She greeted the guests with hugs and kisses, muttered something in Spanish, then slipped back into the kitchen.

Fe translated. "Sorry, Allison. She's counting on all three of you staying for dinner."

"Yes!" Hope pumped a fist.

"No!" Allison groaned. "Can you get me out of it? Tell her I have dinner plans later?"

Fe rose from her chair and stepped inside.

Her three-bedroom house was modest, overstuffed, and always bustling, despite the added space of the in-law suite. She weaved around the oversized furniture and first peeked into her bedroom to check on Gabriela.

Her five-year-old slept deeply, exhausted from the day's PT session. Fe gently nudged her closer to the wall and lifted the bed rail. Gabriela's limbs were still too weak to roll over—but Fe never stopped hoping she'd surprise her one day. She lingered a moment, marveling at her daughter's beautiful, peaceful face, then kissed her cheek.

Diego wasn't in his room. She found him on the front porch, deep in conversation with José, the panhandler, who was polishing off the lunch leftovers Abuela always saved for him.

Her son's serious expression looked too heavy for an eight-year-old.

"So, Mister José," Diego said, frowning, as he studied the man with quiet compassion. "Do you think that if you'd had a nicer dad, your life would've turned out different?"

José blinked, startled.

Fe swooped in. "Hey, honey." She kissed Diego's head. "Go wash up for dinner."

She gave José a wink—he looked relieved—and returned to the house.

In the kitchen, her mother and grandmother set the table, chattering with cousin Glennys in machine-gun Spanish—something about a twist in their telenovela. Fe passed along Allison's excuse and made a quick escape, avoiding the fate of the proverbial shot messenger. Few things upset Abuela more than someone turning down food.

Fe paused on the living room, her gaze drifting to the bedroom where Gabriela lay sleeping. Diego's voice still echoed in her head.

This family—Gabriela, Diego, Mami, Abuela—were her reason. Her why.

If the price for giving them a better life was working with Shawn … maybe it was worth it.

The instant she returned to the back porch, Allison pounced. "Fe, you can't work for Dr. McDevitt. You're terrible at keeping professional boundaries."

Fe crossed her arms with a huff. "I'm not!"

Allison gave her an icy once-over. "You host your clients for sleepovers, while your grandma makes flan for their parents."

One hand on her hip, Fe drew large circles in the air with the other. "Easing the parents' lives *is* part of my work." She threw both arms up. "Allison, you think you're the only one doing psychotherapy? A big part of what I do is handholding—walking parents through their fears, teaching them how to enjoy their kids. Most are overwhelmed by their child's challenges, some even disappointed. It's crucial that the kids don't see that as rejection."

Allison stood and grabbed Fe's flying hands. "Can you please not karate-chop us when you talk? Jeez, woman. You're one Latin stereotype after another."

Joy, quiet until then, said, "I can't believe you got Shawn to agree to attend every session. You have no idea how hard and how late he works. There's no way he'll stick to that."

That had been Fe's hope when she proposed it.

She paced. "I even told him we'd start Saturday morning—early. Figured that would scare him off, mess with his weekend sleep. But nope. He still didn't back off!"

"No need to panic." Allison raised a hand. "Did you sign a contract?"

"He's having his lawyer draft the loan terms and my fees. But we're starting Saturday in the meantime." Fe dropped herself back in her chair.

Allison stepped closer and held her forearms. "You already gave your professional word. I guess you can't back off now. But you need strong boundaries."

"How? What should I do?" Fe asked.

With pursed lips, Allison pointed at Fe's short denim skirt. "First, always dress professionally around him. Send a clear message—this is a work relationship."

Fe nodded. Easy. Dressing up was one of her specialties.

Joy added, "Doctors can discharge patients who don't follow their advice."

"Good point," Hope chimed in. "Add a termination clause. Say you can end the contract if he skips sessions, without penalty for you. And add another saying he must indemnify you if the contract ends because of something he did. That includes inappropriate behavior."

"Yes. That makes sense," Fe agreed. "Anything else?"

Allison narrowed her eyes. "For goodness' sake, keep your family away from him! You know what will happen the minute you turn your back. Your mother will start chatting with him, your grandma will start feeding him Hispanic food—and then your five hundred cousins will invite him to your loud holiday parties."

Fe started to nod, then stopped. "Wait. I *have* to bring Diego to the first teaching session. He's the inspirational story."

Allison sighed. "Fine. But that's it. After that, hide your relatives from him. Understood?"

"Yes! I can do this," Fe said, mostly to convince herself. "Yes, I can."

• • •

Friday at midday, Shawn stopped at the hospital doctor's lounge to squeeze in a flavorless lunch between clinic and rounds.

As he sat down, his mind drifted to Aidan's sessions, starting tomorrow. He hoped the pain would be worth it. His father nearly smacked him for offering so much money to a young speech therapist with none of Marla Desmond's credentials or experience.

He still couldn't decide what bothered him the most about Fe: the fact that she'd refused to date him, or what she'd said about physicians. He hadn't stopped thinking about it.

He glanced at his colleagues scattered around the lounge. Was medicine really stealing their joy of living?

Take his nemesis, Dr. Mark Jones, dictating notes at a nearby computer. With sunken eyes and pasty skin, he looked ghostlike. Tall and lanky, he'd shed even more weight since Shawn had treated him in the ICU months ago for a hypertensive crisis and a bleeding ulcer, both likely triggered by stress.

As if sensing Shawn's gaze, Jones looked up, then stood and walked over.

"Did you hear the news, McDevitt?" he asked. "Both ICU hospitalists walked out today."

"What?" Shawn blinked.

Jones nodded and slicked back his shaggy gray hair, which clashed with his dark, unruly eyebrows. "Until they hire replacements, you and I will split ICU duty every other week."

Jones seemed unperturbed—an empty-nester, three times divorced, with no life outside work. But Shawn dreaded it. ICU shifts felt like walking a minefield with your pockets full of gasoline and matches.

"I'm still on tonight," Jones added. "Your week starts tomorrow."

Shawn flinched. "Uh … I can't arrange childcare on such short notice. Would you mind if I started next week?"

Jones gave him a look of pure contempt. "It's not a big deal. Just get up an hour earlier and plan to be home an hour late. The eICU team takes over at ten p.m."

Yeah. That easy.

Maybe Jones, the seasoned veteran, could breeze through ICU rounds in two hours. Not Shawn. Too much of a perfectionist—and just obsessive enough—he always took much longer.

"Okay, I'll cover." As he turned. Jones rolled his eyes with a huff. "Welcome to another day in *Hell-away* Hospital."

A familiar deep voice rang out behind Shawn. "Oh, I'm sorry, McDevitt. You didn't get the email?" His former boss, Dr. Lee Stewarts—cardiothoracic surgeon and FirstHealth president—poured himself coffee. Despite his neutral tone, he seemed to fight back a smirk.

Unbelievable. Lee Stewarts *never* smiled.

It was striking how much the man had changed in just five years. Shawn remembered a fit, good-looking guy, a couple of decades older than him. Then, Stewart seemed to have aged overnight—half his hair gone, a hundred pounds gained, eyes puffy with exhaustion.

"No, I didn't get any email," Shawn said. "And if I had, I would've made it clear I'm not covering the unit that often."

"We sent several," Stewarts replied with studied calm. "Reddy and Ali gave notice two weeks ago. My secretary must've sent them to your FirstHealth email. She must've forgotten that you deserted us." With that, he turned and walked away.

Fuming, Shawn reached for his hand sanitizer and rubbed it in with short, angry strokes. Stewarts hadn't managed to sue him for leaving the group, but he'd found other ways to make him pay.

His movements slowed, the anger giving way to something deeper.

Was this his future?

Jones. Stewarts. Were they the cautionary tale?

Medicine draining their health, wrecking their marriages, stealing their youth?

Darn it, Fe. Why did you have to say it aloud?

CHAPTER 11

WHEN FE ARRIVED AT RAINBOWS CHILD SERVICES, SHAWN did a double take, thinking he'd stumbled onto a TV star. Then he recognized her—and his jaw dropped.

The bright red lipstick alone drew attention to her sensual lips. Her outfit looked like a sexy secretary costume: a spray-painted knit shirt tucked into a navy pencil skirt—tight and almost too short. A wide belt cinched her waist, exaggerating her curves, in full Jessica Rabbit style. The black pointy-toe stilettos—too high to be practical—belonged more on a dominatrix than a speech therapist.

As if that weren't enough, she'd paired it all with fishnet stockings.

Dr. McDevil jerked awake inside him. He half-expected her to shake out her hair and start dancing on the table, straight out of a cheap erotic film.

He was so stunned, it took him a moment to register she wasn't alone. A tan, green-eyed boy stood beside her. She sent him off with Aidan to the playroom while they talked.

She guided Shawn to a small classroom. A dozen chairs faced a dry-erase board on an easel. She gestured for him to sit, dropped Aidan's thick file on the table, and wrote something on the board.

Session #1 Never believe what a doctor tells you.

McDevil vanished. Shawn half-sighed, half-growled.

What was I thinking when I hired her?

It was bad enough having to watch her dress like a sexual fantasy. And now this?

She turned to him. "This is the first thing I need you to learn: never believe what a doctor tells you."

"Fe," he deadpanned, "*I* am a doctor."

She flinched and raised a hand. "I know. Just hang in there, would you?" She shifted her weight. "Doctors have to slap labels on people. That's how their brains are trained and the only way they can bill insurance companies—diagnosis codes."

He couldn't argue with that.

She pressed on. "The problem is, they forget that *words are magic spells*. Tell someone 'you're sick,' and of course, they'll feel sick. Tell a parent, 'your kid has a problem,' and they'll start obsessing about it. They'll even see issues that aren't there."

"Hang on!" Frowning, he raised a hand. "We don't just make stuff up. Our diagnoses are based on evidence."

She wagged a finger. "But you're human. And you filter that evidence through your own bias."

Losing his patience, he dug the hand sanitizer from his pocket and rubbed it in with force.

Fe turned toward to Aidan's reports and picked up a page. "For example. This evaluator saw Aidan wipe his hands over and over and called it compulsive behavior. But guess what …" She pointed at him, squeezing sanitizer into his palm. "I call that being his daddy's son."

He froze. "Wait. Are you saying *I* have compulsive tendencies?"

Okay, this isn't going to work.

She looked like she was reaching her limit too. "No, I'm saying, 'Give your kid the benefit of the doubt.' Don't let the so-called experts tell you what his destiny is—they don't know it either. You always have the right to refuse a label that limits you."

The master of diagnosis himself, he could barely hide the bitterness in his voice. "So, basically, you're saying, be in denial!"

Her face lit up with the same beautiful grin that had entranced him the first time they met. She stepped closer and placed her hand on his shoulder. "Exactly! Now you get it!"

He stared at her blankly. "That was supposed to be sarcastic."

"Yes, but it's the first step. Your first assignment is to practice *proactive denial.*" She flicked her hand. "We'll still work our asses off in therapy. But while we do, we'll refuse to see Aidan as the label they're trying to stick on him. We'll see him like a completely normal child who happens to have some quirks that need polishing."

Despite his earlier frustration, he couldn't refute her point.

She returned to the table and picked up the file. "Now, I've removed the summary of recommendations that will guide us. What's left here is the judgment. Just pages of evaluator-babble listing the 'not normal' behaviors that led to their diagnosis."

She motioned for him to follow her to a shredder in a corner. Once there, she placed the folder in his hands. "Go ahead. Shred it."

He stared at her, speechless.

When he didn't move, she pulled out the first page and fed it to the machine. It hummed and rumbled, reducing the page to strips. Then she fed another, and another.

She glanced back, smiling. "You're going to miss the fun unless you join in."

When she stepped aside, he moved forward and began adding pages. One after another, he fed them through. With every sheet destroyed, something inside him lightened. Hope swelled in his chest. By the time the last page vanished, he hovered on the edge of euphoria.

Her lips curved, satisfied. "Now, are you ready to go to the end of the world to prove the pessimists wrong?"

He couldn't help but smile as he nodded.

"Good. Follow us," she said, heading to the door. "We're going to the grocery store."

• • •

For the next hour, while strolling the aisles of Walmart, Fe showed Shawn how everything could be a game and a chance to teach Aidan words. Fruit became a lesson in size and color. Red, yellow, and green peppers turned into a sorting game. Aidan's favorite crackers, kept just out of reach, became a reward for interacting—and for learning the "give me" sign, flexing his fingers. Aidan sat so calmly in the cart that the session stretched longer than planned.

And to think, Shawn had assumed Fe just intended to run errands on the clock.

At the end of the session, they stood in line to pay for the crackers and a small treat for Fe's son, Diego—a matchbox car.

"I wanted you to learn that first," Fe said. "Some kids with sensory issues find a shopping cart soothing—the containment, the movement. Aidan clearly does. Taking him to the store like this is something simple you can do to help."

He nodded in awe. Maybe hiring her hadn't been such a bad idea after all.

Diego came running with a box in his hands. "Can I change my mind and get this instead?" He held up a toy microscope.

Shawn leaned down to look. "This says it's for kids twelve and up."

"That's never stopped this boy. He thinks he's forty." She tousled the boy's hair. "I guess maturing fast comes from having to care for his airhead mom."

The pride on her face hit Shawn with a pang of good envy.

Fe raised her hands in a half-shrug. "Sorry, *papi*. The deal was something under five dollars."

Diego rolled his eyes. "You pretend to pay me five miserable dollars for a whole morning as your assistant? That's way below minimum wage."

She leaned in with a playful smirk. "But paying you to work would be child labor. So, on second thought, I should pay you *nothing*, and we should say you did it just to help your beloved mom."

Diego's green eyes narrowed. "That's called extortion."

"No, it's called a motherly guilt trip. Get used to it." She kissed him on the cheek, and he wiped it off with a dramatic frown.

Shawn watched them with longing. Would his son ever speak in words that big—or any words? Would they ever have a conversation like that?

After she paid for the toy car, Fe passed the shopping cart with Aidan to Diego and let him go ahead.

"There's a reason I wanted you to meet Diego today," she said when the boys were out of earshot. "When Diego was two, a doctor labeled him with autism."

He halted, stunned.

She nodded. "The developmental pediatrician based the diagnosis mostly on a speech delay. Looking back, I think he was just confused—growing up in a bilingual household."

Shawn's pulse quickened, new possibilities rising in his chest. He glanced at Diego ahead of them, chatting easily with Aidan despite the boy's silence, then looked back at her.

"That's the rest of the story of how I ended up in this career." She gave a soft smile. "His speech therapist trained me on The Floortime Approach, so I could work with him. That inspired me to go back and finish my degree."

Shawn stood still, absorbing it. It was encouraging to think therapy could've made such a difference in Diego. But something else clicked.

"So that's what you meant by not trusting the doctors," he said. "In his case, the experts were wrong."

A flicker of sadness crossed her face, but she nodded without a word.

• • •

When Shawn arrived home with Aidan, his stomach clenched. Gina's white sedan sat in his driveway, blocking the garage door. The slight woman in navy scrubs and Crocs sat on the front step, waiting for him.

Please, not another scene in front of the neighbors.

The one time he'd called the police on her, she'd morphed into the most cooperative woman alive. He'd ended up looking like the problem. Charm and manipulation were part of the borderline package.

Unable to evade her, he parked and stepped out.

She approached him at once and got straight to the point. "Can you explain what the hell is going on?"

Gina seemed to have aged since the last time he saw her. Her face looked thinner. Worry lines framed her brown eyes, and dark roots streaked with gray grew in her blond hair.

"Hello, Gina."

"Why is the FBI asking to talk to me?" she snapped, ignoring his greeting. "Are you accusing me of trying to hurt you just because of our last argument? Are you using your connections to get me in trouble?"

At least she wasn't yelling. Yet.

He circled the car and unbuckled Aidan, who'd fallen asleep in his car seat. Draping the boy over one shoulder, he kept a cautious eye on Gina.

She followed him up the walkway. "For your information, I'm no longer interested in you. If you thought you needed police help—"

Her voice was rising, so he motioned for her to lower it. "No, this is about something else."

"Something else?" She studied him, frowning, then gasped. "Please don't tell me the threatening letters are back!"

Pointing at Aidan, he shushed her again.

She covered her trembling lips with one hand and clutched his knuckles with the other. "I thought we were free from that nightmare! What happened?"

He slipped his hand away under the pretense of repositioning Aidan. "I'd rather not talk about it here. And if you'll excuse me, I need to get him down for a nap."

She opened her mouth to protest, then reconsidered and nodded. "If there's anything I can do to help, or if you need a friend to vent to, please let me know."

She turned and walked to her car, glancing over her shoulder on the way.

She'd let him off easy this time. Amazing. She must've been taking her meds.

He considered her offer to help. As a phlebotomist, she could pick up rumors and overhear conversations better than anyone at the hospital. But no. Getting her involved would send the wrong message.

At her car, she opened the door, but didn't get in. She stood there, staring at him as he walked to the house.

Her gaze weighed on him as he climbed the front steps and opened the door. Once in, he rushed to lock and bolt the door behind him.

CHAPTER 12

M ARLA WRAPPED THE LAST PICTURE FRAME IN BUBBLE WRAP, placed it in the small box on her desk, then taped it shut. "Well, this is it. The office is now yours."

For the first time, Fe grasped the full weight of what she was taking on.

She'd closed on her commercial loan just last week. Now, she carried two hefty liabilities: the loan and the down payment money Shawn had advanced her. She was expected to repay him with work—an insane number of hours a week. Aidan's speech therapy sessions had started four weeks ago.

"Everything will be fine, Faith. You can do this," Marla said, tapping her shoulder.

Realizing she'd been biting her lip, Fe reached for her lipstick in her purse. Despite the confident front she showed her girlfriends, she feared the business might collapse once Marla left.

"We'll be okay," she finally said.

"Your usual good luck will prevail!" Marla grinned. "Just look at your last lucky shot! Signing Aidan McDevitt as a client is a cash cow! I still can't believe his father is trying to replicate the Smith Center's program with individual providers. Two thirty-minute speech therapy sessions a day, six days a week?"

"And that's just the beginning. We're supposed to increase the time as Aidan tolerates it. I'm also coordinating his OT and behavioral therapy."

"How do you manage that with your other clients?"

"We set the sessions so Dr. McDevitt can attend. One's at noon here at Rainbows, during his lunch break, and the other's at seven in the evening. Since that's outside my regular hours, he offered to bring Aidan to my house. On weekends, we meet at his home on Riverside."

"That's a lot to juggle with his schedule."

Four weeks in, Fe had given up hope he'd flunk his side of the deal and free her from the contract. "The man's maddeningly reliable. If he's even a minute late for the noon session, he shows up with fresh blood-stains on his scrubs, proof he got caught in an emergency. For the evening session, he's so punctual I could set my watch by him. Gosh! He showed up the day after the hurricane! We did the session by candle-light, under the dripping of my leaky roof!"

Marla squeezed Fe's arm. "They're in good hands with you." Then, she wrapped her in one last long hug.

Holding her former mentor's frail body, Fe blinked back tears.

Marla let go, gave Fe a final wink, and walked away carrying her box. It was the end of an era.

Fe stood in her new office, feeling she'd shrunk to the size of an ant. Nearly empty, with just a computer desk, a few chairs, and a bookcase, the place seemed gigantic. The shelves held mostly financial books—the same ones Shawn had reviewed before they signed their contract. She still found them a mystery.

That man was so smart, his brains should've spilled out of his skull. He'd barely glanced at the reports and summarized them in seconds, like he had scanners in his retinas. No wonder he grasped her week-end training sessions so quickly.

And as if her thoughts had summoned him, the front desk girl buzzed through the intercom, "Faith, Dr. McDevitt is here."

She headed toward the playroom, but paused at the observation niche. Through the one-way glass, she watched Shawn's interaction—or lack of it—with his son. Aidan busied himself filling and emptying toy bins. Shawn slumped in the corner chair, motionless, making no effort to play with him. Eeyore from Winnie-the-Pooh came to mind, a gray cloud hanging above his head. He stared at a toy car in his hands, as if he'd forgotten what to do with it.

"God forbid he smile," she muttered. "His stunning face might disintegrate."

• • •

Betty was back at work with a raise. At the end of the noon session at Rainbows, she took Aidan home, and Shawn returned to work. In an unusual break, a new patient cancelled, giving him time to grab lunch with Jay, visiting from Atlanta.

The health food restaurant near Holloway Hospital was decorated to resemble a rainforest. Large fake rocks framed an artificial water-fall on the wall. The moment Shawn arrived, he spotted his father at a table, chatting with Dr. Jones.

Shawn fought not to roll his eyes. A year ago, his father had been forced to retire after a mini-stroke that affected his right hand. But he refused to leave the hospital life behind. He kept himself busy by vol-unteering on bogus committees.

He considered texting Jay, asking to meet somewhere else, when he spotted him at a table with a woman.

Better said, smooching with a woman.

The curvaceous blonde sat on Jay's lap, kissing and groping him, not minding they were in a public place.

Shawn cringed, then cleared his throat. "I'd tell you to get a room, but the closest one available is the hospital morgue."

The woman giggled, but took her time sliding off Jay's lap.

"Can't wait to get together again." She nibbled at his neck. "Call me."

She straightened her dress and walked away without even acknowl-edging Shawn.

Yup. Shawn was used to plenty of women's attention—but stand-ing next to Jay and his ridiculous muscles, he'd resigned himself to invisibility.

"You're not going to introduce me to the lady?" he asked as Jay greeted him with a fist-bump.

Jay slumped into his chair, hazel eyes fixed on his iced tea. "I would—if I remembered her name."

Shawn gave him a blank stare. "Sometimes, you're disgusting."

"I swear I don't mean to be!" Jay sighed, staring at the ceiling. "You know I'm an incurable romantic! Do you think I enjoy women throwing themselves at me, then ditching me when the novelty wears off? It makes me feel so *used.*"

"Oh no!" Shawn pressed a hand to his chest, faking horror. "Poor Jay, cursed with a freaking perfect torso. He's so unlucky that women can't help jumping him." He rolled his eyes and took a seat.

"Wait a minute!" Jay frowned and pinched Shawn's waist.

"Hey!" Shawn slapped his hand away.

"You've lost weight! Are you working out without me?" Jay crossed his arms and pouted. "Have you been cheating on me?"

With a growl, Shawn looked heavenward. "No. I *never* have time to work out." He snatched the menu. "I'm just starving myself. I'm working harder than ever and never have time to eat."

"How come?"

"I'm on call half the time. Dr. Jones and I are taking turns covering the ICU. And the hospital's in no rush to hire new intensivists."

Shawn stood and headed for the salad bar. Jay followed him.

As he layered romaine and grilled chicken onto his plate, Shawn continued, "And on top of that, Aidan's speech therapist makes me attend all her sessions. That's why I've lost weight. To make the noon session, my lunch is whatever I can fit in one hand while driving with the other. Dinner's worse. Last night it was a spoonful of peanut butter and a handful of cereal." He added Caesar dressing and croutons.

Jay poked Shawn's upper arm, eyeing it beneath the sleeve of his scrubs. "You're sure you're not working out without me? Your arms look bigger."

"She makes me carry Aidan constantly. She says it helps us 'bond' and 'get him used to touch.' I don't mind, but he's no light baby anymore." He rubbed his sore shoulder. "She even made me cut his screen time. She's killing me."

They returned to their table.

"I'm spent. I can't use lunch to see hospital consults, so I have to start rounds earlier than ever. And I still have to go back to the hospital most nights after the evening session."

Setting his plate down, Jay clicked his tongue. "She sounds bossy. If I were you, I'd fire her."

"I can't. She's a genius," Shawn grumbled. "It's costing me an arm and a leg and every free minute I've got, but she's my best hope for Aidan."

"What does she do with your kid?"

Shawn sprinkled Parmesan over his salad. "She says kids learn faster when they're invested in what you're teaching them. We're looking for an 'anchor' for the sessions, a favorite toy or game that can hook Aidan's interest. Fe showed him every toy in the world, from a huge toy chest—cars, dolls, Lego. But no luck. The only thing that's caught his attention is a small furry bear he refused to give back. Fe let him take it home. But he doesn't play with it, just carries it around."

Jay's face lit up. "It sounds like fun! I'd love to play with all those toys!"

"It's bittersweet. It brings back memories of playing with my cousins." He tossed his salad, thoughtful. "Did you know they had to teach me how to play? I didn't even know how to throw a ball. My father was always too busy to play with me."

And speak of the Devil.

Seamus McDevitt had just noticed him and waved from his table.

Jay followed his gaze. "Isn't that your old man? Aren't you going to go say hello?"

Shawn mumbled, "It's awkward. He's my competitor's BFF."

Jay raised his eyebrows. "BFF?"

"Dr. Jones trained under him back at Harvard, before Dad left for

UMass. He rubs it in my face all the time that there's no finer physician than Mark Jones."

Seamus strolled over, trailed by Dr. Jones.

"Hey, Shawn! You never answered your mother's message about Friday dinner."

Shawn groaned. "I can't make it. I have Aidan's speech therapy every evening. And next week's worse; I start covering the unit *again*!" He gestured toward Jones. "I really hope the hospital hires new ICU doctors soon."

Something in the gleam of Jones's eyes made Shawn's stomach clench.

"You don't know? They won't. They're dragging their feet on purpose to push you out."

"What?" Shawn gaped at him.

A faint smile tugged at the corner of Jones' mouth. "Lee Stewarts told me. FirstHealth's goal is to make your life hell until you leave town. Having you on call half the time in the unit is just the first step."

CHAPTER 13

SHAWN'S VISITORS OFTEN RAVED ABOUT THE STUNNING VIEW from his lanai: his green yard and the Indian River merging into the infinity pool. But today he barely noticed it. His gaze locked on the woman across from him.

Shawn sat on his new porch swing, listening to Fe, who'd settled into a wicker patio chair. The hour-long weekend session had just ended. Betty had taken Aidan for a bath, and Diego—present today due to babysitting issues—had offered to help.

"You may've heard of sensory integration disorder," Fe said. "It means that kids with special needs have trouble organizing their senses input. That explains some of their daily challenges, like meltdowns at loud noises, intolerance to certain textures or movements …"

Shawn struggled to focus on the lesson. Maybe it was fatigue. But mostly, it was her.

Jaysus! She looks ready for TV cameras.

Lustrous hair, flawless makeup, sexy heels. Today's tangerine dress dipped a little too low at the neckline and was a little too tight in all the right places.

Every time she worked with Aidan, he indulged in the guilty pleasure of staring at her. In his mind, Carlos Santana's "Smooth" played as background music as she walked in, showcasing the day's outfit. Shawn knew nothing about fashion, but he knew her clothes danced right on the edge of unprofessional—without ever crossing it. The little devil inside him spent hours fantasizing about peeling them off.

Fe crossed her legs, and her skirt rode up. He swallowed hard.

"Sensory issues are just an amplified version of normal sensitivities," she continued, unaware of his rising temperature. "We're all different. My friend Allison, for example, hates touch. I call her the porcupine, because she's un-huggable. Me, on the other hand? I crave touch. I can't help reaching for people when I talk. I'm a hugger, I'm always offering back rubs to my girlfriends ..."

The image of her rubbing his back—and more—flooded his mind. Of course, he'd noticed the way she touched him while talking. She had no idea what it did to him.

Distracted, she licked her sensual lips, sending a bolt of electricity through his body. "We all crave or reject certain sensations. Some people love roller coasters and amusement park rides—vestibular stimulation—while others hate them. Others, like me, crave proprioceptive stimulation."

"Proprioception. That's nerve endings in joints, muscles, and tendons," he said, forcing his mind back to the session.

"Exactly!" She nodded. "When I was little, I found a heavy backpack soothing. I loved crawling through cramped spaces. Even now, I love the feeling of being squeezed or squished."

So, she craves being touched and enjoys being squished? I can arrange for that. Dr. McDevil handed him an image: him crushing her under his body weight, right there on the patio couch.

He wrestled his lusty thoughts down before they spilled across his face. "Okay."

She leaned forward, unaware that her deep V-neck revealed a hint of lacy bra. "Oral stimulation is a good example. You've seen people who chew gum nonstop? Or bite their pencils while studying? When I'm distracted, I tend to put things in my mouth—a thread, a pen cap."

McDevil pictured offering something to put in her mouth—his tongue.

Or maybe another piece of his anatomy.

That did it. He needed a cold shower.

"Shawn? Did I lose you?"

Her voice snapped him out of the fantasy.

"Sorry. Got distracted." He scrambled for an excuse. "Can't remember if I turned off my office lights yesterday."

Her usual spark dimmed. "Okay. Let's call it a day."

She rose and began gathering toys, tossing them into her travel bag. He forced his gaze elsewhere to avoid staring every time she bent down.

"Didn't you say you wanted my help reviewing Rainbows' financial reports?" He pointed at the binder she seemed to be avoiding.

She eyed the book like it might leap at her.

"You know, Fe," he said without thinking. "The books are more scared of you than you are of them."

She whipped her head toward him, gaping. "Did you just make a joke? Is that even possible?"

He frowned. "What are you talking about?"

"Honestly, doc, I'm starting to wonder if you're allergic to smiling." Tilting her head, she squinted. "Or, maybe, your inner system is pressurized, like a plane cabin. If you crack a smile, you'll explode. Or deflate … or something."

When he didn't react, she turned serious. "No, really. I'm worried about your expressions around Aidan. Kids on the spectrum are highly visual. He definitely is. And seeing that face of … stoicism can't be good for him."

Shawn knew he hadn't been himself lately. He'd been anxious and depressed. But who wasn't in today's world? The truth was, the so-called *stoic face* was a mask to conceal his lustful thoughts around her.

Instead of answering, he asked, "Fe, how come you dress up so much for the sessions—even on weekends?"

Maybe if you toned it down, I'd stop having erotic daydreams about you.

A subtle tremor passed through her fingers as she tossed a toy truck in her bag. Her pitch rose. "What are you talking about?" She gestured up and down her body. "This is me *toning it down*. You don't want to see the full, unrestrained version of the 'Latin Diva.'" She lowered to scoop up building blocks. "If I could have it my way, I'd wear a tiara to work."

He stared at her blankly. "A tiara?"

"Yes! The only reason I don't is to avoid making others feel under-dressed." The sparkle in her eyes showed she was joking.

"Don't get me wrong. You look …" he hesitated, "… very nice." He cleared his throat. "All I am saying is, it must be uncomfortable to work in clothes and shoes that barely allow you to move."

"Uncomfortable?" She waved the thought away. "Honey, the day you see me not dressed up and wearing makeup, check my pulse—I might be dead." She focused back on the toys. "I'll never forget my *quinces* party. It was the first time I was allowed to wear makeup and heels. Fifteen girls and boys from school and I spent weeks rehearsing this cool dance." She paused. "Only we practiced in sneakers, and then the day of the event, I had to perform in heels. My feet blistered so badly, I spent a week in bed, icing them."

"That's terrible," he offered.

"Are you kidding? It was the happiest day of my life!"

He ventured a guess. "Because you got to wear makeup and heels for the first time?"

She looked around, then leaned in, as if about to confess a secret. Hand on her chest, she sighed, then whispered, "And because I got to wear a tiara."

He suppressed a chuckle.

"Which leads me to my point." She fixed her eyes on him. "Honey, some things in life are worth excruciating pain." She snapped her fingers, popped her hip, and swept her hand around her outfit. "Gorgeous fashion is one of them."

He couldn't help cracking up.

She clapped once and pointed at him. "I knew I hadn't imagined it that day! You *do* know how to laugh!"

He stopped abruptly, surprised she was acknowledging that magical morning they'd agreed to never mention again.

But before he could reply, Diego burst onto the porch, clutching her cell phone.

"Mom! Dad wants to talk to you."

Every muscle in her body tensed. Frowning, she asked the boy a question with her eyes.

He put the device on mute and whispered, "I'm sorry. He called from a number I couldn't recognize, and I picked up." Diego's eyes pleaded. "He wants me to go to his house next weekend, but I'm supposed to go to Miss Hope's hotel with Tommy, Liz, and Ella. Please get me out of it … please!"

Fe mumbled an apology, took the phone, and walked away out of earshot.

Shawn watched her pace the pool deck, jaw tight, phone pressed to her ear. Her scowl deepened, and her shoulders sagged as if she were shrinking by the second.

It hurt to see that man still had so much power over her.

His curiosity about Fe's ex stirred again. The guy must've been extraordinary to get a woman like her. Handsome, successful, rich—probably more attractive than him. Until now, Shawn had resisted the urge to dig around. But now the temptation crept back.

When she returned, all the joy had drained from her face. She handed the phone to Diego. "I'll talk to Hope and see if they can reschedule the trip."

Diego balled a fist and let out a grunt. "Why does he only show up when I have fun plans?" He sighed and shuffled away.

Fe turned to Shawn. Her cheerful spark had vanished, giving way to weary resignation.

"Let's not review the books today. I just want to go home."

• • •

Later that day, Fe sat with her friends at Joy's beach house, where she'd brought Diego for the kids' weekly playdate.

"Is there anything else wrong, Fe?" Joy rubbed Fe's arm with gentle concern from her beach chair. "Usually, it doesn't take you this long to bounce back from one of your ex's calls."

Talking to her ex always dragged Fe down. But today her gloomy mood had another source.

Reclining in her chair, Fe accepted a glass of lemonade from Allison. "Working with Shawn is draining."

"Oh, yes." Hope perked up. "How is it going with—"

"Hope, if you make one more reference to sushi rolls, I swear I'm slapping you," Fe warned.

Giggling, Hope tapped her hand. "I wasn't going to say anything." She bit her lip, clearly struggling to hold back. Then, she blurted, "Think you'll keep your panties on much longer?"

Fe shot her the stink eye. "Please! I'd need to be crazy to be interested in a guy like him." She removed her dangling amber earrings and dropped them in her purse. "I know his type—a workaholic, uptight, humorless. He has a black cloud of depression always hovering above him."

Joy stirred her lemonade, her dark eyes steady on Fe. "Sweetie, don't be too hard on him. Shawn has a great sense of humor. He's just dealing with some rough stuff right now."

"He's obsessed with work." Fe took a long sip. "You wouldn't believe it! We were sitting in his yard, perfect weather, beautiful river view … and he's thinking about *his office lights!*"

Allison struck her trademark pose, hand on chin—her signal that a psychological dissection was coming. "I see. Your female pride is bruised that he's not showing more interest."

Fe waved her off. But the truth was, she'd put extra effort into her appearance, hoping for some reaction. What kind? She didn't even know. But it still stung that he didn't seem to notice.

Maybe he is over me.

"I'm sure Aidan will be fine," she said. "But Shawn needs to chill. He needs to stop fretting so much and just sit on the floor to play with his kid. His stress can't be good for Aidan."

"Stop." Allison shot her a warning look. "It's not your job to cheer this guy up."

Hope snickered. "I know something you can do that would cheer you *both* up."

Ignoring her, Allison went on. "So don't even think to enroll your family in another 'help a parent' operation. You don't need another nudge to get entangled with Shawn."

Fe looked heavenward. "Relax, Allison. I'm not going to do anything!"

Unless it's absolutely necessary.

CHAPTER 14

NOW OCTOBER, THE FBI HAD MADE NO PROGRESS IN TARA'S case. The hate letters kept arriving in Shawn's mailbox. The hospital still showed no urgency in hiring new ICU physicians. Shawn's exhaustion reached unprecedented levels, and his weight loss now teetered between flattering and troublesome.

The worst part: he'd started to doubt Aidan's therapy was worth it.

If he'd ever seen progress—in eye contact, tantrums, or interest in connection—it had vanished. Aidan seemed to be regressing.

At Fe's house, Shawn perched, tense, on the red velvet armchair, clasping the armrests. Aidan had been impossible today. He'd hit Fe over and over, even scratched her and kicked her. She seemed unfazed, but panic rose in Shawn.

He was starting to lose hope in his child.

This therapy is a waste of time.

Dark visions of the future swarmed in his mind.

Across the room, Fe lay on the floor beside Aidan, pretending to throw a tantrum. She scowled at Shawn as she got to her feet.

She rattled off something in rapid Spanish to Diego. Shawn caught only one word: *Abuela.*

Diego slipped out. A few moments later, a short, sturdy older woman arrived. Fe spoke to her in Spanish and gestured for Shawn to follow her outside.

He obeyed, still unsure what this was about.

The warm night air buzzed with crickets. Despite the darkness, moonlight cut across her face, revealing her stern expression.

"Shawn, you have to stop that."

He stared at her, confused. "Stop what?"

"*That!*" She pointed at his face. "Every night you come to the sessions with that … mask of suffering. Aidan's a highly visual kid. He sees that. Worse, *he feels that.*"

Shawn half-sighed, half-grunted. "What am I supposed to do? Put on a happy face? Pretend I'm thrilled my son is *abnormal* and may never amount to anything in life?"

She gasped, then jabbed a finger into his chest. "Never! Don't you *ever* use that word to refer to Aidan, or any kid with special needs!"

He grabbed her finger. "Abnormal. Special needs … what difference does it make? Bottom line, he's not fine! And it's killing me to see it!"

She pulled free. Her scowl softened. "This is good. Use your words."

"What?" Shawn frowned.

"You need to let the fear and anger out, so you don't dump them on *him* every day. Keep talking! Say it! It's hard to have a kid with special needs, isn't it?"

A hand clenched around Shawn's heart. The distant rumble of suppressed feelings rattled him, and then the dam broke.

"Yes! It sucks!" he burst out. "It sucks that my kid throws a tantrum when I try to hug him! It sucks that he bangs balls together when I'm trying to play catch! That I can't have a picnic or a pizza night with him, because he refuses to eat anything that's not dry and crispy!"

She clapped once and flexed her fingers, palms up. "This is great! Keep it coming!"

He turned and punched the mango tree with the edge of his fist. "It sucks, damn it!" he shouted. "I had so many dreams for this child! Dreams of watching him graduate from college, succeed in a career, get married, give me grandchildren …"

His chest heaved. Breathing hurt. He fought the tears clawing at him.

Fe said nothing, just nodded. Her face serene, without pity or judgment. When his outburst quieted and no more words came, she stepped forward and wrapped her arms around him.

He tensed, startled. She was hugging him, rubbing his back, rocking him gently.

"It's okay. It's okay," she murmured.

Inside him, sadness expanded like a cloud of smoke and peaked as physical pain. Just when he thought he'd lose the battle with the tears, the surge began to subside.

The warmth of her body felt delicious, her rocking motion and touch soothing. He hugged her, breathing in the almond-scented conditioner in her hair, drawing in her calm. A strange peace settled over him.

They remained silent, arms wrapped around each other.

Finally, she spoke in a soft voice. "I know exactly how you feel. It sucks. But do you know what? Our children were not born to fulfill our dreams."

Her words seeped in slowly.

She stepped back out of his arms and met his eyes. "Even if Aidan had been a typical kid, no child ever lives up to all their parents' expectations. Especially not a physician's kid! You overachievers lose sight of what's average."

It was true. His own father had never been satisfied with anything he'd achieved.

She stroked his arm. "A kid with special needs forcing you to gain perspective? That might be the biggest blessing that could've happened to you."

"What do you know about that?" he muttered, voice rough. "Your kid is perfect! Diego's speech delay is ancient history." He ran his fingers through his hair, trying to regain his composure. "And the worst part is the guilt. I can't stop beating myself up ... because it's all my fault."

She didn't respond. Just waited, questioning him with her eyes.

Thoughts fell into place as he gave them voice. "I did everything I could to stop Tara from drinking and using drugs while she was pregnant. But I can't stop wondering if it was already too late. Maybe the damage had already been done before I found out. Maybe she still managed to sneak away despite my precautions." The burning surged back in his chest. He swallowed against it. "That's the story of my life. No matter how hard I try, it's never enough."

"Don't do that to yourself!" she murmured, pulling him into another tight hug. "It's not your fault."

This time, the sweet reprieve didn't last. Fe let go, took his hand, and led him away. But instead of heading back inside, she brought him to a small guesthouse tucked at the back of the yard.

The suite held only a bedroom and a bathroom. Near the bed, Diego sat on a chair watching TV.

"You can go now, *papi*. Thanks for helping Abuela," Fe said.

Diego mumbled, "You're welcome," and stood. As he moved, he revealed a second child—a little girl in a wheelchair near the TV.

Shawn stilled. He'd never met Fe's younger daughter before. He'd assumed she'd already been asleep during Aidan's night sessions.

When the girl spotted her mother, her lips curved faintly. Despite her blank expression, her eyes sparkled with love. She was beautiful— honey-brown eyes, tan skin, thick lips, like Fe's—but something was off. She slumped at an angle in the chair. Her legs and arms were thin and frail, almost without muscle.

Aidan's speech delay suddenly felt like nothing in comparison.

Fe opened a drawer in the nightstand and pulled out two tiny nail polish bottles. The girl lit up, wiggling with excitement in her seat.

"Pink or red?" Fe asked.

"B-bink, p-please."

The answer caught Shawn off guard. He hadn't expected vanity— or such clear delight. She grinned as her mother shook the polish, her body buzzing with anticipation.

Fe sat on the bed, beside the wheelchair, and began painting the girl's nails. "This is my daughter, Gabriela," she said. "I've obsessed about what I did wrong, what I could've done differently. I've never touched a cigarette or a drug in my life. I didn't drink a single drop of alcohol while pregnant. I was religious about my prenatal care. I even made sure to have my kids in my early twenties, thinking I'd avoid playing the genetic lottery." She glanced at him. "Turns out, nothing's a guarantee."

Shawn struggled to find words. "What ... what happened to her?"

"Her official diagnosis is cerebral palsy. You know I reject labels." She caressed the girl's hair. "The pediatrician blamed the neurologist. The neurologist blamed the OB. The OB blamed *her*, saying it must be something genetic." She stopped. "For a while I blamed myself ... and sometimes I blamed everyone around me."

Silence fell.

Joy's words from months ago surfaced in Shawn's mind. *The man wasn't even there when his daughter was born.*

And, just like that, he knew. Fe had always wondered if things would've been different if her physician husband had been at her side instead of at work.

The reasons for her mistrust of doctors and the obstacles standing between him and her heart became painfully clear.

"But that's not the point," she said. "I stopped looking for culprits a long time ago. All I care about is helping her get better." Fe looked at Gabriela with deep tenderness. "People think she's my cross, but she's truly my blessing. She's the sweetest soul you'll ever meet. My little angel."

Gabriela sat surprisingly still, watching her mother paint her little nails.

"I'm convinced kids with special needs are our spiritual masters," Fe went on. "They come here to teach us strength. Gabriela's lesson for me is the same one I know Aidan's here to teach you: unconditional love."

She kissed Gabriela's cheek, and the girl giggled, as if tickled.

"My girl may never go to medical school like her father. For her, I may have to adjust my definition of success ... But I'll never tie my love for her to any achievement. And I'll always be her champion. No doctor, or so-called expert, gets to tell me what she can and cannot do one day."

Fe finished the polish. Gabriela beamed at her nails and slowly shook her hands to dry them.

"D-dank you," she said.

"You're welcome."

Smiling, Fe gestured toward her daughter. "Some people say that I'm wasting my time, that she'll never get up from that wheelchair and have a normal life. I dare to disagree. The last word is not spoken until the day we die."

Swallowing hard, he nodded.

Fe stood and turned to Shawn. Her firm tone reminded him of a coach. "So now *you* answer this question: What do you want for Aidan?"

In the past, he would've said he wanted Aidan to become a doctor, like him. Now he replied, "I just want him to be successful at *something*."

She shook her head. "Wrong answer. Try again."

He looked at her, confused.

Leaning closer, she placed a hand on his shoulder. "The right answer is: I want him to be *happy*."

He processed the words, then frowned. "Fe … no one in this world is truly happy."

Her smile widened. "I disagree."

Before he could reply, she turned away, pushing Gabriela's wheelchair toward the door.

He followed her across the yard, down the cobblestone path back to the house. Her words still spun in his mind when they reached the living room.

Fe's hand on his arm brought him back to the present.

"Shawn, look!" she whispered, tilting her head.

He followed her gaze. Aidan snuggled on Abuela's lap, eyes fixed on Diego, who sat cross-legged on the floor, tapping a drum with one hand and shaking two gourd maracas with the other. To Shawn's astonishment, Aidan giggled and held eye contact with Diego longer than he ever had before.

They stood watching in silence as Aidan rocked to the rhythm, mesmerized. It was the longest he'd ever stayed engaged with anything.

Suddenly, Aidan leaped off Abuela's lap, swiped the maracas from Diego, and shook them with delight.

Shawn moved to scold him, but Fe held his arm to stop him.

"Wait!" she said. "We'll work on manners later. I think we just stumbled onto our anchor."

She didn't let go of his arm right away. He dared to cover her fingers with his free hand—and she didn't pull back.

They stood holding hands in the living room, watching Aidan jump and shake the maracas, while Abuela hummed a tune, and Diego beat the drum.

CHAPTER 15

Discovering Aidan's love for music and rhythm was a quantum leap.

In the two weeks that followed, Fe, Shawn, Diego, and Abuela mixed therapy sessions with musical parades marching through the house, playing makeshift instruments to the music on Fe's phone.

Fe made drums out of empty milk jugs and turned glass jars filled with screws into maracas. Shawn had rushed to buy all sorts of musical toys. But Aidan ignored them, preferring the homemade ones.

"What do you want? I don't understand." Sitting on the floor with him, Fe played dumb, so he would tell her what he wanted from the locked toy chest.

"Maraca," Aidan replied.

Fe, Diego, and Gabriela—now often included in the sessions—burst into cheers.

Fe rewarded him with the gourd maraca and glanced at the time on her phone: past eight. The sessions were running longer now that Aidan enjoyed them more.

"Okay. All done today," she said. "Time to clean up."

Like every night, Aidan rushed to gather the toys and toss them in the trunk, humming the "Clean Up" song.

Fe watched him with a mix of tenderness and amusement. He was a smart kid, like his dad, and thrived on routines.

She stood and turned to Shawn, asleep on the couch.

If Aidan impressed her with his progress, Shawn did just as much. Months into the therapy, and despite all her doubts, he hadn't missed a single appointment. But it couldn't have been easy. His recent weight loss and constant exhaustion worried her.

"Should we wake him up?" Diego asked.

"What do you think, Aidan, should we wake up Daddy?"

Holding his tiny, furry bear, Aidan stared at his father in silence. Fe suspected that his refusal to learn the word *Dad* came from a place of unresolved anger. Maybe the little boy could sense and resented that his father wished he were different.

"Maybe he'll wake up on his own," she said to Diego. "Let's feed Aidan dinner and get him ready for bed."

Fe had heard horror stories about Aidan being a picky eater and fighting bedtime. But to her surprise, he cooperated fully. He ate Abuela's rice and beans without protest, and offered no resistance when they bathed him, dressed him in Diego's old pajamas, and brushed his teeth with a new toothbrush.

It helped that an interesting bond was forming between Aidan and Fe's grandmother. Fe wasn't surprised. Abuela's nurturing energy overcame any language barrier.

After Aidan fell asleep on his own in Diego's bed, Fe went to check on Shawn, still deep in sleep. He'd been on call all weekend. His wrinkled scrubs and thickening stubble hinted that he hadn't had time to shower—or sleep or eat much either. She worried about his health.

She placed a hand on his forehead and whispered, "Shawn? Aidan's in bed. Do you want to go home?"

No answer.

Resigned, she crossed to the linen closet and gathered supplies. She slid a pillow under his head and draped a blanket over him, tucking it gently around him. He didn't even stir.

Seeing him like that—so vulnerable, so spent—touched something deep in her. He clearly needed help.

A flicker of defiance sparked inside her against Allison's advice. Maybe she *should* bring Aidan for a sleepover so Shawn could catch up on rest. Maybe she could let Abuela feed Shawn now and then.

She longed to kiss his head, like she always did with her kids. But she stopped herself. Instead, she placed a hand on his forehead and whispered, "*Qué descances.* Rest well."

Then, she scribbled a note telling him to leave Aidan with them and to send the nanny for him tomorrow and quietly retired to her room.

• • •

Midmorning, Shawn rushed out of the ICU to meet Richard in the hospital cafeteria. His schedule didn't allow him to leave the hospital for long.

As he crossed the long hallways, a FaceTime call came in from Betty.

"Dr. McDevitt, you have to see this!" She flipped the camera, showing Aidan, still at Fe's house. He sat calmly at Fe's dining table, wedged between Diego and Gabriela, munching on plantain chips.

"Who is this child?" Betty asked. "Not the same kid who kicked me in the shin yesterday!"

A grin tugged at Shawn's lips. "The little stinker's doing it on purpose. He behaves like an angel over there, so Fe thinks I'm exaggerating."

"Dee-ego, no!" Gabriela muttered from her wheelchair as Diego stole a chip from Aidan's plate.

Shawn chuckled. That little girl had turned out to be much sharper than he'd assumed at first.

Noticing the theft, Aidan smacked Diego on the arm. A slap war started among the boys.

So much for behaving.

Gabriela grunted in exasperation, "D-dats n-not o-okay! S-say you're s-sorry!"

Yup, Gabriela was "The Politeness Police." Shawn had been amused to learn she scolded the other kids in her speech therapy group if they forgot to say "please" or "thank you."

"Thanks, Betty. I've got to run."

He ended the call and kept walking.

A shift had begun in him since meeting Gabriela. Until recently, Fe had lived in his mind as a black-and-white figure—a pendulum swinging from irresistible to infuriating. But lately, she seemed more real—another parent, just trying to make sense of life's setbacks.

Gabriela no longer needed a feeding tube and could speak in full phrases—a testament to Fe's dedication. He clearly had to stay away from Fe. He could find someone to sleep with anywhere. But nowhere in the world would he find another speech therapist like her for his son.

Then why couldn't he stop thinking about her today?

The night before, he'd been too exhausted to move or speak, but he'd felt everything. Her whisper. Her hand on his forehead. The gentleness with which she tucked a blanket around him. Waking up to that memory—and the note she left—had warmed something in him he didn't realize had gone cold.

As he arrived at the cafeteria, he forced himself back to earth. He was no longer the starstruck dreamer who'd once kissed Fe. He knew now they both carried too much baggage to have a real shot at something lasting.

After exchanging quick greetings, Richard led him to a corner table where Keith, his case agent, waited.

Keith, straightening the lapels of his pinstripe suit, said, "We have news. We analyzed the letters and confirmed they came from two different sources."

"What?" Shawn leaned forward.

"The styles and misspellings don't always match." Richard slid a few copies toward him. The highlighted line in one read, *You're doomed.* In another: *Your a murderer.* Others said, *You should've escaped* and *I could of killed you.*

"The letters you received the first year all seem to have come from the same person." Keith rubbed his blond stubble. "We're assuming it's a relative of one of your patients, since they accuse you of being a murderer—say you caused them to lose something they loved, and now deserve to pay." He shifted to a second pile. "Then, partway through year two, a new pattern shows up. Different tone. Cleaner grammar. More vague threats."

Shawn pondered on it. "So, there's more than one person behind them?"

"Either that," Keith said, "or your original stalker found an accomplice—someone else with a reason to scare you. Or hurt you."

"Do we have any idea who's stalker number one?"

"We're reviewing the medical records of every patient you cared for in the past five years who had a poor outcome," Richard replied. "It's taking forever. I knew you were a workaholic, but, jeez, it's worse than I thought!"

Shawn grimaced. "I wish I could help narrow the list, but I tend to forget the details of my cases when someone dies. It's a self-defense mechanism against the guilt. What about stalker number two?"

"We have a couple of theories. A source should be joining us ..." Keith checked his silver watch, then scanned the room. "... right about now."

"Hello."

Gina's voice startled Shawn. He shot a look at Richard, silently questioning him.

Richard said, "Miss Hill recently came to us with a tip I'd like her to repeat in front of you."

Shawn didn't like this. He didn't trust Gina.

Dressed in navy scrubs, she greeted each man at the table with a polite handshake. That unsettled him even more. Gina acting reasonable was like waiting for the other shoe to drop.

She pulled out a chair and addressed him directly. "I overheard a conversation between Dr. Jones and Dr. Stewarts. Dr. Jones said that since you left FirstHealth and opened your own office, his practice has taken a hit. He claims that independent physicians who used to refer patients to him are now sending them to you."

Shawn may not trust her, but he knew that was true. "The man is so busy he can hardly manage. Is he going to complain because some patients don't want to wait weeks to see him?"

"What's the story with this Dr. Jones?" Richard asked.

"He is an institution in town. His practice is affiliated with Mayo Clinic, so it functions like a semi-academic center. He runs clinical trials, has rotating med students … When I first tried to leave FirstHealth, I approached him about becoming his partner, and he turned me down. No wonder he's not thrilled my practice is growing at his expense."

"But that's not all I heard," Gina cut in. "I knew Dr. Jones didn't like you. What surprised me was hearing Dr. Lee Stewarts say horrible things about you."

Richard turned to Shawn. "He's the FirstHealth president trying to sue you, right? You mentioned you two never got along. What's the story there?"

Shawn rolled up the sleeves of the white coat he wore over his scrubs. "Stewarts and I butted heads over a case—yelled at each other in the ICU shortly after I moved here. We've clashed a few more times since. It didn't help that he and my father were competing for the same patients before Dad retired."

After taking a few more notes, Richard and Keith wrapped up and left.

Shawn was about to follow when Gina caught his arm. Tensing, he braced for whichever version of her might show up.

"Shawn, I need to apologize for how I've been acting."

He released the breath he'd been holding. "It's okay. I appreciate you're trying to help."

Her large brown eyes searched his. "Realizing your safety might be at risk has put things in perspective. I sought help. I'm on a new mood stabilizer." She hesitated. "And … I'm seeing someone else."

He hoped she meant it. He'd begged her to seek help more times than he could count before finally ending things. And he genuinely wanted her to move on.

But her eyes clung to his, full of longing. Before she could say more, he dipped his head and walked away.

Her gaze weighed heavy on his back the whole way out.

• • •

After the noon therapy session, Shawn stopped by the physicians' lounge for lunch—and immediately regretted it.

His father sat at a table, amiably chatting with his nemesis, Dr. Jones. Worse, someone else had joined them: Shawn's former boss, Lee Stewarts. A triple dose of eyesore.

"The Devil take me," Shawn mumbled, borrowing his grandma's favorite curse. Would his father ever embrace retirement and stop showing up at the hospital?

Stewarts and Jones stood and shook hands with Seamus McDevitt, then walked away. As Stewarts passed, his eyes met Shawn's. The barely veiled contempt in them sent a chill down Shawn's spine.

Seamus approached and patted him on the back. "Hey, I used to dislike Stewarts when we were competitors, but actually, he's a nice guy. Did you know his son is also a cardiothoracic surgeon?" His eyes glowed with awe.

Figures. Shawn's father had never hidden his disappointment that Shawn hadn't followed in his footsteps. In Seamus McDevitt's eyes, pulmonologists were the support staff for cardiothoracic surgeons.

"Lee said he plans to leave his son his patients when he retires. They share a medical office, isn't that great? That man must be so proud of his son."

As opposed to you, right?

Shawn headed toward the fridge, hoping to cut the conversation short.

"Hey, I talked to Emery," Seamus called after him.

Uh-oh. I know where this is going.

Emery, his younger cousin, had once been his junior resident.

"They just made her program director at University of Miami," his father went on. "She's in charge of all the pulmonary fellows. Isn't that amazing?"

He mumbled an agreement.

"And," Seamus added, "she said they might be hiring at the ICU department there."

Shawn opened the fridge and scanned the shelves for something to eat, hoping his silence would be hint enough.

His father didn't take it. "Wouldn't you love to see your name on research papers? To be tied to a teaching institution? Like Mark Jones. That guy's got the best of both worlds. He makes private practice money, but still gets the perks of academia."

"I'm too busy right now. I couldn't possibly add research or teaching."

Seamus huffed in frustration. "Son, there are things in a man's career worth some sacrifice. You may be content with your little solo practice now, but one day you'll want your name on something bigger."

Shawn froze.

Some *sacrifice*? Little *solo practice*?

His appetite vanished, and he shut the fridge door.

Nothing I ever do is good enough for you. Is it, Dad?

Without a word, he gestured goodbye and walked out.

CHAPTER 16

L ATELY, AIDAN WAS NOT ONLY TOLERATING LONGER SESSIONS—HE was demanding them. Shawn had offered his swimming pool for Gabriela's physical therapy, which gave Fe a chance to squeeze in more time with Aidan on the weekend.

As Gabriela's session ended, Fe stayed on the lawn beside the pool, working with Aidan and Shawn. She was trying to get them to play catch with a soft rubber ball while music played from her phone through a Bluetooth speaker.

Each time Aidan dropped the ball, Shawn flinched—his perfectionism stung by what he saw as failure. Aidan seemed to pick up on it and started dropping the ball on purpose. The tension between them had been simmering for months, and now it crackled in the air between every toss.

Fe had an idea. When it was her turn to toss the ball, she launched it straight at Shawn's head.

"Hey!" he protested, startled.

Aidan burst into giggles, proving Fe's theory right.

She turned to Shawn. "This is going to seem weird, but please bear with me. I promise there's a point."

Ignoring his questioning look, she walked to the pile of pool toys and grabbed two foam noodles. Handing one to the little boy, she whispered, "Go, Aidan! Hit Daddy!"

To show him how, she whacked Shawn with her noodle again and again.

Aidan followed her lead, laughing as he joined the ambush.

"Hey!" Shawn protested between chuckles, ducking and waving his arms to shield himself.

Fe passed her noodle to him, and soon, father and son were deep in a foam-sword duel, both laughing. She stood back watching, delighted.

Then Aidan surprised them. He ran to the toy pile and grabbed two more foam noodles, handing one to Fe and one to Diego, who was lounging by the pool.

"Hit Daddy," he said, repeating Fe's words.

Fe and Shawn froze and exchanged a look. It was the first time Aidan had ever used that word for him.

She obliged, smacking Shawn with her noodle, and signaled Diego to join in.

"What? Three against one?" Shawn gasped, faking outrage. "I'll teach you all a lesson!"

He marched to the toy pile, grabbed a water soaker, and sprayed Aidan, who squealed with laughter. Then he turned to Fe with a wicked grin.

She held up a hand. "I just did my hair. Don't you dare!"

Shawn blasted her anyway.

Fe shrieked and took off across the lawn while Shawn chased her, Aidan giggling uncontrollably behind them.

"I want to soak Mom too!" Diego yelled.

Talk about repressed aggression. Fe had never heard such a maniacal guffaw from her son as he snatched a soaker and joined the attack.

Trying to redirect the chaos, she raised a hand against the streams of water hitting her face. "Hey, Aidan! Let's push Daddy into the pool!"

Shawn stiffened. Aidan seemed to understand the instructions and charged at him. It took Fe a moment to convince Diego to drop the water gun and join her. The three of them grabbed Shawn by the arms and shirt, dragging him toward the pool. He was stronger than she expected—if not for the laughter robbing him of his strength, they'd never have made progress.

From the lanai, Gabriela, wrapped in a towel and seated in her wheelchair, scolded them in her slurred speech. "Dat's n-not o-okay! Y-you all b-behave!"

Her physical therapist wheeled her inside as she kept protesting. Abuela followed, calling the other kids in Spanish to come have a snack.

At last, the three managed to push Shawn into the pool. He hit the water with a splash, and Aidan clapped and cheered. Diego whooped before both boys dashed into the house behind Gabriela and Abuela.

Still roaring with laughter, Shawn resurfaced and climbed the pool steps, dripping wet.

"You're in so much trouble, missy!" he said between chuckles.

Then, he grabbed the hem of his wet T-shirt and peeled it off.

Fe forgot how to breathe. If she had once thought he was getting too skinny, she'd been wrong. He wasn't bulky, but his lean waist emphasized the breadth of his shoulders. Taut and well-defined muscles shaped his chest and upper arms. His shorts teetered low on his hips, soaked and heavy.

And the mischievous glint in his eyes made it clear she was about to pay.

Fe backed away, then bolted.

He prowled after her like a wolf on the hunt. She sprinted across the lawn, flashing back to the morning they met—only now she had no head start and no running shoes. He caught her. His arms wrapped around her waist and lifted her clean off the ground.

She squirmed and kicked, breathless. "Put me down!"

But he was already at the edge of the pool.

She grabbed the belt loops of his shorts and yanked. "If you throw me in, you're coming with me."

Still holding her tight, his voice dropped. "I'm already wet."

And then he jumped, taking her with him.

She barely managed a breath before the water swallowed them both. Her first thought was, *My hair is ruined!*

His arms remained clamped around her waist as they plunged

and sank. It felt like forever before their feet touched the bottom. He bent his knees and launched them upward, aiming for the shallow end.

They broke the surface together, gasping for air. She squealed in protest while he laughed and coughed.

And then it hit her—he hadn't let go. Their bodies pressed impossibly close.

For a moment, the rest of the world vanished. His chest, bare and slick, flattened against her breasts. Her fingers clung to the waistband of his shorts. His hands gripped her hips. His thigh slipped between hers.

His laughter died.

Then her breath caught when she felt it: his arousal against her.

A bolt of desire shot through her. The water between her legs turned molten.

An eternity passed in that suspended moment, their bodies locked, breath mingling, until the sound of children's shrieks from the house snapped the spell.

He reacted first, letting go only to take her hand and guide her up the steps and out of the pool.

She clung to his hand like a lifeline, battling to leave her forbidden desires behind, in the waters' cool embrace.

CHAPTER 17

EVER SINCE THE MOMENT AT THE POOL A FEW DAYS AGO, Shawn had made an effort to keep his distance from Fe. But after a taste of holding her in his arms, his body ached for more.

The image of Fe soaking wet—her shirt see-through, skirt clinging to every curve—was burned into his mind. The memory of her roaming his house in nothing but his bathrobe, waiting for her clothes to dry, lingered like perfume. And the awareness that she'd been naked in his guest bathroom, showering that day, haunted him in his nights of loneliness.

He needed someone to blast him with a hose.

Or he needed to find himself a girlfriend. *STAT.*

He was rushing to the doctor's lounge to grab a bite when Gina intercepted him.

"Hello, Shawn. I have some news." She hesitated.

He slowed so she could catch up. "Something about the hate letters?"

"No. Something personal." She halted and caught his arm, forcing him to stop. "Shawn, my boyfriend, Paul, and I had a fight. He accused me of not being over you. Of using him to make you jealous." She paused. "And I couldn't deny it."

He didn't answer.

Her expression held both nostalgia and a silent plea. "This is taking me by surprise. I thought I was over you. I guess I was wrong."

After all the drama she'd brought into his life, he'd be a fool to reopen that door. He frowned. "I'm sorry if I unknowingly affected your relationship. But there's nothing I can do."

He tried to walk away, but she clung to his arm. "I know I was just a rebound for you. But you were the most wonderful season of my life. If you ever need anything—*anything*—don't hesitate to call me."

Her gaze dropped to his mouth, and she licked her lips. When her eyes met his again, they blazed with desire. For a flash, that reckless spark—the one that had drawn him in back then—flared between them.

She breathed the words. "I know how to take care of you."

The invitation couldn't have been clearer. For a moment, Shawn's body ached with physical need. "How about Paul?" he muttered.

"If you say one word, he's history."

Damn.

Shawn felt like a starving man being offered stale, moldy bread. He'd never consider it in his right mind, but standards could drop drastically in desperate times.

Gently, he slid his arm from her grasp. "Have a nice day."

He walked away. Half of him cried, begging to turn back; the other half knew he'd made the right call.

What a morning! In just the first hour of his shift, he'd admitted three crashing patients to the unit. It was Halloween, and he'd been up since four, rounding by five so he could finish early enough to take Aidan trick-or-treating. Fe had cancelled their evening session to spend the holiday with her kids.

Shawn made it to the lounge too late; the hot food had just been cleared. He sighed, resigned to another day surviving on fruit and yogurt—if the fridge still had any left.

Today, the doctors' lounge was more of an eyesore than usual. Besides his father, still insisting on hanging around the hospital, someone else had joined the crowd. For a second, Shawn thought he was seeing double. Then he realized Stewarts had brought his son to work. The resemblance was uncanny.

In matching scrubs, the two could've been mirror images. The son seemed to be about Shawn's age, but already showed signs of aging poorly—puffy eyes and a receding hairline. Youth still softened his features, but Shawn would bet his bronchoscope that in a few years the guy's looks would catch up to his dad's.

Before Shawn could reach the fridge, Seamus approached him. "Hey, Shawn. Your mother says she's upset you haven't called lately."

"I'll try. We've been slammed in the unit," he said.

"Please do. She's feeling bad we're spending Thanksgiving in Boston with your sister and the baby," Seamus paused. "You don't mind, right? You didn't have any plans for your birthday anyway, did you?"

Shawn shook his head. This year his birthday fell on Black Friday. He was used to people forgetting it, buried in Thanksgiving preparations or early Christmas shopping—another example of his innate bad luck. "I'll be fine. Just send Mary my love."

As Seamus walked off, Stewarts approached with his son. Shawn worked to keep his face neutral. "Hello, Lee."

"I wanted to introduce my son, Liam," Stewarts said, forcing a smile. "Did you hear Mendez is retiring? Our staff would be happy to take on your referrals."

So the man who'd once made his life hell was now playing nice in exchange for patients. Typical. But medical politics in this town were too delicate for honesty.

"Sure," Shawn lied. "I'll keep it in mind." He turned toward the soda machine.

Liam followed him, still grinning like they were old friends. "How's your family, McDevitt? My father mentioned you've got a little one?"

Damn it, now he's trying to bond with me. "Yes, he's three."

Liam nodded. "I've got two boys—a two-year-old with my

current wife and an eight-year-old son with my ex." His smile faltered. After a beat, his voice thinned with reluctance and shame. "And a daughter."

Shawn froze.

In a flash, his brain registered the man's pointy nose and the small gap between his teeth. He'd seen those before.

On Diego.

A jolt shot through him as realization struck.

Liam Stewarts was Fe's ex.

CHAPTER 18

AT JOY'S HOUSE, PREPARING FOR TRICK-OR-TREATING, FE TRIED to persuade Gabriela to wear the final piece of her *Frozen* costume.

"Please, honey! Leave it on. You look beautiful!" Fe said, adjusting the braided strawberry-blond wig. Then she pointed to her own blue gown and platinum wig. "See? You're Anna, and I'm Elsa!"

Like every other attempt, Gabriela announced her refusal with a shake of the head, sending the wig to the floor. People who saw her from a distance—frail and vulnerable—had no idea how strong-willed she could be.

"So how are things going at work?" Joy asked while helping one of her four-year-old twins into a Superman costume. With feathery wings and a pink satin toga, Joy looked every bit the part of an angel—inside and out.

Fe bent to retrieve the wig, avoiding Joy's eyes. "Not that well. Working with Shawn is … awkward."

She wished she could confide in Joy about the growing tension with Shawn. But Hope and her step-kids were due any minute, and the last thing Fe wanted was to add Hope to that conversation.

Joy zipped up Edward's costume, and the blond twin leaped onto the sofa. His older brother Arthur, dressed as the Hulk and absorbed in a video game, let out a startled yelp as the cushions bounced.

Joy turned to help the second twin, dark-haired Alex, into his Ironman suit. "Are you considering quitting?"

Fe tried once more to settle the wig on Gabriela's head—no luck.

"I can't end the contract early without paying a penalty. I'm making progress on the loan, so it's just a matter of hanging in there a few more months. And Aidan is doing so well!"

Giving up on the wig, she rummaged through her purse for scissors. "But he takes up so much of my day, I haven't had time to book new clients. I don't want to end up under-booked when he transitions to the Smith Center." She snipped the two braids off the wig. "Maybe I should start spreading his sessions among other therapists. It would ease the transition and free me to take new clients."

And lessen the temptation that is Shawn.

She used clips to attach a braid to each side of Gabriela's head. The girl offered a weak but satisfied smile—she clearly approved the compromise.

As if the conversation had summoned him, a text from Shawn lit up Fe's phone.

Help. 911

"Excuse me, Joy."

She texted back, *Are you guys okay?*

The phone rang with a FaceTime request. The moment she answered, Aidan's screams pierced through the speaker. A second later, Shawn's face appeared on the broken screen—hair disheveled, eyes wild with exhaustion.

"I'm about to jump through the window!" he said, skipping the greetings. "Aidan's been stuck in a tantrum for forty-five minutes."

Fe removed her wig and stepped onto the back porch for better reception. "Did you go through the usual checklist?"

"No loud noises. No tags. No signs he's thirsty or has a low blood sugar."

"What set him off?"

"He melted down when I put on his Spider-man mask. I took it off right away, but he's still screaming!" He groaned. "I thought he was making progress, but he's going backward!"

Experienced with special needs kids, she was used to the roller coaster—two steps forward, one step back.

She steadied her voice and sent calm through the screen. "Shawn, take a deep breath."

He did.

She stepped back inside and grabbed her purse.

"I'm on my way."

• • •

Shawn hadn't been kidding. By the time he texted Fe, he was seriously considering bolting and leaving Aidan on his own. He'd scrubbed his hands so many times they burned—under stress, he always overused hand sanitizer.

The doorbell rang ten minutes after Fe hung up. When he opened the door, she stepped in, followed by a small parade. Diego, then Gabriela in her wheelchair, pushed by a youthful middle-aged woman, Shawn guessed was Fe's mother. She looked like the exact midpoint between stocky, dark-skinned Abuela and curvy, lighter-skinned Fe. Trailing behind them, in a Superman costume, came a kid Shawn vaguely recognized as one of Joy's twins.

How had they all fit in Fe's tiny car?

Shawn barely registered Fe's Disney Princess dress. A part of him felt grateful she hadn't gone for a sexy costume.

"Where is he?" she asked, cool as a bomb-squad expert on a SWAT team.

He led her up the wide, wrought iron staircase to Aidan's room, where car, truck, and train stickers covered the walls. Aidan lay exactly where Shawn had left him, on the carpet, crying.

Fe knelt beside him and began whispering questions while gently peeling off the Spider-man costume. Aidan resisted every step, but she managed to strip him down to his Mickey Mouse briefs.

"He's stuck in a loop," she said, standing. "The polyester irritated his skin, but now he can't calm down. Help me get him in the tub."

Angling to avoid a kick to the face, Shawn scooped up the screaming boy and carried him to the jet tub in his master bath.

Fe followed, turned on the cold water, and sprayed Aidan. He shrieked louder for a few seconds, then stopped, stunned.

The silence felt like a miracle.

Shawn slumped against the glass shower door and slid down to the floor. "Thank you, Fe!"

"You're welcome." She adjusted the water temperature, warming it up.

Aidan settled in, content to soak. Fe joined Shawn on the spotless floor, her back resting beside his against the glass.

After a few moments of glorious silence—only the sound of running water filling the room—she asked, "Were you guys heading out to trick-or-treat?"

"The plans have obviously been cancelled," he grumbled.

She touched his elbow. "Don't cancel the plans! He's calming down."

"He's beaten me up enough for one day. I don't have the energy."

Her hand stroked his arm. *Damn it!* She still had no idea what her touch did to him.

"Come on, join us. We're on our way to trick-or-treat in Joy's neighborhood. It's more affluent than mine, so people give better treats. And the houses are closer together than in yours—less walking, more candy."

He shook his head. "With my luck, we'll get run over by a truck."

She gasped and slapped his arm.

"Ouch!" he complained, rubbing the sore spot. "What was that for?"

Hands on her hips, she tilted her head. "What are you talking about? You don't have bad luck!"

"Yes, I do!" he snapped. "And don't give me that *luck of the Irish* speech, because it's never helped me."

He growled, pressing his fingers to his temples. "The whole town gossips that I'm a murderer. My old medical group wants to sue me. My ex-boss is making my life hell. And I have this pressure on me for the rest of my life to provide for a child who may never be able to take care of himself."

She stared at him, lips trembling.

And it hit him: Fe had far more reasons than he did to feel unlucky.

For a moment, she just stood there, frozen, as if weighing whether to laugh, cry, or scream. Then something hardened in her eyes.

She rose slowly, her voice hollow, as if something inside her had finally given up. "I quit."

Then she turned and stormed out.

Startled, Shawn scrambled to his feet and chased after her.

• • •

Fe could barely make sense of her own blinding fury as she stumbled out of the master bedroom. She just wanted to go home and forget she'd ever met Shawn. But when she scanned the house from the top of the stairs, her mother and the kids were nowhere in sight. Diego had likely made himself at home and taken them to the pool lanai.

Before she could decide where to go, Shawn caught up and grabbed her arm. "Wait! Wait! I shouldn't have said that."

A wet, slippery three-year-old in nothing but Mickey Mouse briefs, bolted past. Shawn lunged, caught him, and picked him up before continuing.

"I can't believe you dare say you have bad luck!" Fe threw her arms in the air, seething. "Have you looked around? You live in a freaking mansion!"

With Aidan soaking through his scrubs, he shot her a glare. "Please! I'm so sick of people acting like having money means I'm not allowed to complain. I *do* have bad luck."

"No, you don't!"

His voice rose. "Do you know the odds of condoms *and* implantable birth control both failing? One in a hundred thousand." He pointed at Aidan, who squirmed and kicked in his arms. "*This* is a one-in-a-hundred-thousand kid!"

Fe straightened. "Do you know the odds of being born rich, good-looking, American, white-male, with all your organs—and then getting into med school?"

He blinked. "No."

"Well … I don't know either. But I bet you they're even lower!"

Fe's mother appeared in the living room holding a towel. With surprising agility, she rushed up the stairs and took Aidan from Shawn's arms.

Somewhere in the back of her mind, Fe knew her mother had never been in this house and didn't know where Aidan's things were. That didn't stop her. She marched toward the room with car stickers on the door, chatting in Spanish. To everyone's surprise, Aidan let her take him without protest.

Fe headed to the stairs, but Shawn grabbed her arm, stopping her. "I'm sorry, but you're the one who says we have to 'use our words.' So, don't get mad when I tell the truth. My whole life's been a string of stupid bad luck since the day I was born." He shook a finger. "They even spelled my feckin' name wrong on the birth certificate. If that's not bad luck—"

"You should be glad they did," Fe cut in. "If they'd spelled your name 'S-E-A-N,' half the people I know would've called you '*Seen*.'" She turned toward the stairs.

He followed her and grasped her elbow.

"I'm done," she snapped, yanking free and stomping down the steps. "I've had it with your pouting and your sulking, and your endless complaining about the *one thing* going wrong, when you've got a million reasons to be thankful."

He passed her and planted himself at the bottom step, blocking her path. "Name one that's not money!"

She flung her arms wide. "*You can see!* Have you looked out your window? You have a freaking river view!"

"That's nothing," he mumbled. "My father never lets me forget Dr. Jones has an *ocean* view."

Fe nearly choked. "Oh, my word, Shawn. Do you know what view I've got? My fat, old, hairy neighbor in a wife-beater!"

"You rejected me!"

His voice thundered, reverberating in the vast foyer. Fe recoiled, his words landing like a slap.

He trembled subtly. "It was the first time in years I'd felt genuinely drawn to someone. And you—you had to be the only woman in the world who thinks being a doctor is worse than being a terrorist."

They stared at each other in thick silence. His chest rose and fell fast and uneven.

Her anger faded as she moved down the last step and faced him. Her voice softened. "You're right. You do need to use your words. Go ahead, Shawn. I can take it."

Gripping the iron railing, he eased down onto the steps.

"What hurts me the most," he said, "is that the morning we met, I could've sworn there was something real between us. And now I can't trust my instincts anymore."

She said nothing, but she understood exactly what he meant.

"I gave everything I had to show you we could be good together." He looked up at her, eyes heavy. "But it was not enough. Nothing I do is ever enough."

Her chest tightening, she muttered, "Shawn, my turning you down was never about you."

He scoffed. "No, it's always been about your ex." He paused, licking his lips as if weighing whether to go on. "I met him at the hospital today. I wish I'd had the guts to punch him in the face for hurting you, for robbing *me* of any chance with you."

Ah. So that was why Shawn had spiraled back into the memory of her rejection.

He kept going. "I still can't believe the man who broke *you* is the son of the man trying to break *me*. Must be genetic—being an a-hole. Just like his father, he's a jerk. A tool. An … evil … eejit, gobshit, gombeen —" He stopped, trying to grab a hold of himself. "And it sucks. It sucks to know a couple of bullies can hold your future and mine in their fists. Like we don't already have enough to worry about."

Fe hesitated, then sat beside him on the step. At least the topic had shifted from her rejection to the Stewarts. "I hear you, but take it from me. Dwelling on it hurts *you* more than it hurts *them*." She paused. "Shawn, don't give them more power than they have by calling them 'evil.' In my experience, most bullies are either kids in pain or children with special needs."

He looked at her, curious now.

Encouraged, she went on, "Liam bullies me because he can't use his words and tell me he was hurt when I left him. Lee, his father, bullies you because he never learned any other way to interact with people. What I mean is, don't let the haters beat you. Most of the time they're nothing more than scared kids with special needs, staring at something they don't understand, and swinging at it."

Shawn didn't answer for a long time.

Finally, he muttered, "Why do you have to be so deep and kind, damn it? You're like … a freaking Yoda. But you're giving pearls to swine." He rubbed his temples. "All I'm doing while you talk is picturing what's under your clothes—" He winced and bit his lip.

She gawked at him.

His eyes darted away. Clearing his throat, he raked a hand through his hair. "I have no idea why I said that out loud, except that my brain isn't working. I've been up since four, and all I've eaten today is a handful of cheese crackers and two sips of PediaSure." He faced her again. "But if you're quitting anyway, what's the point of being appropriate? Yes, that's how unenlightened I am. I spend our teaching sessions imagining your underwear."

She stared at him, stunned, her thoughts scattering, her body flushing with heat.

"I have some apple juice in my purse," she blurted. "Could you use a boost in your blood sugar?"

He nodded, wordless.

With unsteady hands, she reached for her purse, still at the base of the stairs, and pulled out the juice box. She punctured it with the straw and handed it over.

As he sipped in silence, she lifted her hands in exasperation. "Shawn! You can't be walking around without any food or sleep. How can you take care of so many patients and have no clue how to care for yourself?" She dropped her hands with a sigh. "And you wonder why Aidan is throwing tantrums? He's absorbing your stress! Honey, you need to stop worrying so much."

Still, no answer. He looked so much like his son right now, a sulking three-year-old, stuck in a loop, unable to snap out of his mood. She wished she could plop him in a tub and shock him with cold water too. How else could she shake him?

An idea hit her.

"Shawn, this is going to sound weird. But please bear with me. I swear I have a point." Gathering her long skirt, she gripped the iron scrollwork on the banister and stood. "I'm going to show you my underwear."

CHAPTER 19

I F Fe HAD MUTATED INTO A GREEN ALIEN, SHAWN COULDN'T HAVE been more shocked.

"What?"

"I said, I'm going to show you my underwear."

She reached for the hem of her princess gown just as his apple juice went down the wrong pipe. He choked and coughed. "Wait! Wait! I didn't mean—"

"Hang in there." She cut in. "It's for your own good." And then she hiked up her skirt.

Pulse racing, his first impulse was to squeeze his eyes shut.

"Come on, Shawn. You need to see this."

He cracked one eyelid open. Beneath her skirt and petticoat—lifted to mid-thighs—she wore what looked like … bike shorts? He opened both eyes. Flesh-colored spandex shorts reached to just above her knees.

She grinned, clearly proud. "It's called Spanx shape-wear. The best friend of a pear-shaped woman." She dropped the hem, letting the puffy skirt fall back into place. "Did you really think my waist was that narrow after two kids and my grandma's cooking?"

Too rattled to respond, he just blinked at her.

Beaming, she pointed to her chest. "And this push-up bra is so padded you could stuff a couch with it. My point is"—she sat back beside him again and placed a hand on his shoulder.—"see? You've been torturing yourself over nothing. There's nothing sexy under here. That's what we humans do. We invent imaginary worlds just to suffer in them. And in the end, things are never as big or as scary as we make them out to be." Her honey eyes softened on him. "Same goes for your fears about the future."

As he took in the words, a strange relief washed over him. "I actually do feel better. Thank you."

"Good. Welcome back." She tapped his shoulder. "Ready for the next step?"

"Does it involve taking off more clothes?"

She shook her head.

"Will it make you change your mind about quitting?"

She tilted her head, considering it. "I'll keep working with Aidan. But I'm warning you: I'll be bossier than ever. I'm going to make you chill and stop stressing him out, even if I have to beat you up in the process. Understood?"

Slowly, he nodded.

"If you can't take breaks to eat at work, then pack a lunch the night before," she said, ticking off her fingers. "You need a second babysitter some nights so you can catch up on sleep. And also so you can do something relaxing now and then. What happened to bike riding?"

"Aidan's scared of my bike cart and won't ride with me, " he said. "And I feel guilty about leaving him with a sitter when I'm finally off."

She raised both hands. "Then can't someone watch him early, before he wakes up, so you can ride at dawn?"

He sipped his juice. "I have to be at work before dawn—I can't round at noon anymore, because of our sessions."

Guilt flickered across her face. "I'm sorry. I hadn't realized I'd been stretching you too thin." She pondered for a moment, then stood. "We'll figure something out. Now, let's go trick-or-treating."

He slumped and let out a long breath. "Anything but that. I'm drained."

She offered her hand, a smirk slipping past her stern expression. "It's not a suggestion. It's an order."

Resigned, but smiling, he took her hand and rose.

• • •

Despite Shawn's predictions, Halloween was a success.

Fe had Aidan trade costumes with Joy's twin—Superman didn't need a mask. She dressed him in the costume over his long cotton pajamas, shielding his skin from the scratchy polyester.

They all squeezed into Shawn's SUV and drove to Joy's neighborhood. Seeing so many children, Aidan quickly grasped that something special was happening. Delighted, he mimicked the other kids, ringing bells, and collecting candy—even if, picky as he was, he'd likely never eat it. Within an hour, he'd already learned the words "trick-or-treat."

Now, as Fe confiscated some of Diego's candy to ration out over the next few weeks, she spotted Shawn on Joy's front porch. His gaze locked on Aidan, who giggled, running around with the other kids, his Superman cape fluttering behind him. Adoration and melancholy mingled in Shawn's expression.

She walked toward him.

"Fe, remember the day you said some things are worth excruciating pain?" he asked.

She nodded.

Still watching his son, he muttered, "I'm starting to get it."

A hand clasped her heart. Without taking his eyes off Aidan, he wrapped his arm around her shoulders. The gesture felt so natural, she circled his waist with hers and drew him closer.

They stood there, side by side, leaning into each other and watching the kids play.

• • •

Gabriela and Fe's mother tired first, but when Fe suggested going home, Aidan burst into tears. Hyper from the candy he'd finally tasted, he wasn't ready to stop trick-or-treating.

To keep the peace, Shawn sent Gabriela and her grandma home in an Uber, so Diego and Fe could stay longer. They invited Joy and her kids to join them and rode in Shawn's SUV to his neighborhood. There, houses were so far apart that the last round would surely wear the kids out.

As they strolled behind the children, Shawn and Fe swapped magic stories from Irish and Dominican folklore—from leprechauns to *ciguapas.*

When Joy took over the final shift following the boys, Fe and Shawn rested on the front porch rockers.

"I dread seeing you guys leave," Shawn said. "After all the sugar he's had, I'm not looking forward to putting Aidan to bed. Or entertaining him next weekend, when you're out of town on that hotel trip."

His tired eyes seemed to plead for help.

"Would you like Aidan to stay with us tonight so you can catch up on sleep?"

"In fact, I was about to suggest your whole family move in and never leave, but that might help too."

She laughed, but he seemed serious.

"Let us keep him, we'll call it a sleepover with Diego. It's easier than convincing him it's time to say goodbye. And we've already established that you've been up since four and haven't had a decent meal."

"I'm doing better with that." He pulled a mini-Hershey bar from his scrubs pocket and unwrapped it. "I'm on my third pound of Halloween candy. I'm having the weirdest sugar high right now—I see a halo of light around everything." Chewing on the chocolate, he squinted. "Even you."

She tittered, "It's not your eyes. I've been told I have a radiant aura."

She rose from the rocking chair to fetch her purse and keys.

He followed her inside. "This has been the longest day of my life. Is this really the same day when I started rounds at five in the morning? When three patients crashed in one hour? When Aidan had his tantrum—when you showed me your underwear?"

"About that … here's an idea." She winked. "Tomorrow we blame it on the sugar high and pretend it never happened."

She stole a mini-Twix from Diego's bag on the kitchen counter.

"No, that was great. It cured me of my obsession with your clothes." Licking chocolate from his fingers, he gave her a once-over. "Which is why I feel comfortable asking: why that costume? Why not something more your style? You know ... sexy?"

"I always dress like a Disney princess for Halloween." She beamed, pointing at her head. "It's my one chance a year to wear a tiara."

Chuckling, he grabbed another chocolate. "That explains it."

She peeled off her blond wig, and they nibbled their candy in silence.

"Yes, you *should* let us take Aidan tonight," she said, loosening her hair with her fingers. "Actually, how about we bring him to the hotel this weekend? I'm sure you can use a few bike rides and a couple of nights of deep sleep."

His expression flickered between hope and fear. "You mean ... sending him away the whole weekend ... and not going with him? Can you handle him?"

She shrugged. "Nine kids, ten kids—what's the difference? And how about we make your bike rides a priority?" She considered it. "If you submit proof that you're riding in the mornings, I'll exempt you from the noon session."

His face lit up briefly, then clouded with guilt. "Would it make me a bad father if I admitted that sounds amazing?"

"No, it wouldn't."

Gratitude glowed in his expression. He exhaled. "I could kiss you right now."

She laughed. "After showing you my ugly underwear, I think we're officially cured of that temptation."

He stilled. His gaze darkened, sliding from her eyes to her lips.

The chill of the air-conditioning faded beneath the weight of shared awareness. After a day of nonstop chaos, the silence of the empty kitchen settled around them like a held breath.

"Maybe we should test it, see if the magic is really gone," he said. "It would be for my own good too."

Time stalled. The room felt smaller, warmer.

Despite herself, her eyes dropped to his mouth.

"Is that the Halloween candy talking?" she asked, her voice low, unfamiliar.

He didn't move. "We did say we can blame it on the sugar high and pretend nothing happened."

He leaned in slowly, as if offering her time to retreat.

She didn't.

She waited, breath caught, rooted in place.

Then his lips captured hers.

A thrill rippled through her body, sharp and electric. She trembled at the déjà vú—his soft, warm lips against hers, the instinctive parting of her own, welcoming him in. He tasted of chocolate—mood-altering, addictive. He felt exquisite. The silk of his inner lips softer than the velvet of his tongue.

His arms wrapped around her waist, drawing her close. Her hands threaded through his hair, stroking, anchoring, deepening the kiss. She wasn't sure when or how he'd backed her into the wall.

It was as if no time had passed. They were back at that park, leaning against her car door—kissing and savoring, longing and seeking, licking and sucking, feasting at each other's mouths. As his hands skimmed her curves, heat surged through her, and she arched, aching to fuse with him.

With a small shudder, he broke away and dropped his hands.

Panting, they stared at each other.

"You were right. The magic is gone," he deadpanned. His wrecked voice, wide eyes, and ragged breath said otherwise.

"Bua-bua."

Aidan's voice yanked them out of the moment. He tugged on Fe's skirt, claiming her attention.

Face burning, she cleared her throat and stepped away, widening the space between her and Shawn.

Aidan turned to his dad, repeating, "Bua-bua," and pulled at his hand.

"What is he saying?" Shawn asked.

Fe's thoughts still swirled, slow to organize. At last, she reacted. Familiar with Shawn's kitchen, she retrieved a glass from one of the cabinets. "The night he stayed at my house, I noticed he used 'bua-bua' to ask for water. Just like kids in Spanish-speaking homes. It's a toddler version of *agua* or *abua*." She filled the glass from the fridge and handed it to Aidan, who drank it in large gulps. "Did he ever have a Hispanic babysitter?"

Only then did she notice Shawn—still as stone, shoulders stiff.

"Everything okay, Shawn?" she asked.

He didn't answer right away. His hands shook. "Excuse me." He swallowed hard. "I have to call the FBI."

CHAPTER 20

THANK GOD RICHARD WAS ALREADY ON HIS WAY TO PICK UP Joy and the kids from Shawn's house. Now sitting with him, Shawn said, "It took me a while to connect the dots. Aidan refuses to eat anything I cook, but he ate Hispanic food at Fe's house. He ignores Betty, but listens to Fe's mother and grandmother, who speak Spanish. And now with him saying '*bua-bua*' for water, it makes sense. Whoever took care of him during the year he was missing must've been Hispanic."

Richard rubbed his jaw. "And your friend Jay said the man seen leaving with your wife was dark-skinned. It tracks." He jotted a few notes. "I'll call Keith. We'll focus on Hispanic names on the list of patients with poor outcomes. I'll let you know when we have something for you or your friend."

Aidan ran through the living room, giggling, with Diego close behind. Richard nodded toward them. "Your son seems to be doing better with speech. If we come up with suspects, would you be willing to let us show him some pictures?"

Shawn sank into his chair with a heavy sigh. "I've done everything I can to spare Aidan the trauma of reliving what happened."

"Our best shot is finding out what he remembers," Richard insisted. "Actually, I'd recommend we take him to Gainesville. Let him walk around the area where he was found and see if anything rings a bell."

When Shawn didn't respond, Richard gave his shoulder a quick pat. "Think about it." His phone buzzed, and he glanced at the screen. "Work call. I'll take it outside."

As Richard stepped out, Fe approached, hesitant. Her restless hands and furrowed brow carried a weight of worry.

Shawn motioned for her to come closer. "You okay?"

She took his hand, eyes glistening.

"Fe, are you about to cry?"

She shook her head. "I *never* cry. It ruins the makeup." She sniffled, then she wrapped her fingers around his. "Shawn, why didn't you tell me about the threatening letters?" Her voice and lips quivered. "You could be in danger! You need security!"

He drew her into his arms to soothe her trembling. "It's all empty threats. Whoever's behind them is just trying to scare me. Hiring security in the past was a waste."

Pulling back, she frowned. "Can you be less stubborn?" She sighed. "If there's a chance that Aidan could help the FBI, you should let him. He's stronger than you think. And he's such a bright child. I believe he can do it."

"Maybe I'm the one who's scared of going back to Georgia," he confessed with a helpless shrug. Even now, he still had nightmares about identifying Tara's body in that Gainesville morgue.

Fe studied him, like she had more to say.

"Anything else?" he asked.

"Shawn, if Aidan spent the last year with a Spanish speaking caregiver, do you know what that means?"

His mind, dulled by exhaustion and tangled emotions, drew a blank. "What?"

She tightened the grip on his hand, holding his gaze. "His speech delay may not be real."

He staggered back as if a gust of wind had hit him.

"The experts may've been wrong about his diagnosis," she said gently. "He could just be a regular, quirky kid confused in a bilingual household—like Diego."

Hope surged, wild and overwhelming … but quickly gave way to fear. What if she was wrong? What if he let himself believe again, only to crash in disappointment?

• • •

Allison hadn't answered Fe's emergency text yet, but she couldn't wait. After leaving the kids in bed, and her mother and grandma tucked in front of the TV watching their telenovela, Fe headed to Allison's condo.

After ringing and knocking for a while without an answer, Fe tried the doorknob and found it unlocked. She pushed the door open.

"Allison, are you home?" The lights were on, suggesting she was still awake. She inched into the living room, calling her friend's name, then she spotted her on the white leather loveseat.

No wonder she wasn't answering. Allison sat in half-lotus, headphones on, with a black beauty mask splattered across her face and cucumber slices over her eyes. Her hair was wrapped in a white terry cloth turban that matched her robe.

"Allison?" Fe repeated, approaching with caution.

When she got no answer again, she touched Allison's knee with one finger.

Allison screamed and leaped off her seat.

In an instant, Fe lay chest down, pinned to the carpet, her arms twisted behind her in a judo hold.

"Wait, wait! It's me!" she rushed to say.

"Are you trying to scare me to death?" Allison let go of Fe's arms and yanked off her headphones. It was the first time Fe had seen her express any emotion.

"I'm sorry! You didn't answer my text, but I had to see you! It's an emergency!"

Allison helped Fe up, grumbling, "You made me crack my Dead Sea mud mask. And now I lost the relaxation from my guided meditation. I'll have to start this chapter all over!" She walked into the tiny kitchen, where a glass bowl of water sat in the sink.

"Chapter?" Fe asked.

Allison used a wet washcloth to wipe the mask from her face. "For my next book, *Resisting the Pressure*. It's a relaxation plan to help single women stay calm over the holidays, so they don't second-guess their choice to be alone. What's so urgent?"

Fe followed her into the kitchen. "I couldn't go to Joy or Hope with this. Ever since they've happily paired up, they've become like fanatic preachers trying to convert people to couple's life. You're my last hope to talk some sense into me." Her body trembled out of her control. "It's a disaster! The last thing I need is another scandal in the medical community in town. And the last thing I want in my life is another workaholic!"

Without a word, Allison grabbed a spray-bottle from the counter and sprayed Fe in the face.

Fe yelped at the cold splash. "What was that?"

"Ice water. Good for shrinking facial pores." She grabbed Fe's arms and made her hold still. "You're doing it again. Your speech is turning ultrasonic, and your hands look like you're flagging down a helicopter to rescue you from a deserted island. Calm down and start from the beginning."

Fe pulled a tissue from her purse and dried her face. "I was ready to skip the next couple of decades and go straight to being like my mother and grandma: men-less women living together, supporting each other." She quivered. "But then one day this cute respiratory therapist I liked crashed his bike and landed on me." Her pitch hiked, her words speeding up. "And then he started talking about his Irish grandma … and then he said he wanted to kiss the Chihuahua … and then he ended up being a doctor …" Her voice became shrill.

Allison grabbed the bottle and sprayed her again, shocking her. "Woman, get a hold of yourself. I saw too many people cry at my practice today. I don't need another one."

Fe glowered. "I never cry. It gives you wrinkles."

"Get to the point."

"Shawn kissed me tonight!" Fe blurted. "And I kissed him back!

And it was so good I couldn't stop. I didn't want him to stop! And then I found out he might be in danger! And now I can't stop thinking about him!"

Allison sprayed her again.

Fe glared at her. "Is this the way you treat your psychotherapy clients?"

Impassive, Allison set the bottle down. "No. But they *do* pay me." She clasped Fe's arms above the elbow. "Listen, falling for that man would be a financial disaster. Have you forgotten that ending your contract means you owe him a penalty? Not to mention the money he loaned you. You can't throw away your business dreams for a spark of infatuation. We both know the magic eventually fades, and you'll be bored with each other."

Still shaking, Fe asked, "What can I do, then? How do I fast-forward to when the magic is gone?"

Holding her chin and narrowing her eyes, Allison tapped a foot on the floor. "Desperate times call for desperate measures. I'm going to reverse my previous advice and ask you to do the opposite."

"The opposite?" Fe blinked.

Allison nodded. "Go back to dressing like you normally do. Better yet, let Shawn see you dressed like a slob. Forget professional boundaries. Let your family be as friendly to him as they please, like they've done with every other client. Go ahead and give him a full dose of the real, unrestrained, un-retouched Fe Hernandez."

Her thoughts tumbled, trying to make sense of it. "I don't get your point."

"It's simple." Allison stepped closer, her blue eyes sharp. "Attack him with the ultimate weapon to kill the magic." She paused. "You have to friend zone him. Big time."

CHAPTER 21

RIDING HIS BIKE EVERY MORNING, LIKE FE HAD SUGGESTED, felt like taking a shower in well-being. Shawn slept more deeply, woke up refreshed and energized, and finished work more efficiently. His mood improved so much, not even Stewarts' latest attack—replacing the ICU doctors' computers with slower ones— managed to bother him.

That Saturday after Halloween, he'd awakened late to three reassuring texts from Fe. Photos of Aidan in the hotel with her. God bless her. Aidan looked happier than ever, splashing in the water park with the other kids.

Maybe it was the extra sleep, but that afternoon, as he pedaled his bike along his favorite path, his brain felt sharper, brighter than it had in months.

Now, in November, while the rest of the country braced for the winter, Florida entered its golden season. The humidity dialed down, the air turned crisp, and the temperature hovered at perfect. The sky shone deep blue, and the trees lining the path looked greener than ever.

His racing thoughts unraveled ahead of him with rare clarity.

She kissed me back.

But it felt different than the first time.

His physician's brain pieced the clues together.

The tenderness of her touch that night. The way she trembled in his arms after learning about the threats. The effort she'd made to help him rest by taking Aidan. Her steady stream of reassuring texts.

What does all that mean?

His inner voice whispered the diagnosis, *She loves me, too.*

Shawn pedaled harder on the way home, neither resisting the thought nor dwelling on what he meant by *too.* The cool wind tempered the heat blooming on his face as the realization sank in.

For the first time since the crash months ago, when fate had steered him into Fe, he gave himself permission to open the gates. The dreams he'd once filed as delusions made their way back, flooding him.

Yes. He wanted her, but not for one night. He wanted her all the way—from Paris, to grandchildren, to growing old together. That morning they met, he'd seen it so clearly, he feared he'd gone insane. Could those visions be an echo from a different dimension? A potential future he still could slide himself into?

Did he dare tempt his luck?

He left his bike in the garage and went straight to his home office. From a desk drawer, he pulled out a leather-bound notebook and wrote:

Step #1. Find another speech therapist for Aidan.

On his desktop computer, he searched for the email he'd been avoiding all week. His contact at the Smith Center had mentioned a position opening soon in its four-year-old program. Aidan could join after his birthday, February fifth.

Shawn had dragged his feet, hesitant to disrupt Aidan's progress by transferring him to a new team—and reluctant to lose his daily excuse to see Fe.

But now things had changed. Ending their professional relationship had become essential.

He typed a short reply: "Yes. Please save that position for Aidan. If anything opens earlier than that, let me know."

Click. Email sent.

He turned back to his notebook.

Step #2. Prove to Fe I'm not a workaholic. Find a business partner so I can work fewer hours.

He picked up his phone and searched his contacts for Dr. Emery Love, then dialed.

"Hi, cousin!"

The voice on the other end came flat. "What do you want, McDevitt?"

"What do you mean?"

"You only call me 'cousin' when you need something."

He gasped. "Come on! Seriously, can't I call my family …?"

Sighing, he leaned back in his chair. "Okay, fine. I admit it. I need help. Dad said you're working with fellows-in-training at the University of Miami. I need to hire a business partner. But I don't have time to deal with recruiters or screen CVs. Can you recommend someone from the fellows about to graduate?"

She paused. "Let me ask around. I'll call you back later."

He ended the call and scribbled:

Step #3. Expose whoever's sending the threatening letters.

Shawn had a hunch. Too vague to justify it to the FBI bureaucrats, but too strong to ignore. He emailed his private detective to schedule a call: *I need you to help me investigate a few people, starting with Lee Stewarts and his family.*

Send.

Then, he wrote:

Step #4. Seduce Fe.

He turned toward his paper calendar on the wall. With a red marker, he circled February 6th. If he'd managed to keep his hands off her for months, he could definitely wait a little longer.

He smiled at the calendar.

"Enjoy the coming weeks, Fe," he said aloud. "They're the last of life as you know it. On February sixth, I'm coming after you with everything I have."

CHAPTER 22

"LET ME SEE IF I'M GETTING THIS RIGHT."

At Fe's office, Hope narrowed her eyes and counted on her fingers.

"This guy's spending weekends with your kids, and you with his. He's falling asleep on your couch. He's hanging out with your family all the time—even your grandma. Now you're also *feeding him* ... and you're *not* sleeping with him?"

Fe rolled her eyes. "No, Hope. I'm not."

Rotating a hand forward, Hope concluded, "So, you've made Shawn into your husband, except you guys don't have sex. All the work of a marriage, with none of the perks?"

Hope didn't need to know that Fe was doing everything possible to friend zone Shawn—from receiving him at her house dressed like her best version of a slob, to treating him like one of her girlfriends.

"You make it sound worse than it is," Fe said. "First of all, what's the big deal about feeding him? You know Abuela; accepting food from her the first time is like signing up for a cult."

"And he got fed the first time because ..." Hope gestured for her to complete the phrase.

Because I found out he was skipping dinner to make it to the evening session.

"He was practicing his Spanish with my mother and mentioned he'd gotten a taste for Hispanic food when he trained in Miami. Abuela made him try her marinated chicken, and the rest is history."

Hope's slanted look screamed her skepticism. "He's supporting your practice financially."

"No, he's not!" Fe protested with a gasp. "Don't forget the down payment money was a loan!"

"And how about all the clients he's referring to you for speech therapy? And the doctors calling, wanting to hire your grandma to cater food to their offices?"

Fe played with the paperclips on her desk. "I was mortified that he insisted on paying for groceries when Abuela feeds him, so I tried to repay the favor by getting my relatives to help babysit Aidan so he could go on his bike rides. This is his way of paying back *that* favor."

Gosh, Fe could never one-up Shawn! Her last attempt to thank him was inviting him and Aidan to Thanksgiving dinner when she learned his parents would be out of town. Instead, he insisted on hosting them all at his house—even the extended family. The poor guy had no idea what he was getting into.

Like every morning, Shawn's picture-text arrived, and Fe's heart jumped in anticipation. Lately, the selfies he sent to prove he'd been on his bike rides had evolved into snapshots of beautiful views. Yesterday, it was a sunrise over the ocean. Today, the view from the top of the causeway.

She loved it. As usual, he included his right hand, showing his Celtic ring, as proof he'd been there.

"What are you grinning about? Who's texting you?"

"Nothing. No one." Fe cleared her throat and lowered the phone. "How about you finish your idea for my mother's new business?"

Hope opened a binder and flipped to a set of drawings. "I'm calling it 'For-profit Meals on Wheels.' Every day, there's one fixed lunch option that changes daily, for variety. Abuela and your mother get to do what they love—cooking in bulk—and your brother Junior handles deliveries in his van. People sign up ahead of time, so there's minimal waste. We start with Shawn's doctor friends, since they're already asking. As it grows, we could move to an industrial kitchen and bring in some of your aunts to help cook."

Fe stared at her in awe. Only Hope could design a plan that supported not just her mother and grandmother, but half the family.

"Could we put that industrial kitchen in the empty office at Rainbows?"

"Zoning would not allow for food services. But I've got another idea for that empty space I wanted to run by you."

She opened a second binder. "Remember when you asked me if you could borrow my step-kids for Aidan's sessions?"

Fe nodded. "He behaves better with other kids around, trying to copy them. I've been planning group sessions with typical peers as role models."

"So, here's my proposal: charge parents to enroll their kids in your playgroup."

At Fe's skeptical expression, Hope added, "You know how your clients keep saying they wish you worked with all their kids—even the ones without delays? This is their chance."

"Speech therapy for kids who don't need speech therapy?" Fe frowned.

"Not therapy. Just what you do at your famous sleepovers—educational games, music, art ... Call it an after-school club. Or a 'developmental enrichment group'—something fancy for parents who want something more than screen time for their kids. T.J. and I would endorse you. My step-kids have never behaved better than when they're with you."

Fe clasped her hands. "I love it! The kids with special needs get role models. The typical kids have fun and learn compassion for people who are different."

"And even if you charge less than your one-on-one rate, you'll still earn double or triple per hour. I'll help you research licensing and compliance."

A hopeful feeling fluttered in Fe's chest. These two business ideas could mean freedom from her ex for good.

A FaceTime request lit up her phone, and she beamed. "It's Gabriela again!" Only God knew how those tiny hands—still too clumsy to hold a spoon—could tap a screen with such precision.

She picked up. Her cracked, blackened screen flashed Gabriela's triumphant smile for a second, then flopped to show the floor.

"Hi, *mi amor!*" Fe waved. "I'm so proud of you for learning how to call me. And I love that you do it ten times a day. But that phone isn't for playing."

"Where did Gabriela get a cell phone?" Hope asked as Fe ended the call.

"Shawn bought it for Mami and Abuela and added them to his family plan. It's to make sure they can reach him when they're babysitting Aidan. But they're terrified of it, and only Gabriela uses it. She calls me and Shawn—the only two numbers saved in it—like a hundred times a day." Shaking her head, Fe giggled. "Thank God Shawn's such a good sport!" She couldn't stop herself from grinning.

Too late, she noticed Hope's smug smirk.

"Oh, sweetie," Hope snickered. "You're so eating that sushi roll!"

• • •

After Halloween, an undeniable change had occurred in Fe's mother and grandma. It was as if they'd been restraining their affection for Shawn, and suddenly, they couldn't hold it in anymore.

It started with offerings of fresh fruit juice and espresso. Then came effusive greetings with hugs and kisses, followed by attempts at friendly conversation. Then, one unforgettable evening, Abuela officially began force-feeding Shawn.

He tried to refuse politely at first. But Abuela rattled away in some strange Dominican dialect—Fe called it *Cibaeño*—making it impossible to get a word in. When he finally gave in and accepted the meal—rice, beans, and marinated chicken—his elated expression erased the need for language.

He was hooked, and so was Abuela. The beaming old woman received his delight as a standing ovation and request for an encore.

Two weeks and five pounds later, he negotiated a deal with her: If she allowed him smaller portions, he'd pack the rest for lunch the next day. Ever since, he'd become the envy of the hospital lounge. While the other doctors endured their tasteless meals, Shawn reheated his leftovers in the microwave, filling the room with the glorious smell of home-cooked food.

"What are you smiling about?" Mark Jones asked as they left the telemetry unit at the end of the day.

Shawn struggled to suppress his grin. "What's *not* to smile about?"

Jones' dark, bushy brows knitted. He sent Shawn a cold glare. "Are you kidding me? Our lives are a nightmare. Too much work, not enough pay. Medicare's always cutting reimbursements; FirstHealth keeps hogging the patients, and you're even worse off than I am. I have no idea why you're in a good mood."

Shawn pressed the elevator button. The doors opened immediately. "Morning bike rides and soul food can really cheer up a man." They stepped in.

Shawn kept to himself his other reason for his good mood: looking forward to seeing Fe at the evening therapy session. Regaining energy had come with one downside—his body was craving her again.

Lately, she'd relaxed the fashion show. The first time he'd seen her in a snug tank top and cutoff jeans, he almost fell flat on his face. No room for Spanx under those.

Last night, she'd greeted him in *pajamas*. Did she have no clue how a lusty man's brain worked? She'd sat on the floor, her shorts riding up, revealing more and more skin. Her top's spaghetti straps kept sliding down her shoulders, the flimsy fabric threatening to fall any second. The memory of that body in his arms was so fresh, he'd bet he could recognize her by touch, blindfolded, among a dozen other women.

A ding brought him back. The elevator had reached the bottom floor. He beamed at Jones. "Look at that. Express service today. Maybe my bad luck is giving me a break."

As they exited, Jones said, "Man, I'm tied to this town because my exes and my kids live here, but you're young and free. If I were you, I'd send it all to hell and move back to Miami. It must suck to know so many people in town want you gone."

Jones' hollow eyes fixed on him, making clear he was one of those people.

Shawn stopped. "What do you mean, 'so many people'? Mark, do you know about the letters I've been getting?"

Blinking rapidly, Jones took a step back.

Was that a flicker of guilt?

Gathering himself, Jones said, "Your father told me about the letters." He scoffed. "Speaking of someone who wants you gone from this town." Then he turned and strode off, glancing over his shoulder once before disappearing through the main doors.

Shawn stood there, the words settling.

His father had once urged him to move, to put Tara's scandal behind him. Lately, he kept encouraging him to apply for academic jobs elsewhere.

But Dad would never go so far as to send those letters.

Would he?

It made no sense. Jones was probably trying to distract him from suspecting him. He'd better talk to Keith.

His phone announced a FaceTime call from Emery. He sank into one of the lobby chairs and answered.

Emery's striking face filled the screen. As a kid, she'd been funny-looking, thanks to her unusual racial mix. But her features had grown into themselves, starting with her reddish hair, which now obeyed the laws of gravity.

On the screen, Emery chewed the tip of her pen. "Well, Shawny,

I spread the word about your job offer. It's not looking good here with the fellows."

His enthusiasm deflated.

"But," she added, "there's one remote possibility."

"Who?"

"Me."

He thought he'd misheard. "You?"

"Yes. I just started dating a cute lawyer I met online, and he happens to live in Fort Sunshine."

A flash of excitement surged through Shawn. "Emery, you'd be the perfect business partner! Do you remember what an awesome team we made when I was your senior resident and then your fellow?"

"Whoa! Curb your enthusiasm." Emery lifted a hand. "I'm not ready to move to Dead-town-in-the-middle-of-nowhere, Florida, especially not for a guy I just met." She fiddled with the stethoscope hanging around her neck. "I'm talking about the future. I don't know … two or three years from now, if things work out."

Shawn fidgeted in the chair. Despite her dramatic streak and tendency to take everything too seriously, Emery was one of the best doctors he could ever hope to hire. "Let's do this. Next time you visit Fort Sunshine, let me take you around, show you the hospital. We'll start there."

She hesitated. "Okay. I'll email you the dates I'm planning to visit."

"I'm going to make you fall in love with this town, Emery." Shawn grinned. "Give me one weekend, and you'll be begging me to make you my partner."

Emery shot him a skeptical look. "Goodbye, *McDevitt*."

"See you soon, *Love*." He ended the call.

"Who's that Emery you're talking to? Why are you calling her *love*?" Gina's voice startled him.

Shawn looked up from his phone and met her baffled expression. She must've overheard only the end of his conversation. He saw no point in clarifying that Emery was his cousin, or that her last name was *Love*.

"I'm sorry, Gina, that's none of your business."

Rage sparked in Gina's eyes. Her breathing quickened, and her lips trembled. Shawn braced himself inwardly for the inevitable lash out.

"Are you sneaking around with yet another woman?" she shrilled. "Gosh, Shawn, is one not enough?"

Tense, he stood. "What are you talking about?"

"It's a small town; things can't be hidden for long. A friend told me you're involved with your son's speech therapist. She's always at your house."

So, Gina still had contacts among his neighbors, feeding her intel. But he wasn't worried about himself, only about the trouble those rumors might cause to Fe.

"Not that it's your business," he said with studied calm, "but Ms. Hernandez is a professional and deserves all my respect."

Rage and panic rippled across her face. He expected an explosion, but she held on. Thank God for mood stabilizers.

She stared him down. He held her gaze.

"You deny being involved with Fe Hernandez, but you didn't deny your involvement with this Emery."

He didn't answer. Let Gina stay disenchanted. It might be safer for everyone.

"May I help you with something?" he asked. "I'm on my way out."

Flushing with anger, she gave him a slow once-over. "I came to give you my latest piece of information about your case. But I've just decided I'm done helping you." She raked him with a final stink eye, then turned on her heels and stalked toward the elevator.

Shawn suppressed a sigh of relief. He'd known her politeness wouldn't last long.

As he headed for the parking lot, he checked his phone.

A bunch of random emojis from Gabriela—those always made him smile—and one text from Jay inviting him out.

He was still debating his answer when he spotted his car—and his blood froze in his veins.

Spider web-shaped cracks radiated across the windshield. Scratches and dents wrecked the doors and hood, cut deep into the paint. Slashed tires sagged against the pavement.

Dread clamped down on his chest at the sight of the envelope tucked beneath the windshield wiper. He grabbed it with shaky fingers. The familiar typewriter font across the front twisted his stomach into knots.

But this one had something new.

Dark red smudges streaked across the paper.

It took him a moment to register what they were.

Bloodstains.

CHAPTER 23

S HAWN HAD FILED SO MANY POLICE REPORTS IN THE PAST TWO years that he could now do it in record time. Richard and Keith met him at the station. Once they were done, Richard helped him get his car towed to the body shop and then drove him home.

Now seated in Shawn's living room, they reviewed a copy of the letter in silence.

"Do you see what I mean?" Shawn asked, more dispirited than anxious. "This letter describes my morning bike route. It mentions when I stopped for gas. It even details what I had for lunch. Richard, this person is really stalking me."

Narrowing his eyes, Richard loosened his tie. "Wait, they described your lunch? So they were at the hospital with you around lunchtime. Were any of our suspects there? Jones, Stewarts, your ex?"

"I can't remember. But vandalizing my car is such a drastic move, I'm starting to doubt anyone I know would do it."

"Didn't you say your ex-girlfriend had a psychiatric history?"

"I was with Gina in the lobby shortly before that."

Richard removed his dark jacket. "We don't know exactly when the damage occurred. She could've met you afterward on purpose to steer suspicion away from her. I wonder if that's also why she's calling me."

"What do you mean?"

"She left me a message yesterday, saying she had a tip. She claimed she overheard Dr. Jones talking to someone about wanting to buy your office building—and that you refused to sell. What's she talking about?"

Shawn took a moment to recall. "When I first tried to leave

147

FirstHealth two years ago, I bought a commercial building. I own my suite now, instead of renting. Also lease out other offices, so it brings some income." He paused. "Now that you mention it, Dr. Jones did offer to buy the building back then."

Richard concluded, "So, he's not just interested in eliminating you as a competitor, he has another motive."

"But Jones wouldn't resort to vandalism or crime!" *Would he?* Shawn rubbed his temples. "What do we do next?"

"As a friend and as an agent, I strongly recommend you hire private security. And I urge you to reconsider your decision not to involve your son. Also … I'm afraid your morning bike rides have to end."

"What?" Shawn whipped his head toward Richard. "But this is the best I've felt physically in ages!"

A loud knock on the door, followed by frantic bell ringing, interrupted them. Richard lifted a hand to stop Shawn from rising and walked to the door himself.

"Uh, Shawn?" he said, peering through the peephole. "Are you expecting a visit from a wrestler or something?"

"A wrestler?" Shawn stepped over to look and froze at the gleam of a brass chest plate. A Roman soldier in full uniform stood at his door.

"*What the feck?*"

He shifted, angling for a better view of the man's face through the peephole.

It was Jay.

Still confused, Shawn opened the door.

Jay rushed in and hugged him. "Are you okay? Sorry it took me so long to get here. I was at work when I got your message."

Shawn took in the bright red feathers on Jay's helmet, the chest armor, the sword at his belt, and his muscular legs poking from under a tunic that looked more like a short skirt. "Please don't tell me you're a male stripper now."

Jay gasped. "What? I'm *not* a stripper—" He cleared his throat and mumbled, "*anymore.*" Another throat clear. "This is for a photo shoot for my company's website."

Richard stared blankly. "Your company?"

Before Jay could answer, Shawn waved it off. "Don't get him started. Richard, this is my friend Jay. He thinks he's an entrepreneur and life coach—whatever that means."

"I am. Seriously!" Jay said, shaking Richard's hand. "The problem is, Shawn doesn't respect any career that doesn't come with a framed diploma."

"My difficulty respecting your job has little to do with your credentials." Shawn gestured at the costume. "It has more to do with things like … this." He sighed. "I can't believe you're my best hope of identifying the man Tara ran away with!" Holding his forehead, he returned to the living room.

Jay removed his helmet and ran a hand through his short, dark hair as he followed. "I've done my best. I've been working with the FBI for months, going through photos. But I've never been a visual person."

As Jay's massive frame dropped onto the couch, Shawn could've sworn the rest of the furniture bounced.

Sitting back in an armchair, Shawn looked at Richard with pleading eyes. "I'd hate to give this person the satisfaction of ruining my days. Is there any way around it, so I don't have to stop my bike rides or spoil them by dragging a bodyguard along?"

Begging seemed to work; Richard hesitated. "You'd have to promise never to go alone. This person might not intend to hurt you, but don't tempt them by riding in the dark by yourself."

"I'll go with you whenever I'm in town!" Jay offered.

Richard eyed Jay. "Perfect. You'll scare people off better than a paid thug. I'll try to cover when you're not here." He turned to Shawn. "But now we need to make a phone call."

Shawn gave a single nod.

Richard dialed Gina's number and placed the call on speaker. "Ms. Hill? This is Agent Fields returning your call."

"Thank you so much for calling me back." As usual, Gina's voice softened into sweet politeness when speaking to law enforcement.

"You mentioned a tip?"

"Yes, but please don't tell Shawn I called. We had an argument earlier, and … it would hurt my feminine pride if he knew I was help-ing you."

"In your message, you mentioned something about Dr. Jones?"

"Actually, I have something else to report now," Gina replied.

"What is it?"

"Some mutual acquaintances saw Shawn trick-or-treating with his son's speech therapist on Halloween." Her voice lowered. "She's Stewarts' ex-daughter-in-law, and, apparently, he's livid that they had the nerve to parade around town arm in arm."

Shawn's breath froze in his lungs for a painful moment.

Richard raised his eyebrows, watching Shawn. "Dr. Lee Stewarts?"

"Yes," Gina replied. "I heard him say that Shawn had gone too far, and this was *the last straw*."

Shawn and Richard exchanged a worried look.

CHAPTER 24

THANKSGIVING GOT OUT OF CONTROL.

It began as a simple dinner invitation from Shawn to Fe's immediate family—then one cousin remembered an aunt, who remembered a godmother, who remembered someone else "who would feel left out." Even José, the town's homeless guy, somehow made the guest list.

When it became obvious the crowd wouldn't fit around Shawn's dining table, Fe tried to cancel. Shawn refused, hiring an events company to set up a buffet and tables in his backyard. Fortunately, Florida's weather made an outdoor Thanksgiving possible.

And then, after dinner, Uncle Tony produced a stereo out of nowhere and declared, "A party without music is no party." Ten minutes later, Shawn's yard was hosting the loudest Latin rave his spiffy neighborhood had ever witnessed.

After kicking Aunt Juana and cousin Glennys out of the house for snooping around the guest rooms, Fe collapsed on the family room couch and covered her eyes with both hands. She needed a nap. Or a chance to do someone's hair and makeup. Immediately.

"You okay? Need an aspirin?" Shawn's voice startled her.

She lowered her hands and forced a smile. "I'm fine. Just had to step away from the noise for a minute."

He offered his hand. "If you want to hide, let's do it right."

Puzzled, she followed him upstairs. Away from the hum of the servers, the sitting area already felt like an improvement, but that wasn't his plan. Shawn disappeared into his room and returned with an armful of supplies: noise-canceling Bose headphones, a sleep mask, a pillow, and a blanket.

"Here, we do things properly."

He settled her on the plush couch and draped the blanket over her. It was the softest thing she'd ever touched, probably cashmere.

"Man, you know how to live!"

"Wait. I'm not done."

He vanished again and reappeared carrying a portable cooler, which he set on the coffee table. "Some alcohol, in case the nap isn't enough." He pulled out two beers. "Guinness or Presidente?"

She blinked, impressed he'd stocked Dominican beer too. "Neither, thank you."

"I see. You need something stronger." He produced Coke and rum, scooped ice with a plastic cup, and in no time had improvised a Cuba libre.

She eyed the Brugal bottle. "Where did you get the rum?"

"I confiscated it from your Uncle Tony." He passed her the drink. "Make sure he gets his liver function checked, like I recommended."

Fe accepted the cup and studied Shawn. Handsome and classy, in formal charcoal pants and a fitted aqua shirt that made his eyes look lighter, he seemed worlds away from the chaos downstairs.

She wished she could disappear. No need to parade her lack of refinement in front of him. Her former in-laws had spent years reminding her of it.

"I'm sorry for the disaster downstairs," she blurted. "I'm sorry, Abuela insisted on bringing rice and beans. I apologize for all my relatives asking for free medical advice. Please tell me my cousin Glennys didn't try to show you her weird butt mole!"

Shawn's lips quirked with barely contained amusement. "No, she asked me to invest in her beauty salon."

Fe cringed and sank deeper into the couch. "I'll get them all out as soon as possible. I just need to improvise a whip and a torch."

He chuckled. "What are you talking about? Your family is adorable."

"No, they're a disgrace." With a groan, she flopped back and took a sip of her drink. "They have no concept of boundaries. They guilted me into inviting them, and now they're all drinking heavily and throwing a loud party in your yard."

"Do you think guilt trips, overbearing families, and heavy drinking scare me?" He huffed. "I'm Irish! We invented that!" He made himself another Cuba libre, took a long sip, and settled into the armchair. "The problem isn't your family, it's mine."

Uh-oh.

Fe had thought he'd be thrilled when his parents showed up—she'd even helped arrange it, when Shawn's mother reached out through Betty. But apparently, it'd been a mistake. She'd never seen Shawn look tenser than when his father sat beside him at dinner.

Tentatively, she commented, "You must be honored your parents cancelled their plans to visit your sister to spend Thanksgiving with you."

"I'm not surprised. In my family, bad news trumps joy any day." He lifted his hands like a set of scales. "A cute baby on one side ..." He lowered the left hand. "A murder, a lawsuit, threatening letters, and an autism diagnosis on the other ... I win!"

She winced. "Rough year, huh?"

"Can't wait for it to be over." He drained his drink in one gulp.

"But we're not here for you to cheer *me* up," he said, refilling his glass. "Looks like today you're the one who needs a pep talk." His turquoise eyes pierced her, soft and unrelenting. "What's going on, Fe? You're the most cheerful, family-oriented person I know. Why are you hiding from the party?"

She smoothed the flutter sleeves of her rust-colored dress, gathering herself. "It's not my family's fault. I spent the morning on the phone with my former in-laws; they couldn't decide if they wanted Diego at their dinner." *Always Diego alone, never Gabriela.* Talking to that family was somehow more exhausting than talking to Liam directly.

"This kind of party is exactly what used to make them cringe." She took a long sip, the rum burning even through the Coke. "I spent years reining in my noisy family, terrified of embarrassing my ex and his parents in front of their doctor friends."

His gaze drifted over her, slow and deliberate, sending a shiver across her skin. "You could *never* embarrass anyone."

"Don't you know me at all, Shawn?" She groaned. "I'm not exactly *normal*. I'm the woman who gives unsolicited back rubs, and that's just the beginning. I spend my life holding back, keeping the loud, passionate, full-throttle me under wraps." She gestured at herself. "What you see now is me toned down."

"You couldn't tone it down if you tried, Fe." He leaned forward, his gaze enveloping her. "People need sunglasses to look at your smile."

She winked. "Trust me, honey. If I wasn't toning it down, they'd need *eclipse glasses*."

He laughed.

She finished her drink with one last swallow. "I'm too much. That's my blessing and my curse. People who love me call it 'endearing' and overlook my eccentricities. But Liam and his parents? They had a way of making me feel like ..." She faltered, searching for the right words.

"Like the girl who came back to school with an accent after a year away?" he offered.

She blinked. He still remembered that story, and he was dead right. "Exactly." She nodded. "How do you know?"

His smile faded as he took her glass and mixed another drink. "Let's just say I have an advanced degree in dealing with people who make you feel inadequate. My father can't help reminding me I'm a disappointment."

She studied him—every inch of flawless beauty—and traced an

invisible outline in the air with her hands. "Which part is a disap- pointment? The sky-high IQ and heart of gold? The absurdly good looks? Or maybe the MD degree and thriving career?"

Oblivious to the praise and the teasing, he handed her the fresh drink. "The fact that I went to UMass instead of Harvard, like he did. That I'm not a cardiothoracic surgeon like him. But mostly, that I run a 'little solo practice' instead of being an academic physician."

The music downstairs relented, leaving behind the welcome hush of voices and clinking glasses. He tipped his head toward a set of French doors and led her to the deck overlooking the Indian River. She leaned on the railing beside him, savoring the cool air and the low hum of conversation drifting from below.

Floodlights washed over the yard, revealing Aidan running and giggling alongside Fe's little nephews. Behind them, Diego pushed Gabriela in her wheelchair so she could have her turn at being "it."

Shawn gestured with his drink toward the table where his par- ents sat, chatting with Doña Carmen, Fe's mother. "Dr. Seamus McDevitt—legend at Harvard, former director of Thoracic Surgery at UMass. Nothing I ever did could measure up."

Fe stayed quiet, unsure what to say.

He winked. "And of course, the day I told Richard that story, his answer was, 'Cry me a river. My father was an alcoholic who used to beat me up.'" Shawn's smile returned, eyes glinting. "So, see? Not even my traumas are good enough."

She burst out laughing.

They drank in silence for a while. Then, she said, "I wish I could say I know how you feel, but my father wasn't famous, or even ed- ucated. He was just a convenience store owner in Washington Heights." Nostalgia swelled, then clarity struck. "So that's why I'm not myself today!" She tapped her forehead. "Holiday syndrome! Ever since *Papá* passed, I get the blues at every family holiday." The reali- zation felt almost like relief.

"I bet you had a wonderful father."

She nodded with energy. "You would've liked him. He was a little like you, the hardest worker you'd ever meet. I think that's how he wrecked his health. Even after his kidney transplant, he worked the bodega late into the night. I just wished he'd spent more time at home." She tasted her drink, easing the bittersweet ache.

Shaking herself, she stomped a foot. "Okay. Enough pouting. I'm ready to drag everyone out by the ears."

"Please don't leave yet!" He caught her wrist. "Not until my parents leave!"

"Uh … about that." She glanced up from under her eyelashes. "Your mother's not planning to leave until midnight. We're supposed to surprise you with a birthday celebration."

He flinched as if slapped and released her wrist. For the longest time, he just stared at her.

"Three more hours with Dad?" he finally said.

"I'm so sorry." She winced.

He blew out a breath, dragged a palm down his face, and paused at his mouth. She braced for a recrimination, but instead, he gave a hollow laugh.

He laced his fingers with hers and smiled. Every skin cell touching him sang with joy.

"If I'm stuck here until midnight, so are you." He nudged her shoulder with his. "Let's make the most of it."

• • •

Shawn was determined to enjoy the night—and he did. The whole event was worth it just to see Fe's wide-eyed shock at his salsa and merengue skills—thanks to his Cuban college roommate and years in Miami. Later, he and his parents coaxed her into trying Irish step dancing, and of course, she moved as if she'd been born doing it.

At midnight, Fe appeared with presents and balloons, and the party broke into "Happy Birthday." He blew out the candles on his favorite dessert—a Key lime pie his mother had brought—then laughed as they sang it again in Spanish and made him blow out the candles on a flan. As if he hadn't already binged on turkey and pumpkin pie.

Now, at the end of the evening, Shawn stood on the driveway, waving as his parents' car disappeared down the road. The second it was gone, he sighed in relief.

"You're slacking, man."

The voice behind him startled him. Shawn turned to face José, the vagrant, scratching his underarm in a filthy, powder-blue tuxedo with a torn bowtie.

"Excuse me?" Shawn asked.

José pointed toward Fe, farther down the driveway, walking the last of her relatives to their car. "Your girl. I saw you staring at her like a hungry wolf while dancing."

Shawn shook his head, baffled. "Fe's not 'my girl.' She and I—we're not a couple."

Impatient, the man huffed. "Exactly my point!" He poked Shawn's forehead. "Man, she's Latina, like me. Take my word for it, you need to get yourself some *cojones* and take a bold step."

Shawn gaped at the man, but the rumble of a motorcycle approaching cut off any reply.

Jenny, José's friend, sputtered up the driveway on a decrepit Honda.

"Hello, hottie!" She flashed her rotten teeth at Shawn. "Those thyroid pills you prescribed are the bomb! I even gained weight." She pinched her skeletal arm.

He gave her a weak wave in return.

José kept eye contact with Shawn as he backed away, frowning like a reprimanding mentor. Then, he slung his sack of leftovers over his shoulder and mounted behind Jenny. The motorcycle backfired and coughed as it disappeared down the road.

"Finally! My last cousins are gone," Fe announced. "Where are Mami and Abuela?"

Shawn shook himself from his daze, took her arm, and walked

her back to the house. "I sent them home in an Uber a while ago. The excuse was putting Gabriela to bed, but my real goal was stopping them from cleaning."

In the foyer, she tilted her head toward the stairs. "Diego helped himself to a guestroom after Aidan went to bed. All the dancing and running finally wore him out."

"Let him sleep; Betty can take him home tomorrow."

Their gazes locked, a tense silence swelling between them. He wished he were as bold as José suggested, bold enough to ask her to stay too.

Where is Dr. McDevil when I need him?

"Okay." She cleared her throat. "I'll get going then."

She reached for her purse and keys on the coffee table, but he caught her wrist to hold her a moment longer. "Thanks for the presents. The gallon-sized hand sanitizer pump might be my favorite gift ever."

Giggling, she swung the purse over her shoulder. "I played it safe. What do you give the man who already has it all?" She inched toward the door, mirroring his reluctance.

"It was great meeting the rest of your family. I still can't believe how our parents hit it off."

"I know." She gave an eager nod. "What could they even talk about? My mother barely speaks English."

"And mine speaks even less Spanish!" He held the door and followed her onto the front porch. "I suspect my mother was interrogating yours about whether we're dating."

She winced, bracing herself against the cool night air. "Your parents must be terrified of that."

"Are you kidding?" He laughed. "After Tara and my ex Gina, they'd *die* to set me up with a hard-working, nice Catholic woman like you."

She stopped, her mouth curving in a half-smirk, her eyes filled with skeptical amusement.

Guessing her thoughts, he stepped closer and brushed a lock of hair from her face. "Never believe anyone who says you're too much. You're your own kind of perfection. Don't ever tone it down—the world needs you exactly as you are."

Her expression softened. Then, she forced a grin and gave him a playful shove. "You're trying to make me sob, but you're wasting your time. I *never* cry. It ruins the makeup." Her voice wavered. "But … thank you."

He stepped closer still. "No. Thank *you*. This has been the best birthday I've ever had. I can't think of anything that could've made it better." His smile faded, and his gaze slipped from her eyes to her mouth. "Well … maybe one thing."

His eyes asked the question without words. She seemed to understand, her attention sliding to his lips.

"Tomorrow, we'll blame it on the Cuba libres and pretend nothing happened." She dropped her purse to the floor, stepped forward, and pressed her mouth to his.

He jolted at the touch, but the surprise quickly gave way to a blast of joy. He held her tight and delved into her soft, exquisite lips. Her arms looped around his neck as she deepened the kiss. The faint taste of rum on her tongue paled in comparison to her other flavor: a contagious, insatiable hunger.

The world fell away. The crickets hushed. The cool November breeze vanished in the heat of her body, pressing against his. Breathing in her perfume, he let his hands trace her curves.

Her fingers slid through his hair, stroked his back, while her mouth teased and tortured his, inciting him. Waves of desire rocked him with every kiss. He gripped her hips, pulling her flush against him, letting her feel the depth of his hunger.

A loud thud split the night. He broke away, heart racing, and instinctively shielded her with his body. Confusion clouded him as he glanced around for the source.

"Shawn, look!" Panting, she pointed at the floor.

A brick wrapped in gift paper lay on the porch. Someone had launched it at the window—one that would've shattered if not hurricane-proof.

He clasped Fe's arm and rushed her inside, then stood at the threshold. Scanning the dark, deserted street, he bent to pick up the brick. A familiar blood-smeared envelope was taped to it. He studied it as he re-entered the house and closed the door.

Inside, a single line:

"You'll be dead soon."

CHAPTER 25

THE BRICK BECAME THE LAST STRAW. Fe HAD TO BEG, BARGAIN, and threaten, but she finally convinced Shawn to let her and Aidan work with the FBI.

The Saturday after Thanksgiving, they joined Keith and Richard on the 6:00 a.m. flight to Atlanta, and then drove an hour to Gainesville. All morning, they let Aidan wander the area where he'd been found.

Now, taking a break, Fe sat in a café FaceTiming with her friends. Hope had propped her phone on the table to free her hands while wrapping Christmas presents. Fe's busted screen showed them all gathered at Allison's condo—the official hiding place for gifts, since she was the only one without children.

"I hope they're paying you for all those hours," Allison mumbled, a marker cap between her teeth as she wrote gift tags.

Fe leaned the phone against a napkin holder to stir sugar into her coffee. "Yes. I worked out a flat fee for the day with Shawn."

Next to Allison, Hope forced a casual tone, but couldn't hide her smirk. "Are you spending the night there?"

"No, Hope. We fly back at nine tonight. And drop it."

Hope snickered. "Someone's prickly!"

Fe hadn't meant to sound edgy. But surrounded by FBI agents, she and Shawn hadn't had a private moment since their kiss. Not that she expected he'd mention it—she had implied from the start they'd pretend it never happened. Still, a new awkwardness hung between them.

"I can't believe Fe 'Bargain-shopping-queen' cancelled her Black Friday spree!" Joy called from the background.

"I had to. I spent most of yesterday making scrapbooks with Aidan, teaching him to point at photos and say names. My plan is to repeat it when the FBI shows him suspect pictures."

Allison scoffed. "Again, I hope they're paying you *double* your rate."

"Speaking of rates, that's why I was calling." Hope reached for a folder. "I have everything ready for your pilot trial of the after-school playgroup next week." She held a report up to the phone. "After taxes and paying an assistant, your hourly income will be two hundred fifty percent of what it is now."

Fe frowned at the screen. "In English, please."

"This number here"—Hope tapped a line—"is what you'll be making for the two-week pilot camp."

Fe's jaw dropped.

"With Shawn's help, we enrolled ten kids," Joy added. "So you'll either have to split them into two groups or hire someone to help."

"And the pilot trial is next week?" Fe had forgotten her friends were organizing that after-school camp. "There's no way I'll be ready."

"Why not?" Hope asked. "You'll be doing the same thing you do when you volunteer to watch all of our kids—only this time you'll get paid. And you won't be dealing with insurance."

"Ms. Hernandez, Aidan just took off. We need you."

Jay, one of Shawn's friends tied to the case, interrupted. Fe said goodbye to her friends, dropped some cash on the table, and grabbed her toy bag.

She and Jay rushed to catch up with the group. Aidan sprinted down a street as if he knew exactly where he was going—as if he recognized it. Three blocks later, they reached a playground he seemed to know well.

"This kid has an amazing sense of orientation," Jay commented as Aidan climbed the slide.

"It comes with his condition," Shawn said in a somber tone. "Do you remember the movie *Rainman*, where the main character was a genius with numbers? That's an exaggeration, but disproportionate strength in left-brain skills often comes with autism and Asperger's."

Fe elbowed Shawn. "But we don't put labels on Aidan." She turned to Jay. "We all just have different strengths. Aidan is a very visual kid."

Jay exhaled through pursed lips. "I'm not. That has been my handicap in helping the FBI. They want me to identify the man who left with Aidan's mother, but I've never been good at remembering faces. Not even hypnosis has helped."

Aidan jumped off the swing and bolted from the playground.

As the group followed, Fe said to Jay. "Then the FBI should focus on your strengths, not your weaknesses. If you're not a visual person, what about trying to remember sounds and smells from that day?"

Striding beside them, Richard shot her a curious look. "I've never heard of that."

Jay nodded. "It's worth a try! I'll tell my hypnotist."

They followed Aidan into a beaten-up neighborhood he clearly remembered. After a few turns, he stopped at a vacant storage place. He walked straight to a hole in the drywall and reached inside, as if searching for something. When he pulled his hand out, he held a moldy, tiny teddy bear.

Fe gasped. "He's been here before."

Richard gave her a quick nod. She grabbed her toy bag and sat on the floor with Aidan for a floor-time session.

• • •

After the storage unit, Aidan took them to a motel—the same one where his mother had been found. That hurt Shawn. It proved Aidan had stayed there at some point, and only God knew what he'd seen. It also left them at a dead end: they already knew the room had been rented with a fake ID.

Fe had been working with Aidan for an hour, searching for any memory he might've had in that place. She must've noticed Shawn's tension, because she suggested he take a break and leave her and Keith alone "to help Aidan focus."

Now, sitting with Richard and Jay at a local restaurant, Shawn checked the time on his phone. "I'm counting the minutes till five o'clock. I so need a drink. Or a bike ride." He turned to Richard. "You're coming with me tomorrow, aren't you?"

"I can't believe you'd rather get killed than give up your bike rides." Richard huffed. "Does stubbornness come with being Irish?"

Jay scooped a handful of peanuts from the plate. "It's the same at his job. He'd die in the ICU from overwork rather than quit. That's not Irish, it's obsessive."

"Obsessive?" Shawn scoffed. "Says the man who stalks women."

With a grunt, Jay rolled his eyes. "For the thousandth time, Shawn. I don't stalk my ex-girlfriend!" He cleared his throat, then muttered, "anymore." Another throat-clear. "But speaking of women. Didn't you say you hated Aidan's speech therapist? Fe's so nice!"

"He doesn't hate her." Richard snorted. "He's dying to screw her."

Shawn choked on his water. He'd never told Richard a word about Fe. Faking offense, he protested, "I'm not!"

"You always pause a second before saying her name, and drop your pitch on that syllable. That ain't the way you say Betty's name."

Damn Richard with his sharp FBI agent eye.

Shawn signaled their waiter. "You must be sensing my stress about the money I'm paying her. She's costing me an arm and a leg."

Richard gave him a skeptical once-over, and Shawn sighed in resignation. No point in hiding from him. And maybe he didn't want to. The fact that Fe had stuck to her suggestion and refused to mention their kiss was killing him.

After the waiter delivered their drinks and took their snack orders, Shawn turned to Richard. "When research fails me, I resort to a mentor. You're the only man near my age I know who's truly happy with his woman. How do you woo a woman who doesn't want to be wooed?"

Silence settled over the table.

With a straight face, Jay spoke first. "Well, when I want a woman's attention, I just find an excuse to take off my shirt. Never fails."

Shawn shot him a dirty look. "Thank you, Mr. Abs-of-Steel, but not all of us kayak to work and do one-arm push-ups while answering emails with the other hand." He rolled his eyes, then turned back to Richard. "Any pearls of wisdom?"

Richard considered it. "Man, I'm not into holding hands and giving paternal advice. But maybe you should take a step back. Let her be the one who comes to you."

Jay raised an eyebrow. "You mean, play hard to get?"

Ignoring him, Richard continued, "It wasn't easy winning Joy over. She'd been through hell with her late husband. She had PTSD against relationships …"

Encouraged, Shawn leaned in. "That's it! With Fe, it's complicated enough—she works for me. And if I handle it wrong, she'll quit, and Aidan will lose her. On top of that, she has her own PTSD from her ex. What did you do?"

"It was dumb luck. Since I was undercover, I had to fake not being interested in Joy. I ended up being the only guy she could let her guard down with. I'd push a boundary now and then—flirt, test the water— but I always backed out before she even noticed. And before long, *she* was the one making moves on me."

Shawn mused, "So, the trick is, make her feel safe. Then wait until *she* makes a move?"

Jay tossed back a handful of peanuts and mumbled around them, "Or, just take your shirt off."

• • •

The next day, back in Florida, Shawn and Richard went on a late afternoon bike ride. It was another perfect Florida fall day—cool, crisp, and rare enough to be treasured.

Outside the convenience store, where they'd stopped for water, José sat on his usual bench, this time his arm draped not around Jenny, but a new homeless woman. When he spotted Shawn, he winked and gave him a thumbs-up.

"Oh great," Shawn groaned. "Even the town bum has a girlfriend, and I don't. Maybe I should've listened to him and been bolder with Fe."

Richard eyed the man from a distance. "Well, he reeks of piss, and his girlfriend is a toothless skeleton. I'm not sure you want his advice." He rested a hand on Shawn's shoulder. "Stick to the plan, man. Make her feel safe."

On the drive home, Richard asked, "So you're paying Fe a small fortune. What exactly does she do with Aidan?"

"She's a genius. She turns anything into a chance to teach Aidan new words. She teaches me to use his favorite toys and games to hold his attention."

"So, basically, you're paying this woman an arm and a leg to teach you how to play with your kid?"

Shawn shook his head. "It's more than playing. It's called The Floortime Approach, and occupational therapy for sensory issues. We teach him words through play. We go to playgrounds, we make him bounce on a large rubber ball—" He stopped short. "Oh my God, you're right! We're just … playing with him!"

The realization hit, and it all came into focus. His father had never spent time with him. All his attempts to bond with Aidan came from imitating idealized TV fathers. Without these therapy sessions, Aidan would've grown up just like him—with the same hollow love-hate relationship he'd endured with his emotionally absent father. Either a self-flagellating overachiever like Shawn, or a waste of a human life like Tara.

If Aidan had any hope of breaking that cycle—if any of Shawn's future children did—it was thanks to this autism scare.

Maybe Fe was right after all. Even what he'd seen as a tragedy carried a hidden blessing.

That night, after Betty left, Shawn watched Aidan play with the little teddy bear he'd stolen from Fe's toy trunk. Sitting on the floor, the boy made the bear tap a tiny drum, just like Fe had taught him. Then his eyes lifted and met Shawn's.

A deep peace settled over Shawn, and with it came a strange certainty: Aidan would be fine. This scare had been God's way of shaking him awake, forcing him to grow.

Aidan held his gaze much longer than usual. Wordless communication seemed to flow between them, as if the boy understood and accepted his peace offering.

"It's bedtime, buddy," Shawn said.

To Shawn's surprise, Aidan didn't resist. Still clutching his little bear, he slipped his small hand into Shawn's and walked him to the bedroom.

CHAPTER 26

S OMETHING STRANGE WAS HAPPENING TO SHAWN, FE COULD
sense it. Lately, he'd been respectful and polite to the point of
annoyance, always keeping his distance. Was he compensating
for their kiss on Thanksgiving?

Or had she misread everything, and he was already over her?

Luckily, for the next two weeks, the after-school program kept her
too busy to dwell on it.

Now, with the last of the new kids gone, she updated Joy over the
phone.

"The pilot trial was a success!" Fe said over speakerphone, tidying
the improvised playroom. "Parents are begging me to make it permanent. And the sessions worked for my original idea, too."

"So, Aidan made progress from interacting with other kids?"

Fe smiled as Aidan eagerly packed away leftover materials from
the Christmas ornament craft. "He's thriving! His new milestone is
echolalia—he repeats everything he hears. There's still a gap between
mimicking language and using it appropriately, but it's a sign of improvement, and I'm thrilled."

"Aunt Joy! Listen to this!" Diego faced Aidan. "My name is Aidan."

"My name is Aidan," the boy echoed.

"I'm a green elf."

"I'm a green elf."

"I eat worms for breakfast."

"Diego—no!" Fe warned.

Diego batted his lashes. "But he sounds so cute in that tiny voice!"

"D-dat's n-not n-nice!" Gabriela scolded in her slurred speech.

Aidan repeated, "That's not nice."

"D-don't b-bock me," Gabriela huffed.

"Don't mock me," Aidan parroted.

"Hey, gotta go, girl." Fe laughed into the phone. "My kids are turning Aidan into a toy recorder." She ended the call and wheeled Gabriela away.

When she turned back, two men had entered the playroom. Her stomach dropped. Broad-shouldered, ruddy-faced, with upturned noses, Liam and Lee Stewarts—her ex and his mirror-image father—stood waiting.

Adrenaline spiked. Heat and nausea surged. What were those two workaholics doing out of the office at four?

Her pulse hammered as she clasped the handles of Gabriela's wheelchair and forced a steady tone. "May I help you?"

Liam pursed his thin lips, looking down at her. "You haven't answered my calls. I got worried."

Worried I don't call about the missing child support?

She swallowed against the urge to gag. At least she could finally hope never to beg him for money again.

"I'm fine. I imagine you'd like to see Diego." She didn't bother to remind him how often he left Gabriela out of the visits—she wasn't brag-worthy enough. "*Papi.*" She turned to her son. "Why don't you take your dad and grandpa to the ice cream shop and plan your next weekend together."

Gabriela sat quieter than ever in her wheelchair. Did the girl even remember her father? Fe placed a gentle hand on her shoulder, sending her love and reassurance. Then she kept her gaze averted from Liam—a silent sign the conversation was over.

Reluctantly, he turned to Diego. "Come with me."

"Y-you b-bogot t-to s-say b-bleese."

At Gabriela's slurred protest, Liam frowned, baffled. "What did she say?"

"Y-you b-bogot t-to s-say b-bleese."

Aidan blurted, "You forgot to say please."

Bittersweet warmth filled Fe's chest. With all his challenges, Aidan still tuned into Gabriela better than her own father.

Diego slipped his hand into Liam's and walked him out.

Unfortunately, Stewarts senior lingered. "Faith, I'd like to talk to you about something that worries me. I haven't told Liam."

Fe reached into her purse and began brushing Gabriela's hair. "How about you email me?"

"Are you dating McDevitt?"

She froze, brush in hand. The question blindsided her. "Of course not." *And it's none of your damn business.*

His puffy hazel eyes raked her face. "It's a small town. People talk. I heard you spent Thanksgiving with him. Friends said they saw you together on Halloween. At the airport too, as if you two were traveling."

A hand on her waist, Fe straightened with feigned confidence. "I'm his son's speech therapist. That's it."

His eyes narrowed. "It would be awkward for my family if people thought our former daughter-in-law was … sampling all the doctors in town."

Thank God for olive skin that hid her blush.

"I have nothing to hide."

We're only friends, she told herself. Yet the memory of their kisses branded her a liar.

Paternal concern laced with condescension in Stewarts' expression. "Believe it or not, I care for you, Faith. People are starting to notice. You should be careful."

She knew better; it was a warning.

He leaned in. "You wouldn't want rumors spreading that you're *involved* with the father of one of your clients. Think of the damage to your professional reputation."

Fe's gut twisted. Behind his politeness lay the threat. His family would gladly start that rumor. They could blacklist her, like they did before.

Will I ever get rid of these people?

• • •

It took Fe a couple more hours to finish work after the unexpected visit. Lee's vague threats kept replaying in her mind. Should she quit her job with Shawn to avoid provoking the Stewarts family? But then, wouldn't that only confirm Lee's suspicions? His accusations about her and Shawn were lies!

Weren't they?

The memory of their last kiss burned through her. *Damn it.* She'd neglected to talk to Shawn about defining what they were to each other—she, the one who told everyone to "use their words."

Was something actually happening between them? His recent withdrawal hinted he was done with her. But was he? If she explained everything and tried to quit, would Shawn try to talk her out of it? A part of her wished he would.

After dropping Diego and Gabriela off with her mother, she texted Shawn, asking if she could stop by. When he agreed, she drove to his house.

Her ancient phone froze and lost signal again. At a red light, she powered it off and back on. By the time she rang Shawn's bell, another message came through, delayed: *"I hope you don't mind I have a visitor."*

Too late to back out. The door opened. Instead of Shawn, a young woman stood in the threshold with Aidan on her hip.

"Hi. May I help you?"

Pain twisted Fe's gut. The woman was one of the most beautiful she'd ever seen.

A visitor, my butt.

CHAPTER 27

THE WOMAN AT SHAWN'S DOOR FLAUNTED A STRIKING BLEND of Asian features, shocking green eyes, and full African lips. Her low-cut dress clung to generous curves. Either she was the work of genetic engineering or a stellar plastic surgeon.

To make things worse, she wore the most stylish outfit and ankle boots Fe had ever seen.

Damn. She has good taste too?

"Hi! May I help you?" the woman said in a musical voice, setting fidgety Aidan down. He gave Fe's legs a quick sideways hug before darting into the house.

The woman still waited for an answer, so Fe snapped out of her trance. "I … I'm Fe," she managed.

Shawn appeared behind the visitor, phone pressed to his ear, and motioned Fe inside. He greeted her with a kiss on the cheek, held up a finger, mouthed, *hospital call*, and walked away.

"I'm Emery. A friend of Shawn's from Miami," the woman said, twirling a lustrous lock of auburn hair. "You must be the miracle-worker speech therapist! I've heard so much about you!"

To Fe's surprise, the woman hugged her.

Oh no, she's affectionate too!

"Sorry! I'm a hopeless hugger," Emery said. "Shawn told me all about the wonderful work you've done with Aidan. Isn't he the most adorable little boy? We had so much fun on the swings in the backyard. And tomorrow I hope they take me to the beach."

Tomorrow? She's spending the night?

Fe's eyes searched for Shawn, pleading for an explanation. But he was still absorbed in the call.

"Shawn's giving me a tour of the town, trying to convince me to move here," Emery explained.

Fe finally found her voice. "So … Miami. You guys know each other from training?"

Emery giggled. "Well … we've known each other a very long time. We have some … *history.*"

A clamp tightened Fe's throat and chest. As the shock ebbed, a wild, unreasonable woman surged inside her, ready to rip Emery's head off.

"So," Emery said, her eyes boring into her with eerie intensity. "How can we help you, Fe?"

Sudden self-consciousness flooded Fe over her consignment-store clothes.

"I … I forgot this here." She snatched her sunglasses from the coffee table, mumbled an apology, and bolted out.

• • •

When Shawn returned to the living room, Fe was gone. Emery was back to cuddling Aidan against his will.

"Where's Fe?" he asked, disappointed.

"She just stopped by to pick up her sunglasses." Emery tilted her head toward the door. "So, that was the famous Fe, huh?"

When his cousin smirked like that, nothing good followed. "What about her?"

"You think I was born yesterday? It took me one second to figure out you like her."

Shawn changed the subject. "So … do you think Aidan looks like you?"

Emery gasped and spun the boy to study his face, eager. "Do you think so?" She showered his cheek with kisses while he squirmed, desperate to escape her arms.

Shawn couldn't remember if Emery was his first cousin or fifth, but one thing was certain: they looked nothing alike. Her mother, a former super model, was famous for her exotic beauty—a mix of Korean and Jamaican roots.

On second thought, Emery was his aunt's stepdaughter. She shared no DNA with the child she passionately hoped resembled her.

Still, today, he'd play the family card, as if she were a sibling.

Pouring creamer into his coffee, Shawn begged, "Emery, you're my only hope. Please say you'll come work with me."

Emery tightened her grip as Aidan wriggled harder. The fact that he wasn't throwing one of his infamous tantrums counted as progress. "I can't make promises. Ken and I are in a new relationship. I shouldn't relocate until I know where it's going."

Shawn fluttered his eyelashes in mock pleading. "But you said you're ready to say yes if he proposes."

Emery grimaced. "Buddy, I'm ready to say yes to Bigfoot if he proposes. My biological clock isn't just ticking—it's screaming. I almost don't care who I marry as long as I can have a baby. STAT!" She kissed Aidan's cheek again.

He finally slipped free and dashed upstairs.

Emery's mischievous smile returned. "So, this girl, Fe ... You're drooling over her, aren't you?"

He puffed, but didn't bother denying it. "A useless exercise, considering she wants nothing to do with me."

"Don't be so sure of that." Emery snickered. "I ran a little experiment while you were on the phone. Trust me, the girl's into you."

Hope swelled in Shawn, so strong it made him dizzy. Just as quickly, caution returned. "Emery. You've read too many romance novels. Please don't get me in trouble."

• • •

"*Oh! We have history! I wanted to murder her!*"

In Allison's living room, Fe hit the clown-shaped inflatable punching bag Hope had bought for her nephews. "I wanted to scalp her, scratch her face, claw her eyes out. And then strangle her with her own silicone boobs!"

Sitting on the couch, her friends watched in wary silence.

When Fe had texted the girls about a support meeting, she meant to vent about her ex and his father's visit. But a more urgent crisis had taken over.

"Now I get why Shawn's been acting weird lately!" Fe wagged a finger at the clown, then poked its eyes. "Here I am, worried sick, thinking he's overwhelmed with the threatening letters, or feeling awkward after our kiss—"

"Wait!" Hope bolted upright. "What kiss?"

Ignoring her, Fe went on "—and the truth is he's sneaking around with other women!" She slammed the bag, growled, then gave a bitter chuckle. "I'm such an idiot! Turns out he only flirts with me and kisses me on days he's bored and out of other options?"

Hope's eyes widened. "Wait! *Days*—as in plural? Don't I get included in the juicy news anymore?"

With her usual impassible mask, Allison turned to Hope. "No. We're all fed up with your double entendres and dirty mind." She shifted back to Fe. "So, in summary, you're jealous."

Fe froze, hand still raised to strike the clown. "No, I'm not." Her squeaky pitch betrayed her lie.

Allison gave her the "cut the act" look. "Fe, let's be honest. You're infatuated with Shawn. You've been taking him for granted, and it burns to realize you're not his only option."

Hope translated. "Infatuated means: *you have the hots for him.*"

Fe dropped into the armchair, trying to gather herself. Gosh, her fiery Latin temper again. No wonder the Stewarts had called her a family shame.

"I'm fine now." She straightened her clothes. "Everything happens for good. Now I know I was imagining things. There's nothing between Shawn and me."

At her wavering tone, Joy rose and hugged her from behind. "Sweetie, are you about to cry?"

"No, I'm not!" Fe blinked fast, fighting back the tears. "I told you I never cry. It—"

"It ruins your makeup and gives you wrinkles," Allison finished with an eye roll.

"Wait," Hope said in a weak voice. "Can we rewind to the kissing part?"

Fe brushed off the question. As Joy released the hug, she continued, "I'm actually relieved. Now I know I was right to stay away from Shawn. He should be nothing more than the father of one of my clients. And I always knew I should never date a doctor."

Her phone rang again—the third time that hour—from Abuela's number. Fe sighed, resigned to yet another call from Gabriela.

She answered, "Hello?"

"Fe, *corazón*."

Her stomach clenched at her mother's voice. If Mami had overcome her terror of cell phones to call, something serious had happened.

"Sweetheart," she said, her usually steady voice trembling. "It's Gabriela."

CHAPTER 28

S HAWN'S RINGTONE YANKED HIM FROM THE DEPTHS OF SLEEP. He muttered a curse, fumbling for the phone on his nightstand. Wasn't the eICU covering the unit? Who the hell would call at this hour—two in the morning, maybe?

Without opening his eyes, he pressed the phone to his ear. "Hello?"

"Sorry, Shawn. Did I wake you?"

Fe's voice slipped through layers of drowsiness. Another dream? The kind where she asked him to join her in bed?

"I wasn't asleep." His yawn betrayed the lie.

"I'm so sorry to bother you. Could you do me a favor?"

Okay. The usual dream. "Yes?"

"Would you call in some antibiotics for Gabriela?"

His eyes drifted open. The clock read 9:15 p.m. He'd gone to bed at eight, drained from work and a day of showing Emery the town before dropping her at her hotel. He could've sworn it had been hours.

"Fe, if she has a virus, antibiotics won't help. Can you bring her to my office tomorrow so I can examine her?"

"Tomorrow is Saturday."

I'm in bed by nine on a Friday night. Pathetic. "Then bring her here tomorrow when you come for Aidan's session."

She hesitated. "I … I'm not sure it's safe to wait."

Something in her tone snapped him fully awake. He sat up. "Do you think you should take her to the emergency room?"

"I … I'm trying to avoid that."

Dread and fear mixed in her voice. He jumped out of bed and strode to the closet. "Tell me her symptoms."

Her voice trembled. "She's coughing nonstop and refuses to eat or drink. Her breathing seems labored—the usual first signs of her aspiration pneumonia."

In the walk-in closet, he wedged the phone between his shoulder and ear while pulling on a pair of jeans. "Any fever?"

"No."

"I'm coming over to check her. Do I have time to call Betty to stay with Aidan?"

Her silence answered for her.

"Never mind, I'll bring him with me." He shifted the phone from his ear long enough to shrug a T-shirt over his head. "Promise me you'll call nine-one-one if she gets worse before I get there."

• • •

The doorbell rang, and Fe hurried to answer, praying it was Shawn. A minute earlier, she'd nearly called 911—Gabriela seemed less and less responsive.

The peephole revealed Shawn standing at the door with Aidan asleep in his arms. Her hands trembled as she unhooked the chain and worked the locks.

"I'm so, so sorry, Shawn! I didn't mean to bother you this late." She rushed to take the sleeping boy from him.

Shawn skipped the greetings. "Where is she?"

"On the couch."

Gabriela lay sprawled across the sofa, chest rattling with harsh, uneven breaths, her eyes rolling in half-consciousness. While Shawn pressed a stethoscope to her lungs, Fe tucked Aidan into bed with Diego.

When she returned, Shawn was finishing his exam. "She's wheezing," he said. "Does she have a history of asthma?"

Fe struggled to gather her thoughts. "She's needed nebulizer treatments during pneumonia, but she was never officially diagnosed."

Too agitated for English, Mami burst into a rapid rant in Spanish. The cough had begun after a neighbor started cutting trees and mowing the lawn. Shawn switched languages to question her. Had Gabriela ever had an allergy to trees or pollen? Possibly. Had she been exposed to anyone sick? No.

"I doubt it's pneumonia," Shawn said at last. "No fever. I suspect asthma, likely triggered by an allergen. Let's take her to the ER."

Fe cringed. "Do we have to?"

His beautiful teal gaze wrapped her as he reached for her hand. "What's the problem with that?"

She hesitated. "The ER gives me flashbacks … from all the times I had to take her there before."

His brows rose, and after a pause, his hand slipped from hers. "Let me grab something from my car."

He stepped outside and returned with an inhaler and a spacer. Holding the mask snug against Gabriela's face, he gave her two measured puffs. In a calm, coaxing voice, he instructed her to breathe deeply. Then, he stayed with her, stroking her hair, while phoning prescriptions to the nearest twenty-four-hour pharmacy.

When he hung up, he lifted her frail body in his arms. "Fe, please help me install Gabriela's booster seat in my car. We're going to run a couple of errands."

• • •

Gabriela's fragile health made any illness dangerous. Shawn wanted at least a chest X-ray, blood counts, and cultures. Could he manage it without sending her through the ER?

He drove Fe and Gabriela to his office, where he picked up his pulse oximeter to monitor the girl's oxygen levels and his portable oxygen tank—just in case. From the driver's seat, he guided Fe through another inhaler treatment for Gabriela in the back.

At the hospital, he slipped them in through a back door with his badge and keyed an X-ray order into the first computer he found. A radiology tech he knew on night shift helped him cut through the red tape.

"Won't you get in trouble for this?" Fe asked behind him.

"Nah. They've got her insurance; they'll get paid." He turned to wink at her. "Worst I'll get is a slap for using after-hours staff on out-patient orders."

Minutes later, the X-ray was done. It had been years since he'd last read a pediatric film, but the radiologist on call reassured him nothing had changed from the previous studies.

He called in a favor from his friend Steve, an ICU nurse, who met them in radiology to draw blood and bring flu swabs. Shawn rushed the samples to the lab with a STAT label before heading home.

Inside, he was sweating. Normally, he'd never risk managing such a fragile patient outside the hospital. But the gratitude in Fe's eyes made it worth it.

• • •

Fe marveled at how quickly Shawn had taken charge and at the calm and authority he radiated.

While waiting for the labs to rule out an infection, they moved Gabriela to Abuela's guesthouse, away from the other kids. There, Mami insisted on relieving Fe so she could change out of her work clothes.

When Fe returned, in her pajamas, Shawn was still there with her mother, giving Gabriela the medications cousin Glennys had picked up at the pharmacy.

"Now, this is a steroid," Shawn explained, squirting syrup from a syringe into the girl's mouth. "It may make her hyper, maybe even keep her from sleeping, but it's our best chance to decrease the swelling in the bronchial tree."

Fe insisted on taking the first shift. After kissing Gabriela and Fe good night, Mami slipped out.

Shawn assembled the nebulizer, breaking open the ampoules and pouring in the medication. "I'm going to give her another treatment. In four hours, you'll need to repeat it. If she's not much better after that, we'll have to head to the ER."

Fe nodded. "Don't you have to go back to … your guest?"

Shawn fastened a mask over Gabriela's face. "Emery's in a hotel." His hands froze, eyes flicking to Fe as if he'd just realized what she'd assumed. A suppressed smile tugged at his lips. "Now we just wait for the meds to kick in."

He pulled a chair beside the bed. Fe imitated him.

Only the hum of the nebulizer broke the silence. Shawn watched over Gabriela closely, brow furrowed. Just his presence was enough to soothe her.

"I must say you have an amazing bedside manner," she said softly. "I'm so thankful you're here. Really—someday I hope you let me repay you."

"Your obsession with repaying favors makes me wonder if your family is tied to the mafia," he teased.

She lowered her voice. "Actually, my cousin Cheo in the Bronx *may or may not be.*" She winked. "That's how I might be of help someday. You may have friends in high places, but I have cousins in low places."

They chuckled together. The release of tension felt good.

Shawn listened to the sleeping girl's lungs and sat back. "She already sounds better."

Relief spread through Fe's chest. "Thanks, for real, Shawn. I'm so glad she's not in the hospital, so I don't have to call her dad and notify him. Not that he'd bother to visit."

Shawn studied her in silence before asking, "Is he bothering you again?"

No point in burdening him after all he'd done tonight. "Nothing new. Being divorced from Liam is a pain in the neck—but it still beats being married to him."

She'd meant it as a joke, but his expression sobered. "Was it that bad?"

A fountain of melancholy sprang inside her. "He had control issues. He couldn't stand that I wanted to continue my education, or have friends and interests outside the house."

He nodded, his full attention wrapping her like a warm, heavy robe.

Almost against her will, she went on. "I really tried to make him happy. I tried to be the perfect arm-candy wife who's always seen and never heard. But it was killing me."

When he didn't reply, she pushed forward. "I guess if the relationship had been healthier, we would've found ways to compromise. But by then the connection was gone, even the friendship." She paused. "It's hard to stay friends with someone who's never there."

His eyes held nothing but understanding. "He was always at work and never with you—just like your father."

The words struck deep. Pain welled up, burning her eyes with tears. "Yes. Just like *Papá*." So many years and self-help books later, it was the first time she'd made the connection.

Sobs broke loose before she could stop them. Everything hit at once. Lee and Liam's ambush visit, meeting Emery, the terror of Gabriela's illness, and the long ache of her past. The child craving attention from a workaholic father, the odd Latina girl returning to school with an accent. The pride of catching a wealthy med student's eye—and the heartbreak of never being accepted by his family. And worst of all, the pain of having to give up on all of them, and say goodbye.

Shawn reached for her hand and held it steady. His calm expression radiated quiet peace. A subtle sway in his body hinted he was debating whether to hug her. He chose instead to tighten his grip.

With her free hand, she grabbed a napkin from the coffee table and dried her eyes and nose. What had come over her?

Trying to lighten the mood, she forced a chuckle. "Gosh! What did you do to me? Do you hypnotize your patients to extract information?"

Smiling, he nodded. "It's called the doctor's spell. Most of what we do is let patients tell us what worries them. Saying it aloud means the work to fix it is already half-done."

"You use the magic of words too!" She stared at him, amazed. "How come I never saw that before?"

His smirk was both divine and devilish. "You *think* you know doctors, but your ex was *a surgeon.*" He rolled his eyes, the word *surgeon* carrying an insult. "Surgeons aren't trained to talk. They prefer their patients unconscious."

"I never thought about it that way." Awe filled her voice.

He released her hand. "And that's why doctors tend to be melancholic. We suck the sadness and fear from each patient, like drawing poison from a snakebite, and end up carrying it. We're professional worriers. Patients don't have to fret anymore, because we're worrying for them."

She gasped, seeing his dark moods in a new light. "You're right! I feel like you sucked the worry right out of me!" She paused, reflecting. "Medicine seems to have advanced so much, but you're telling me it's like ancient witchcraft—exorcising bad spirits, infusing cleaner energy."

He nodded eagerly. "Exactly. We're constantly transferring energy to patients. That's why we're so drained at the end of the day. The physical exam is more healing touch than data collection."

He hovered his hands over her. "I didn't give you a physical, so you missed the full treatment. Trust me, it feels good."

She laughed.

His smile slipped away. He dropped his hands, and his voice came out deeper, rawer. "Yup … You won't believe how good I'll make you feel when I finally get my hands on you."

Her jaw fell.

Fire blazed in his eyes, awakening goose bumps across her skin.

Wait. Am I imagining this?

Swallowing, she braced herself. "Shawn, who's Emery?"

His gaze locked on hers. "There's nothing between Emery and me. She's just—"

Mumbles from the bed announced Gabriela was awake.

Shawn rushed to her side, beaming. "You're awake, my little ninja!" He ran his fingers through the girl's hair, eyes brimming with tenderness.

"What did you just call her?" Fe asked.

He lifted the tiny girl onto his lap. "I secretly call her 'Little Ninja.' She looks defenseless, but she never lets anyone push her around. She may not have much muscle, but she's learned to whip her arm like a lever, just enough to give Diego a good smack if he tries to boss her."

Fe was impressed he'd noticed. Tittering, she covered her eyes with a hand and shook her head. "I shouldn't celebrate my daughter's violence, but I can't help feeling encouraged when I see signs she's getting stronger."

Shawn straightened the strap of Gabriela's nightgown. "The other day, Aidan yelled 'Jaysus!' in front of Betty, and I was so happy he'd learned another word, I celebrated it instead of scolding him for swearing. You should've seen Betty's face."

They laughed together.

"D-dat's n-not n-nice," Gabriela mumbled with a scowl. Apparently, she'd understood they were making fun of Aidan.

Chuckling, Shawn kissed her cheek. "You're terrible, my politeness police. But I'm so glad you're doing better." He showered her face with kisses, making her giggle.

The sight hit Fe like a punch to the stomach. Gabriela had never seen even a fraction of that sweetness from her own father. She took in Shawn's loving gaze, the playfulness in his voice, the gentleness of his hand brushing her daughter's hair aside.

How had she ever compared him to her ex? How had she ever doubted he was different?

The realization struck—and flattened her—like a truck on the highway.

She'd been wrong. Shawn wasn't, nor could he ever be, just another client. And Hope and Allison had been wrong too. What she felt for him wasn't infatuation. It wasn't "the hots." It wasn't lust.

It was love.

I love him.

I so love him.

Shoot. I'm in so much trouble.

CHAPTER 29

THE BLOOD COUNTS CAME BACK NORMAL, AND THE FLU SWAB test was negative. With no fever and a clear chest X-ray, Shawn ruled out an infection and the need for antibiotics.

Gabriela had bounced back, waking up hyper and asking for food. Yet fatigue won, and she fell asleep again after her 3:00 a.m. snack. Abuela and Doña Carmen insisted on relieving Fe for the rest of the night.

Now out of excuses to stay longer, Shawn announced he was leaving. Aidan slept so deeply that they agreed to let him be until the morning.

As Fe walked him to the main house door, she said, "Hey, you should send me a double bill. Tonight was therapeutic … *for me*. You improved my opinion of doctors."

He pressed a hand to his chest with a dramatic gasp. "Are you saying you like my kind now?"

She grunted. "Let's not exaggerate. I just dislike your kind *a little less*."

Laughing, he reached for the doorknob, but her hand on his arm stopped him.

Her slouched shoulders and lowered eyes carried an apology. "No, seriously. Tonight, you proved what I've always suspected: your work is pretty awesome. And I was a horrible witch for not understanding that sometimes doctors have to neglect their personal life in order to save others."

Her words touched him. Admitting that couldn't have been easy.

"No, you were right. We doctors are a bunch of neurotics not worth your mental space."

"Really?" Her eyes lifted to his.

"Oh, yes. You're lucky you aren't one of us." He waved it off. "We're just overachievers obsessed with grades, desperate to impress our impossible-to-please parents."

His aim was to make her laugh, but her expression turned serious. "The next time your father complains about your solo practice, tell him, 'Shut up. Fe says I'm the best damn doctor in the whole freaking galaxy.'"

Heat rushed to his face, delight mingling with emotion. Before he could thank her, she threw herself in his arms.

He tensed for a beat, then surrendered, holding her tight. Eyes closed, he breathed in her scent. Her flimsy pajama top offered no shield between her breasts and his chest. He savored the warmth of her body pressed against his, her neck hooked with his, the silk of her back beneath his fingers. Stopping himself from kissing her took every ounce of strength.

She drew him tighter, erasing the last sliver of space between them. Every inch of his body pressed against hers throbbed.

And he knew; it was a signal. She was inviting him.

Two paths split open before him, leading to parallel realities. In one, he resisted temptation, and everything stayed the same. In the other, he gave in, ravished her mouth, feasted on her curves, released everything he'd bottled up. After the confessions of this night, after her gratitude, she wouldn't resist. It would take four steps to make it to her bedroom; five seconds to peel away her scanty clothes; six to shed his own. And after so much deprivation, seven minutes to be done.

She pulled back, eyes brimming with the same longing. Without words, she urged him—begged him—to take the next step. Her lips parted, summoning his mouth.

God, he wanted her!

But this wasn't right. Not like this. Not tonight.

Harnessing every shred of restraint, he eased away. "I should get going."

She gaped as if he'd spoken in another language. "What?"

"It's been a tough night. You need rest."

She shook her head hard. "I'm perfectly fine!" She stepped forward, but his arms kept her back.

"No, you're not." He pressed a kiss to her forehead. "I'll send Betty for Aidan tomorrow. Good night, Fe."

Shock lit her face, but before she could answer, he turned and strode out—faster than he needed to, afraid he'd change his mind.

• • •

"He wouldn't kiss me! I practically threw myself at him, and he rejected me."

No shouting. No hand-waving. No tears. The day after Gabriela's illness, Fe sat slumped on her living room couch, staring through the casserole and flowers her friends had brought.

Joy slid beside her and wrapped one arm around her. Hope perched on the other side and clasped her hand.

"I'm such an idiot," Fe whispered. "I spent months with him, and only now do I realize I love him. I should've never rejected him that first day. I should've never taken Aidan's case, painting myself into a corner. I should've quit—set the record straight the moment we kissed on Halloween."

Joy hugged tighter, and Hope leaned in.

From the armchair, Allison sat back, arms crossed.

Joy tipped her head toward Fe. "Come join the hug, Allison. Fe needs to be connected to our love."

Allison leaned away. "No, thanks. My love is wireless."

Joy and Hope glowered. With an exaggerated sigh, Allison stood, stretched out a hand, and gave Fe's head a half-hearted pat.

They sat in silence until Fe spoke again. "I'm pathetic, aren't I? Pining for a man I had my chance with—and ruined it."

"Maybe it's not too late," Joy murmured, releasing the hug.

Fe shook her head. "I think he's over me! Ever since Thanksgiving, he's been so … *appropriate*." She spat the word like a curse. "Maybe it's time to admit this is never going to happen."

"Or …" Hope arched a brow and smacked her lips. "Or maybe it's time to up your game and hit him with everything you've got."

Fe blinked, stunned, but her chest loosened—Hope's words lit something inside her.

"I have to be the voice of reason—again," Allison said, returning to her chair. "Fe, even if it's not too late, have you forgotten your ex and his father threatening to blacklist you? Or that you swore off workaholics? Didn't you promise never again to choose a man who doesn't put you and your family first?"

Damn it. Allison had a point.

"Please!" Hope flicked her wrist. "It's not like Fe's planning to marry the guy!" She rose from the couch. "Let her start by screwing him first, then she'll figure out the rest." She hauled Fe up and pierced her with her dark eyes. "Fe, can you arrange that?"

Fe groaned. "I don't think I could ever seduce a man. I'm a modern woman, but I was raised by two conservative Latinas. I still have this ingrained idea that men should lead."

"Nonsense." Hope scowled. "Men love it when we take the pressure off them and make the first move."

"I disagree," Allison cut in. "Men are wired to be the hunter. That comes with their tiny Neanderthal brains. If you want one in your life, you have to play dumb and let them think they're seducing *you*. I hate that game. That's why I'm alone."

Fe turned to Joy, the tiebreaker.

Joy shrugged. "I don't like generalizations. Men aren't all the same."

"Gosh!" Fe sighed. "It's a pity that my three brothers are such disasters of retro machismo. I wish I had a male consultant to ask questions like this."

Joy considered it. "I'd say, give him clear hints. Men struggle with insecurity too. Wear your prettiest outfits, make eye contact, touch him lightly. Subtly let him know he won't be rejected if he makes a move."

"Subtly?" Fe winced. "Huh. Subtlety's a concept I've never practiced before."

CHAPTER 30

S HAWN COULD'VE SWORN FE WAS TRYING TO KILL HIM. FOR THE past two weeks, she'd worn her sexiest outfits and touched him more than ever. One day, he complained of back pain, and she offered a *back rub*. Damn it. That'd been so good.

She even volunteered to trim his hair in cousin Glennys' salon next door. There, she'd sent him into a trance—rubbing his scalp while washing his hair, then running her fingers through it as she cut. He kept his eyes closed, fantasizing about throwing her into an empty chair and taking her right there.

But he couldn't ruin it now. He had thirty-six days to go before he could end their professional contract and start his seduction plans.

Now, on December 30, he sat with Richard and Keith at his house, getting the latest update on the case.

"We interviewed some of the parents at the Gainesville playground Aidan showed us," Keith said. "Two women recognized his picture. They said the boy had been in town just a few weeks, usually with a Hispanic woman they assumed was his nanny. They never saw Tara or the man she ran off with."

The news was a relief. Shawn hoped Aidan had spent as little time as possible with Tara's killer. He prayed daily that the man hadn't formed any attachment to his son.

Richard added, "Fe's idea of having your friend Jay recall smells and sounds has paid off." He flipped through a file. "Under hypnosis, Jay remembered the smell of weed coming from the white van the man drove. Combine that with your cleaning lady's statement that Tara left

191

'with the lawn guy,' our theory is she actually said, 'with the *grass* guy'—the local drug supplier for the neighborhood teens."

Shawn frowned. "Tara wasn't into weed. Her addiction was opiates."

"This guy seems to have retailed all kinds of drugs," Richard said. "It won't be easy to get anyone in your neighborhood to admit they know him, but it's a start. And Fe's been helping every day, showing Aidan pictures of suspects. So far, he calls every Hispanic woman 'Abuela' and hasn't shown any interest in the men."

"Any progress on the second person sending letters?"

Keith answered, "Besides securing your house, we installed cameras in places where letters have appeared—the hospital mailroom, the garage … Next time someone tries to drop off one, we'll catch them."

When the meeting wrapped and Keith left, Richard lingered.

"How was your Christmas?" he asked.

Shawn grunted. "I was on call, stuck at the hospital most of the day. Poor Aidan would've had a miserable time if Fe hadn't offered to bring him to her house."

"Ouch. I hope you paid them double babysitting hours."

"I did. I also asked Betty to pick out gifts for Diego and Gabriela when she bought Aidan's presents. I was too swamped at the unit for shopping."

Damn it. He'd officially become his father—present for his family only through money. Great way to prove to Fe he wasn't a workaholic.

Excusing himself, he shot a quick text to Emery, urging her to consider his job offer.

As Shawn walked Richard to the door, Richard asked, "Any plans for New Year's Eve?"

"Fe's mom and grandmother offered to host Aidan for a sleepover, so I can go out."

"That sleepover's the event of the year," Richard said. "Arthur and the twins are going. Joy and I have been counting down the days—though first we have to make an appearance at some party with her girlfriends."

"Yes. The Latin music club. Fe's cousin invited me too, but I haven't decided."

Shawn didn't explain his hesitation. He still wanted distance from Fe, but the longing for her was eating him alive. Turning her down the night he cared for Gabriela still burned. Maybe the next thirty-six days would be easier if he could steal one more kiss.

Just one. He could blame it on champagne, then pretend the next day it hadn't happened.

Only one more kiss.

• • •

The New Year's Eve party exceeded everyone's expectations. Joy and Richard dazzled them all with their dancing. Fe had honestly thought Joy was using a euphemism when she said she gave him lessons in the bedroom. Even Hope's fiancé, shy Tom, honored the dance floor.

Allison refused to come, claiming she'd never attend a party where Agent Fields was present. Left unpaired, Fe and Shawn danced together all night. Between the rock songs, the silly "Electric Slide," and the inevitable "Macarena," he impressed her again with his moves on salsa and merengue—even on pieces as challenging as bachata and perico.

At the start of the evening, Hope had sworn they'd dance until sunrise. By 10:30, though, they were all feeling their age and doubting they'd even make it to midnight. Fe had been counting on Joy, who never drank, as her designated driver—but Joy and Agent Fields disappeared early, still in their honeymoon phase. By eleven, Hope whispered she and Tom were slipping out too, so Fe asked them for a ride. Shawn tagged along.

Fe dozed in the car and was half asleep when Hope tapped her shoulder and said they'd arrived. Only after the car pulled away did Fe realize she wasn't at her house—she was at Shawn's.

She yawned. "Why'd they drop me off here instead of home?"

"They're heading to Orlando tonight. Stopping at your neighborhood would've added an hour. I told them I'd take you."

His clumsy hands fumbled with the door keyhole.

She giggled. "You're not in any condition to drive."

He finally managed the lock. "Neither are you. That's why we'll make coffee and sober up first. It's almost midnight anyway—we don't want the New Year catching us on the road."

The kitchen was out of coffee, so Shawn led her upstairs, where he kept another coffee maker.

Fe's steps wobbled on the staircase. She gripped the railing with one hand, his arm with the other, though he seemed just as tipsy, and hardly better support. Laughter echoed, and only after a moment, did she realize it was hers.

At the top, she let go of him, uncertain who'd been holding up whom. "I'd better get an Uber. Coffee or not, you can't drive me—you're drunker than I am!"

Starting the coffee maker, he winked. "Not really. I'm just exaggerating how drunk I am, so I'll have an excuse to be inappropriate with you."

She chuckled.

It was a joke … right?

Shawn opened the French doors to the deck facing the river and leaned over the railing. She followed him into the cool night.

Across the dark water, the lights from Highway US1 gleamed, and a few fireworks flared in the distance.

He pointed toward the horizon. "Every year at midnight, some family over there sets off gigantic fireworks. I don't even think they're legal."

He crossed to another set of French doors, opened them to his bedroom, and flicked on the TV. After tuning into the New Year's countdown, he angled the screen toward the deck. When he came back out, barefoot and carrying binoculars, the coffee scent was already drifting from inside.

They settled on the outdoor couch, trading the binoculars to scan the stars. She slipped off her shoes and tucked her feet beneath her, tugging the hem of her red dress over her legs. From the TV, the noise of a street party poured into the night.

"You grew up in New York City," he said. "Ever been to the Times Square New Year's Eve celebration?"

She lowered the binoculars. "No. My parents and brothers were too overprotective. How about you?"

His eyes lost in the stars, he nodded. "Yeah. Years ago, in my twenties."

"How was it?"

He shrugged. "Meh. Too crowded. The only perk is plenty of strangers willing to kiss you."

"Why would you want to kiss a stranger?" She made a face.

He turned to her. "Because next to Valentine's Day, the worst night to be single is New Year's Eve—not having anyone to smooch at midnight is pathetic." A playful smirk bent his lips. "Why do you think you're here? You're my New Year's kiss."

Normally, that line would have flustered her, but that third glass of champagne had done wonders in lubricating her brain. The spark in his eyes was devilish. Was he teasing or actually flirting? Interestingly, she didn't seem to mind either way.

He grabbed the TV remote and switched to a music channel playing an old slow tune. "Come on." He helped her up from the couch. "Let's dance one last song."

He wrapped his arms around her waist, cheek to cheek. Almost on instinct, her arms slipped around his neck.

Moving to the music felt hypnotic. For all the dancing they'd done that night, this was their first slow piece. The space between them shrank until it vanished. His hard body pressed against hers, and her hips soon aligned with a different kind of hardness. Her core turned to butter, melting slowly. It took her a moment to recognize that golden blend of bliss and restlessness as arousal.

Their gentle rocking was less about the music than about holding each other. His lips brushed her neck, flooding her with delight, as his hands slid down to clasp her bottom.

She jerked, but her clouded mind found his boldness amusing. "Shawn McDevitt. Are you daring to grab my butt?"

He moaned in affirmation. "Tomorrow, I'll blame it all on being drunk, and we'll move on, pretending this never happened. In the meantime, let me enjoy it. I'm in heaven."

She giggled. "Your heaven is a butt?"

Still swaying, he mumbled, "You have no idea how much I've fantasized about this since the day we hit the ground together." He squeezed her tighter, crushing their hips.

She gasped, then laughed. "Shawn! What's going on with you tonight! This is not you!"

He pulled back to study her face. "You think I'm the most harmless man in the world, don't you? If men came in degrees of alcohol, I'd be close to a virgin drink, right? That's what you think?"

His gaze unsettled her. Maybe she'd thought herself the hunter when she was actually the prey. "No … I mean, if you want to charm a woman, talking about her butt is too blunt. Compliment her eyes, for example."

His expression softened. "Of course, I've dreamed plenty of those too."

He kissed her neck, then locked gazes with her again, his voice a whisper. "I fantasize all the time about looking right into your eyes while I blow your mind in bed."

Her brain short-circuited, all wits gone.

Just then, fireworks burst over the river.

His brows lifted. "Happy New Year, gorgeous."

The instant his mouth claimed hers, the last thread of clear thought vanished.

She kissed him hard, desperate, like a survivor who'd crossed the desert and finally found water. But no matter how much she drank, each sip only fueled her thirst.

Encouraged, he deepened the kiss. Their tongues tangled, their hands turned reckless. It became a daring game, each raising the stakes, the other matching and exceeding the bet. His hands slid beneath her skirt; hers untucked his shirt. His palms trailed up her legs; hers pressed against his bare chest. When his fingers slipped inside the back of her Spanx, touching skin, she moaned into his mouth.

She never knew exactly how they'd made it to the bedroom. The TV still played slow music, yet they reached the bed fast. His shirt disappeared first, then her dress, then his pants.

Even drunk, something held her back from stripping away the last layer. He seemed hesitant too. So, she still in her Spanx and bra, he in his boxer briefs, they indulged instead in driving each other wild. They rolled and turned in bed, tangled in the blankets—kissing and biting, grinding and rubbing for a delicious eternity.

Then, a flash of clarity broke through. She pulled away, breathless. "Wait! Stop!"

To his credit, he let go instantly. "What's wrong?"

Panting, she struggled to sit up in bed, tugging the blanket up to cover her bra. He sat up too, eyes begging.

She tried to steady her thoughts. "If we keep going, we'll feel terribly guilty tomorrow."

Blinking fast, he raked a hand through his disheveled hair, then gave a slow nod. "You're right. Absolutely right. But—" He hesitated, then half shrugged. "We've gone so far already, we'll feel guilty tomorrow *anyway*. Shouldn't we at least make it worth the guilt?"

Her champagne-clouded brain fought his logic—and lost.

She lifted a finger. "Excellent point."

Then, without another word, she shoved him back onto the bed and leaped on top of him.

CHAPTER 31

WHEN SHAWN WOKE ON NEW YEAR'S MORNING, HIS FIRST thought was that he'd drunk too much. As sleep's anesthesia wore off, he braced for headache and nausea. Fortunately, both were milder than he feared.

Instead, something in his body felt different in a good way—lighter. Like he'd been hauling a sack of bricks, and someone had swapped it for a bag of feathers.

Then, it hit him.

He turned sharply, heart racing, only to find the other side of the bed empty.

Had it all been a dream?

Sitting up in bed, he examined the spot beside him the way he'd tackle an elusive diagnosis: a shallow dip in the mattress, wrinkled sheets, makeup smudged on the pillow.

Oh Jaysus.

Oh shite.

He flopped back, vivid memories flooding in. Fe in his bed. The bliss of her body pressed to his. Their limbs tangled like that day they fell together—except this time, no layers stood between them. Her kisses. His. Taking her over and over in a string of fantasies come true, each more unreal than his wildest dreams.

Janey Mack.

The clock on his nightstand read 9:52.

Aidan!

He'd promised to pick him up by ten.

Shawn bolted out of bed, deciding he'd shower later. He yanked on jeans and a light blue T-shirt, then sprinted to his car.

As he drove, the self-scolding began.

Way to be subtle, man! Just five more weeks—you couldn't wait? Now what?

Her scent clung to him, summoning flashbacks.

His mouth on her body. Her mouth on his.

Oh, cripes.

No one answered at Fe's house, but the nosy neighbor was quick to oblige. Doña Carmen and Abuela had gone to visit relatives. Everyone else had just walked to a friend's bakery nearby, hoping it might open despite the holiday. If he hurried, he could still catch them.

Following the woman's directions, he strode deeper into the scuzzier parts of Fe's neighborhood. A few blocks later, he spotted them— Fe holding Aidan's hand, Diego pushing Gabriela in the wheelchair.

He quickened his pace and called her, "Fe!"

She froze. Slowly, she turned to face him.

He closed the half-block gap, then stopped six feet away.

Their eyes locked, but neither of them spoke.

What was in her gaze? Was it longing? Contempt? Shyness? Disappointment?

He had so much to say. First, he wanted to thank her and admit that last night had surpassed his wildest dreams. Then apologize and reassure her he was usually gentler—that maybe he'd been drunker than he'd let on.

He wanted to hold her, kiss her, beg her to swear last night had been their first, but not their last. More than anything, he needed to know what she was thinking. Had he met her expectations or let her down?

But he stayed still, silent. Waiting for her to speak.

What now? Did they have a plan? Did last night mean she was willing to give him a chance? Did it mean she could no longer work with Aidan?

Would she acknowledge it, or pretend again that nothing had happened?

They both opened their mouths at once.

"Sorry, you go first."

"No. You first."

They stumbled over each other again, both trying to yield.

She cleared her throat, looking away. He studied his shoes, scratching his arm. She shifted her weight, then glanced at the sky. He raked his fingers through his hair and sighed.

Dang, this was awkward.

Now, he understood why serious talks should happen *before* the first time in bed.

He finally raised his eyes to her face—

But before he could speak, Diego blurted, "Mom! Where's Aidan?"

Fe's head snapped toward Diego. Only then did they realize Aidan was gone.

"Aidan? Aidan! Where are you?" she called out.

They split up, searching for the boy.

"Aidan?" Shawn spotted him far ahead, darting down an alley. He tore after him, shouting his name. Fe and Diego followed.

It was a blessing that the streets were deserted on this sleepy New Year's morning. The boy bolted through alleys and streets, making sharp turns, as if he knew exactly where he was going.

"Where is he headed?" Shawn asked Fe, who ran close behind him. Even with her runner's stamina and his much longer legs, they struggled to close the gap.

Diego called out, "He's taking the shortcut to the playground!"

"What playground?" Shawn asked, his breathing growing ragged.

"The one at the park," Fe replied.

Sure enough, Aidan reached the playground and went straight to the swings, like he'd been there before.

Shawn stopped, bent over, a hand pressed to his chest, heart racing, lungs heaving after the sprint. Fe and Diego were breathless too.

That had been terrifying. If not for the light traffic, Aidan could've been run over.

Fe told Diego to head back for Gabriela, left behind in her wheelchair. Then, she turned to Shawn. "He seems to know this place. Have you ever brought him here?"

"No. I assumed you had."

She shook her head.

Shawn's pulse had barely steadied when Aidan hopped off the swings and ran to a large oak tree. He crouched and stuck his hand inside a hole in the trunk.

Déjà vu jolted Shawn. He'd seen Aidan do something like this before. Where?

Georgia. At the storage place he'd taken him with the FBI.

Aidan rummaged inside the trunk for a moment longer. When his hand emerged, it clutched a moldy, tiny teddy bear.

Fe and Shawn both gasped.

"He was here before!" Fe said. "It must've been around the time he was lost."

Shawn yanked his phone from his pocket and dialed his case agent. "Keith, is this a bad time?"

But Aidan bolted again.

Fe and Shawn sprinted after him, struggling to keep up.

As precise in his sense of direction as ever, Aidan zigzagged two blocks before stopping at a run-down building. He charged up the stairs to the second floor, straight to an apartment door, and knocked.

A middle-aged Hispanic woman opened. When she saw him, she gasped, her face lighting up.

"¡Adancito? ¿Eres tú?"

Aidan squealed, opening his arms wide. "*Tía!*"

CHAPTER 32

F E KNEW THE SITUATION WAS SERIOUS WHEN A FULL FBI TEAM showed up in record time—even on a holiday.

Noemí, the woman Aidan called "*Tía*," spoke only *Cibaeño*, so they asked Fe to translate.

"Noemí took care of Aidan the year he was lost. First here, then in Georgia," Fe explained. "She says her younger brother, Ramón, showed up one day with his new woman and the boy. All she knew was that the boy's father was someone Ramón held a grudge against."

"And his way to get even was running off with the man's wife?" asked Keith.

Fe asked Noemí, then translated, "At first, providing Tara with drugs was a personal vendetta against her husband—Shawn. Yet Ramón had 'never been well in the head' and soon became obsessed, wanting her for himself. She says he seduced Tara, and she ran away with him willingly. Over the next weeks, though, it became clear that 'the gringa was even crazier than Ramón,' and couldn't care for Aidan, so Noemí took over."

"Was Ramón ever close to Aidan? Any risk he might want him back?" Shawn's tight jaw betrayed his anxiety.

Fe translated, "She doesn't think so. At first, Ramón paid some attention to Aidan, but he soon lost interest. After Noemí took over, Aidan only saw his mother briefly, on her good days."

Relief softened the tight lines on Shawn's face.

Fe added, "She says after Tara's death, she dropped Aidan in front of the police station, but he must've wandered away. She seems to care for him."

"And he was quite affectionate with her," Keith agreed, tentative, his eyes probing Shawn's. "She must've taken good care of him."

Shawn rubbed his temples, the tension of months unwinding. He nodded. "Good to know he wasn't suffering."

• • •

Shawn couldn't believe it—they were one step closer to ending his nightmare. Now they had a name: Ramón, or Raymond Blandino. It took the FBI a few short hours to trace him as the son of one of Shawn's former patients.

Re-reading her chart brought it all back. A woman in her sixties, brain-dead after a car accident. Four of her five children had agreed to withdraw life support. One son refused. As chair of the ethics committee, Shawn had been part of the ruling in favor of the majority. As the ICU attending, he had given the order to disconnect the ventilator.

Only now did he remember how painful that case had been. The man's accusations still echoed—calling him and the other doctors "murderers."

His gaze shifted to Fe, sitting with Aidan on his lanai, a scrapbook spread across their laps. After everything that had happened, he and Fe hadn't had a chance to speak alone.

"What are we doing?" he asked Keith, uneasy.

Keith hushed him. "Fe's showing Aidan the same scrapbooks they'd worked on for weeks. Only now we've slipped in pictures of Noemí and Ramón Blandino."

They stood behind and watched in silence.

A strongly visual kid, Aidan quickly recognized Noemí as "*Tía*," winning Fe's praise.

Fe turned the page, and the suspect's face stared back.

Aidan lit up, as if recognizing an old friend. He jabbed his finger at the photo, and his next word hit Shawn like a blow.

"*Papi.*"

• • •

It had been an intense day for Shawn, Fe knew it. She could only imagine the pain of hearing Aidan call another man *Papi* after refusing to call him Dad for months. And the thought of a suspected killer's hands on his son must've been terrifying.

Yet an even darker shadow haunted her: the man was still out there, unstable, and a danger to Shawn.

She suggested they take the next day off from therapy. Shawn must've misread it as a request for space, because he made no effort to contact her. When sessions resumed, Betty brought Aidan alone at noon, but Shawn didn't text the usual picture. By the time of the evening session, Fe was quivering with anticipation to see him. Yet he walked in tired and distant, his gaze sliding past hers.

She took the hint. That night between them had been a drunken impulse, and like their previous kisses, should never be mentioned again.

The thought devastated her. First times were usually awkward, but that night had been amazing. And now he was pretending it had never happened?

For the first time in her life, Fe couldn't find a silver lining. Burying her sobs in her pillow so she wouldn't wake Gabriela, she cried herself to sleep.

CHAPTER 33

THREE DAYS INTO THE NEW YEAR, SHAWN WAS BURSTING INSIDE. He couldn't believe Fe was pretending nothing had happened between them.

No amount of hand-scrubbing or bike riding could slow the storm of dreadful thoughts flooding his mind. Had he been a fiasco in bed? Was that what this was about? Had he fallen short *again*?

Even José, the town's hobo, seemed to glare at him from his eternal bench, contempt and disappointment in his eyes.

Shawn was angry with Fe—but even more furious with himself. He'd been working so hard to prepare everything for them. He'd even convinced Emery to return for a formal job interview. Were all his plans ruined? Was it worth confronting Fe?

"Are you okay?" His father's voice pulled him back to the physician's lounge, gentler than usual, genuinely worried.

"No. But it's not your fault." Shawn picked up his tray and carried it to the trash can. Oblivious to the storms between him and Fe, Abuela kept packing his lunch every night. Today, he couldn't bring himself to eat it.

Seamus followed him out of the lounge. "Is there anything I can do to help?"

Shawn gave a bitter snort. "Sure. Get me a time machine to undo stupid things."

Remembering his previous talk with Dr. Jones, Shawn stopped walking and turned to his father. His family steered clear of confrontations and unpleasant topics, but his current frustration pushed him over the edge. "Dad, did you tell Mark Jones you wanted me out of this town?"

The flicker of guilt in Seamus' face was undeniable. "I … I just wanted you to have a chance to start all over somewhere else—maybe an academic job."

Shawn steeled himself. "Have you had anything to do with the threatening letters?"

"What? No! Are you crazy?" Seamus shuddered. His shock seemed sincere. "I'm so worried about you, I can't even mention those threats aloud—not even to a friend!"

"Wait." Shawn frowned. "Jones said *you* told him about the letters. Didn't you?"

Seamus' baffled expression answered for him. Before Shawn could press further, his phone rang.

It was a call from his private detective, so Shawn picked up and resumed pacing. "What's up, Del?"

"Big news. I found juicy dirt that may finish the Stewarts' family."

Shawn stopped walking. He'd nearly forgotten about hiring his PI to dig into them.

Apparently overhearing, his father shot him an inquiring look. "What news did Del find?"

Scanning the area, Shawn signaled Seamus to follow him to the physician's library—always deserted. He closed the door, settled at one of the studying tables, and put the call on speaker. "Go ahead, Del."

"I had an interesting talk with Larry McGuire, Faith Stewarts' lawyer."

It took Shawn a moment to connect the name. "You mean *Fe Hernandez's* lawyer?"

"Yes, he's been trying to convince her to report Liam Stewarts for late child support. He has everything ready, just waiting for her approval."

Shawn frowned. "How come?"

"The guy has a bad habit of withholding child support for months at a time. Then he starts paying it again, but never catches up with what he owes. The amount's now high enough to qualify as a felony. And when you factor in that he never paid Faith her share of the profits from selling their marital home—well, if she wanted, she could report him and send him to jail."

For a fleeting instant, the thought of punishing Fe's ex tasted sweet. But the satisfaction vanished as quickly as it came. "That's never going to happen," Shawn said. "He'll just produce the money and pay it all at once."

The detective snickered with the glee of gossip. "That's the best part. Liam Stewart is not as liquid as you'd think. Between his new wife's addiction to designer clothes, their oceanfront property, and the boats he never uses. To raise that kind of cash now, he'd need to move assets or borrow."

Seamus nodded. "That matches what Mark told me."

Del lowered his voice. "And Larry says Judge Cail, the family law judge likely to get the case, has an old grudge against Lee Stewarts and won't pull his punches. Liam could face it all: accounts frozen, medical license suspended—maybe even time in jail, if the judge decides to teach the family humility."

Shawn raised an eyebrow. "That would be fun. But it wouldn't finish them."

Seamus raised a hand. "I give it a fifty-fifty chance they'll leave town. Lee mentioned Liam's wife has been pressuring him to move to a bigger city. A scandal like this could be the last push. Lee can't sustain the practice on his own. If his son leaves, he'll retire."

"But there's one obstacle," Del said. "Liam Stewart's ex refuses to sue. She's too proud."

The words left him numb. Not long ago, the chance to make these bullies pay would've given him cause for rejoicing. Right now, if he couldn't have Fe, nothing else mattered.

• • •

When Fe thought things couldn't get any worse, Betty spilled the beans: Aidan was starting at the Smith Center in a few weeks.

Did this mean Shawn planned to fire her and hadn't even had the courtesy to tell her? Was all he wanted a night in bed, only to toss her aside like a used rag?

Fe longed to vent to her girlfriends, but she had to be careful about what to share. If Hope caught the faintest whiff of what happened on New Year's Eve, Fe would need to wave a flaming torch to get her off her case.

Luckily, the spotlight would shift elsewhere for now. Joy had just called for emergency support after a huge fight with Agent Fields. For a while, the friends had treated that on-again, off-again relationship like a time bomb. Apparently, the bomb had just gone off.

On the drive to Joy's, Hope muttered revenge plans against Fields if he dared break her sister's heart again. Fe doubted the fight would last, so she kept her opinions to herself.

Allison, by contrast, seemed to be having the best day of her life. Even the layers of Botox that froze her smile couldn't mask her glee.

Fe carried the ice cream; Hope had the tearjerker movie and Kleenex. Allison brought champagne.

They rang Joy's bell so many times without an answer, they assumed it was broken and started knocking. When that failed too, they called her phone—still no response.

At last, unsteady steps shuffled inside, and the door opened.

Joy stood at the threshold, glassy-eyed, hair wild, mascara smudged. A terry bathrobe hung loosely from her shoulders. Towering behind her loomed Agent Fields—his face smeared with lipstick, hair sticking up, shirt half-undone with three buttons fastened in the wrong holes.

He smirked at Allison with a mix of amusement and defiance.

"Hi, girls!" Joy said, breathless. "Didn't anybody get my text?"

Hope huffed. "You took him back *already*? No emergency support meeting? No raiding your closet for hand-me-down clothes? That's no fun!"

Wincing in apology, Joy let them in. "I sent you all a group text saying everything was fine, that you didn't have to come." She checked her phone, then grimaced. "Oh … I forgot to hit send."

Her elation vanished, Allison had gone speechless. Fe couldn't decide whether to cringe or laugh it off.

Joy guided them into the living room. "I'm sorry, girls. It was my fault; I overreacted. I should know the drill by now. Every time this relationship moves forward, one of us freaks out a little."

Agent Fields—Richard—nodded hard. "I don't know why she worries. She should've learned by now the only way she'll get rid of me is by paying someone to kill me."

Allison mumbled something about volunteering to do it for free.

"The relationship moving forward? Wait a minute!" Hope squealed, seizing Joy's hand. "Is this an engagement ring?"

Beaming, Joy lifted her hand. "Yes! And it's quartz! Richard knows me so well!" She rose on tiptoe, tugging him down for a kiss on the cheek. "He knows I have ethical concerns about diamonds and that I love quartz, because I'm into energy clearing. Isn't that thoughtful?"

Allison cleared her throat. "And conveniently cheaper."

Richard pivoted, scowling. "I'm getting tired of your attacks. You don't want to mess with me. I know more of your history than you think, Allison." His tone dropped cold. "Or should I call you *Grace*?"

Allison's blue eyes shot darts at him. She straightened her back and, in her heels, made herself nearly as tall as he was. "I have nothing to hide about my name change, Agent Fields."

He narrowed his eyes. "I also know your real age."

Fe had never seen Allison so tense.

Richard smiled. "Relax, Connors. I'm not the enemy. Give me a chance, and I know I'll grow on you."

She eyed him with contempt. "Yes. Like a malignant tumor."

"Okay, enough," Joy cut in. "Allison, calm down. You act like

Richard's competition for my time and attention, but he'd never stop me from hanging out with you guys."

"On the contrary!" he said. "I love that you take her to all the girly stuff—shopping, manicures, chick flicks—so *I* don't have to." He wrapped an arm around Joy's waist and squared his shoulders. "And you, ladies, should stop seeing me as a rival and start seeing me as an asset. I'm … your external consultant. Your insight into the male brain."

Hope arched a brow. "Funny you mention it. We were recently saying Fe can't trust her brothers' advice. And my T.J. is a proudly self-proclaimed beta male—not the typical man."

She studied Richard for a long beat, squinting. "All right, Fields. Prove your worth. Earlier, Fe told us how her love interest's been acting strange—aloof, avoiding her."

Heat rushed to Fe's cheeks.

Hope pointed at Fe with her open hand, eyes still on Richard. "Go ahead, impress me with your wisdom."

Without missing a beat, Richard motioned Fe to take the armchair, then settled on the loveseat with Joy beside him. Hope and Allison perched on the couch, watching.

Over the next few minutes, Fe gave Richard the sanitized version of her heart drama. She'd once turned Shawn down—a choice she now regretted. Lately, she'd been sure something real was budding between them. They'd shared "a few kisses." And then, he'd gone cold.

Richard listened in silence, his expression serious until she finished.

"Let me tell you something about us men," he said. "We're much simpler than you think. Women keep trying to read between the lines and second-guess everything. But we usually mean what we say, and say what we mean."

"For goodness' sake, Fields! Cut the act." With a grunt, Allison sprang to her feet and faced Fe. "You don't need a man's brain insider, there's not much inside their brains. *I* will tell you what!"

In a rare display of emotion, Allison paced the living room, clenching her fists. "You give men more credit than they deserve. Fields got *one* thing right: men are simple. They're nothing but sex-obsessed creatures, slaves to their testosterone. If your man seems cranky, or if he's getting complicated, the answer is easy." She threw her arms up. "*He needs food or sex.*"

Richard studied her, brows raised, eyes brimming with amusement.

"Allison, that's an unfair generalization," Joy protested.

He raised a hand. "Actually, angel, Connors has a point. Keep your man fed and satisfied, and you'll have a much simpler human being in a far better mood." He turned to Fe. "So, what's the deal with Shawn? Still not putting out for him?"

This time, Fe's olive skin couldn't hide her blush. Richard, meanwhile, showed no trace of self-consciousness.

"Actually … Uh." She twisted a strand of hair, avoiding his eyes. "We kind of … did it. On New Year's Eve."

Joy gasped, slapping a hand over her own mouth. Allison's no-longer frozen eyes went wide.

With a shudder and a guttural squeal, Hope shot up and flung her arms overhead. "What? You ate the sushi roll and didn't tell me!"

Richard fought to keep from laughing. "And you wonder why he's cranky and difficult? Clearly, he's hoping for more, and he hasn't gotten it."

He leaned forward, his eyes heavy with paternal concern. "Girl, trust me. You ladies want men to be nice, talk to you, woo you, before you want sex. But we men are the opposite. Only *after* sex can we open up, be vulnerable. Only then can we connect deeply, treat you the way you deserve."

He drew a deep breath and straightened. "It's my consultant's opinion there's only *one way* to get unstuck from this mess." He tilted his head, as if prompting her to supply the answer.

Hope leaped closer to Fe. "So … if I'm hearing this correctly, I've been right all along! If you want Shawn to talk reasonably, you need to drop everything, go find him …" she paused for effect "… and do him. *STAT.*"

CHAPTER 34

ORE THAN A WEEK HAD PASSED SINCE NEW YEAR'S, AND Fe still avoided him. It drove Shawn crazy. And now, Betty claimed she'd overheard Fe talking about quitting?

What? Had he been such a disappointment in bed that she couldn't stand to see him anymore?

Couldn't he catch a break? Sure, he hadn't been on top of his game—he'd been drunk. But wasn't he worth a second chance? It was his life story: no one ever cut him slack.

He knew he had to confront her face-to-face, but dreaded confirming his fears. While he gathered the nerve, he forced himself to go out with Jay tonight—anything to quiet his mind.

Fresh out of the shower, he was finishing dressing when a text chimed on the nightstand. Apprehension struck at the sight of Richard's name on his phone so late at night. Could this be about the investigation?

He sat on the bed, thumbed the message open, and read it.

"About that debt I owe you for saving my life in the ICU. Just paid an installment. You're welcome."

Shawn was still puzzling over the words when his bedroom door swung open.

Fe stood in the doorway, staring at him, expression unreadable.

He didn't rise, didn't move, waiting for her to speak.

Finally, she broke the silence.

"Take off your clothes and get in bed."

Her voice trembled, soft but unmistakable, yet the words hit him like a foreign language, impossible to comprehend.

"What?"

She unbuttoned her tan leather jacket. "Aidan's spending the night at my house, and I gave Betty the rest of the day off. And now, you and I are going to have sex."

Shawn's brain shut down—operating system frozen. He couldn't move, talk, hardly even breathe.

Without looking at him, she dropped the jacket on his reading chair and unzipped one of her knee-high camel boots. "I'm angry with you, and I know you're angry with me." She tugged off the first boot and sock, then moved to the other foot. "I'm not even sure I'll enjoy this, but that's irrelevant. We have to get it done so we can finally talk like adults. Completely sober. No Halloween candy to blame. No pretending tomorrow that nothing happened."

Finished with the boots, she reached for the hem of her dress, ready to lift it.

Is this another of my recurring dreams?

It couldn't be. In those dreams, Fe was a mellow kitten eager to please, not this tense, determined woman.

What on earth had gotten into her? He opened his mouth to ask, but in a flash her dress was off, and he choked on his own breath.

Jaysus! No Spanx today

She stood before him, all curves, in satin gold bikini panties and matching push-up bra.

Shite! She wasn't kidding!

She frowned. "What? Do you need help with your own clothes?"

Instantly, he whipped his shirt over his head, ignoring the buttons. His clumsy, shaky fingers rushed to unfasten and unzip his pants. His mind raced at its usual lightning speed, but the thoughts came scrambled, senseless fragments that refused to line up.

He almost tripped stepping out of his pants, then flung them aside.

Standing in his boxer briefs, the last thread of coherence managed to crawl from his brain to his lips. "Fe … can you explain what's going on—"

He never finished, because her mouth was on his. She wrapped him in her arms and pressed the length of her body against him, almost with anger.

The last shred of logic dissolved, and he kissed her too.

Never mind! He didn't need an explanation.

He pulled her down with him onto the bed, and words became irrelevant.

· · ·

Fe wanted to be bold, passionate—even angry—but Shawn wouldn't let her. When she bit his lips, he kissed her softly; when her hands clenched with force, his turned to silk, touching her with such reverence she almost cried.

He refused to be rushed. He took his time, gently kissing every inch of her body, murmuring admiration for her beauty.

She never knew exactly when her own caresses turned sweet. She wasn't expecting it when his mouth, trailing kisses up her neck, reached her ear and whispered, "*I love you.*"

She jolted, sure she had misheard him. But he rolled her to her side, looked into her eyes, and said it again, this time louder. "I love you."

Her first instinct was to run. He seemed to know, because his hands tightened on her arms. He kissed her again and again, repeating the words until she stopped fearing them. "I love you." He kissed her face. "I love you." He brushed his lips along her neck. "I love you." He kissed her shoulder.

Her tears and sobs caught her by surprise. "I love you too."

Never had his smile looked more beautiful and his eyes brighter. "I know. I knew it long before you did." He claimed her lips again, with the best kiss they had ever shared—a kiss of celebration instead of guilt, of joy instead of fear.

Their lovemaking now was nothing like the frantic stumbling that their first time had been. It was a slow dance, every touch a declaration of love. She stopped fighting it and surrendered to his tenderness. For a while, their kisses and caresses were all softness.

Until they weren't.

CHAPTER 35

F E AWAKENED SLOWLY AND ONLY THEN REALIZED SHE'D FALLEN asleep. The most pleasant warmth in the world enveloped her and, at first, she couldn't place it. Then she remembered where she was.

She curled under the blankets. Shawn wrapped her with both arms and one leg; she used his chest as a pillow. Every fiber of her body relaxed. Every cell hummed.

Gosh, that had been even better than the first time! This mix of exhaustion and accomplishment reminded her of the day she rode thirty miles on her bike.

Maybe Allison and Agent Fields had tricked her. Making love wasn't just about "helping ground your man by keeping him satisfied," it calmed *you*, the woman. Suddenly, the grudges she'd clung to hours earlier no longer seemed a big deal. It felt like the opposite of PMS—maybe its antidote.

Shawn gently turned her and wrapped his arms around her from behind. His low voice brushed her ear. "I'm your slave now. I'm still not sure exactly what you came here looking for, but whatever it is, it's yours." He kissed her neck, raising goose bumps on her skin. "Want me to sign over the title to this house? My practice? My 401(k)?" He kissed her shoulder. "Want us to go shopping for shoes or get a facial? Whatever you want, you got it. Just promise me we're doing this again tomorrow. And the day after … and the day after that."

She giggled and squirmed to face him. "I had a detailed agenda of topics to discuss, and I can't remember a single one."

She sat up, clutching the duvet to her chest. Under the blankets, she groped for her underwear tangled up in the sheets and slipped them on—she needed a shred of dignity for this conversation. Once her bra was fastened, she turned to him and blurted, "Why are you firing me?"

He snatched his boxer briefs from the floor and pulled them on. "Because I don't want you to be Aidan's speech therapist anymore ..." He sat on the bed and met her eyes. "I want you to be his stepmother."

She froze, clutching the dress she was about to put back on.

"I've been trying not to freak you out," he said. "I've been ready to ask you to marry me practically since the day we met. It's killed me to have you so close, yet so far, all these months. And the more I've gotten to know you, the surer I am—you're The One."

Fe's brain sparked and smoked; all her wits were gone. She was still reeling from having acknowledged they loved each other.

"I admit I've been suffering too, wanting you," she conceded. "But my mind never got past us making it to bed. I never tried to imagine a future or the big picture of blending our complex lives. *Getting married*?" She shuddered.

"I know being married to a doctor was traumatic, and you're dreading the wrath of the Stewarts family." He gestured between them with his hand. "But wouldn't it be stupid to let that get in the way of *this*?"

"It's more complex than that." She straightened, drawing a steadying breath, though her voice still trembled. "Shawn, you have no idea what you're getting into. Remember my family? *I'm worse.* I'm clingy. I'm whiny. I'm jealous of my man's time. I can't stand being second—"

He cut her off with a long kiss that slowed the frantic thrum of her thoughts.

Then, holding her face, he said, "A wise woman told me once: 'Some things in life are worth excruciating pain.' Guess what." He kissed her again. "*You* are one of those things. And I want the chance to prove I am too."

She blinked her tears away. "Shawn, I've worked so hard to stand on my own two feet. I'm scared that if you and I ..." She couldn't get herself to say the words *get married* yet. "If we became a … permanent couple, I'll always feel in your shadow, indebted to you. I'll be back to feeling powerless, afraid I have no say in our life."

He flinched, as if she had slapped him, and let go of her face. "Fe, it hurts me that, after all this time, you still see me through the filter of your ex." Slowly, he pulled back with a tired sigh. "I hate how much he still affects you. And that you won't report him for the money he owes you." He paused. "It makes me fear that you still care for him."

"No!" Startled, she reached for his hand. "I swear it's not that. It's …" She stopped, searching for the right words. She was still trying to understand it herself.

"Liam's the one failure in my life," she said at last. "The one that shakes my belief that even the hardest case can turn around. It still hurts that he's the only person I ever gave up on."

"Did you, Fe?" His gaze pinned her. "It seems to me you're *still* trying to rescue him. Still hoping he'll prove he's changed."

She opened her mouth, but no answer came. Shawn had a point.

His expression softened. "Why are you afraid? Haven't you been telling me not to fear the future, to trust that everything happens for good? Why not have faith this could turn out for the best—even for him? A lesson he needs to grow."

She processed his words for the longest time. "You mean, reporting Liam would be like practicing tough love with a kid—stop rewarding his tantrums."

Shawn nodded. "And then, you step out and let the lawyers handle it."

Covering her face, she groaned. "But I don't want his money. It's poisonous."

"Then don't use it for yourself—use it for your kids. Save it for Diego's future. Or better yet—" His mouth curved into a devilish smile, as he leaned in. "Start a college fund for Gabriela. Didn't you say people call you delusional for believing she'll improve enough to go to college? What can be a better vow of trust than beginning her education fund?"

Fe went speechless. Finally, she muttered, "Darn it, you're a smart man."

After a long pause, she reached for her bag on the floor and texted her lawyer. *"Hi, Larry. Okay. Pull the trigger with Liam."*

The reply arrived in less than ten seconds—one word, with clapping hands and balloon emojis: *"FINALLY!"*

She turned to Shawn. "It's done. The lawyers can deal with it now. My promise to you is to leave the past behind and cut the last ties with my ex."

He leaned forward to kiss her, but she pressed a hand to his chest. "Now I need a promise from *you.*"

He stilled, eyes locked on hers.

"I need to know you'll be there for us," she said. "My biggest fear is to discover that work's an addiction for you, like it was for him. And if I'm leaving my past behind, at least I should learn from it." She paused, choosing her words. "My marriage to Liam didn't fail because of fights, big or small. It failed because we never spent enough time together to sustain *a friendship*. I don't want that to happen to us."

Nodding slowly, he drew her into his arms. "My promise is to cut back my hours. To be home as much as possible. You and the kids will always come first."

Fresh tears stung her eyes. That was exactly what she'd always longed to hear.

"So that's it?" he asked, beaming. "We figured out our biggest obstacles. Are we official now?"

He tried to kiss her, but she caught his face. "Wait, I'm still Aidan's speech therapist. I can't risk rumors that I'm involved with a client's father."

His joyful expression dimmed. "I don't want him to lose you before he starts at the Smith Center, but I've been waiting so long for this." He hesitated. "What should we do in the meantime?"

"Let's keep things under wraps." She stroked his cheek. "We've waited this long; we can keep our hands off each other for a few more weeks. On February sixth, Aidan transitions to the Smith Center. I'll be at his intake evaluations, but after that, my work with him is done. Then, I'll be free to be his father's girlfriend."

His face lit up. "Isn't that also the day your after-school program opens? Perfect. Let's celebrate both by going somewhere nice. After all these months, and everything we've shared, I've never taken you on a real date."

He kissed her, and joy burst in her chest. Could everything truly be lining up in their favor?

His lips trailed from her mouth to her chin, then down her neck, as he murmured, "How serious were you about keeping our hands off each other?"

She laughed.

He claimed her mouth again, and the way he kissed her left no doubt—they weren't going anywhere for a long while.

CHAPTER 36

N EVER IS A KISS MORE ENTICING THAN WHEN IT'S FORBIDDEN. Shawn and Fe's attempts to keep apart for the rest of their contract only fed the fire. Every spare minute during sessions, he'd push her into a powder room or closet for a quick, searing kiss that left them breathless. Desire built over the week until they gave in to temptation in hurried, guilt-ridden encounters far from home.

He had never enjoyed himself more than when they were breaking their own rules. Maybe he needed therapy—someday. For now, the guilt was too much fun to give up.

He forced himself to stop grinning as he walked the hospital halls after rounds. Not even the thought of meeting Richard and Keith for a case update rattled him. Even his search for a new business partner looked promising. Emery had just finished her formal interview. He'd given her a tour before she left for Orlando to spend the weekend with her new boyfriend.

"So, it is true, Shawn. You're involved with that woman Emery."

Gina's voice cut through the lobby. She must have heard about Emery's visit.

Maybe it was the euphoria of requited love, but today he wasn't afraid of Gina's volatility.

He turned to face her. "I don't owe you any explanations."

"The telemetry clerk says you were parading around the hospital with some Emery clinging to your neck and kissing your cheek."

Shawn held back a smile. Emery was always overly affectionate, and that day, even more so after confiding her suspicion that her boy-friend, Ken, was about to propose.

He'd rather Gina fixate on Emery than sniff around him and Fe. "I will say it again, Gina. *None of your business.*"

"McDevitt, do you have a minute?"

Dr. Jones, walking toward them, was a welcome interruption—unexpected, since the man rarely acknowledged Shawn's presence.

"Sure, Mark," he said, sending Gina a pointed look. "The lady was just leaving."

Gina shot him a murderous glare and strode off, her Crocs smacking against the vinyl floor.

It was always hard to read Jones's mood, given his eternal scowl. "McDevitt, is it true that you're interviewing candidates to hire a partner?"

So, he already knew why Emery had been there. That was fast. Shawn hadn't dared jinx himself by talking about hiring Emery yet, not even with Fe.

"I am. Why?"

Jones' frown deepened. "Have you lost your mind? This town isn't big enough for three independent pulmonologists. FirstHealth already monopolizes most of the patients."

Shawn resumed walking, Jones trailing him out. "I need help. And I can't wait forever for the hospital to hire ICU specialists."

They reached the parking lot elevators. Shawn pressed the call button, hoping the gesture made it clear the conversation was over.

"Afraid of hard work?" Jones said with a huff. "Kid, I don't know what's wrong with your generation. What are you even doing in Florida? At your age and with your stamina, you should be making a million a year working in Alaska, or some other underserved place. If you're not chasing a name in academia, at least go chase the money."

Shawn eyed him from head to toe. "Your hurry to kick me out of town—is it really about patients? Or is it about my office building?"

For a split second, surprise flashed across Jones' face. But he said nothing.

"And by the way," Shawn added, narrowing his eyes. "I caught you in a lie. My father never told you about the threatening letters. How did you know?"

Jones seemed to steady himself. "My mistake. I must've heard it elsewhere." He paused. "Maybe Lee Stewarts told me." With that, he walked away.

Shawn stepped into the elevator, turning that answer over.

But Stewarts doesn't know about the letters.

Does he?

He mused on the exchange for a while.

But not even that awkward encounter dimmed his mood. He hummed a tune as he drove to meet Richard and Keith at his private office.

This had better be quick. Today, the clinic was busier than usual, catching up after time off for Emery's tour and for Aidan's fourth birthday party over the weekend. He'd have to head back to the hospital that night to finish his rounds. He dreaded it, but he couldn't let work pile up. Tomorrow was February 6—Aidan's transition into the Smith Center and also the opening of Fe's after-school program. He had a big night planned with her and didn't want anything to spoil it.

Richard and Keith were already waiting when he arrived. After the greetings, they settled down to talk.

"The latest debriefing with Noemí Blandino turned up something worrisome," Keith said. "She claims that her brother Ramón wasn't acting alone. He had a financial sponsor, someone with a grudge against you, trying to punish you."

Not grinning became easier for Shawn. "That backs your suspicion that the letters came from two different sources—not all Blandino. But who?"

"We're still pursuing the same theories," Richard said. "Maybe someone wanted to scare you out of town. It might be time for another round of interviews with the doctors on our list. But that's not all."

"What else?"

Richard glanced at Keith, who hesitated before speaking. "Noemí maintains her brother was 'sick from the head' and wanted to punish you, but that he actually cared for Tara and would never have killed her."

"Of course she'd say that. He's her brother." With a dismissive wave, Shawn reached for the gallon-sized hand sanitizer pump—Fe's birthday present—on his desk.

Concern flickered in Richard's eyes. "But if she's telling the truth, do you realize what that means?"

Shawn's scrubbing slowed and his chest tightened as the answer sank in. "If Blandino didn't kill Tara, and she was instead murdered by the other person sending the letters—then the person stalking me is more dangerous than we thought."

CHAPTER 37

A FTER THE TWO-HOUR MEETING WITH THE SMITH CENTER, Fe was drained, but satisfied. Hopefully, Aidan's transition would be smooth. She still planned to keep working with him after hours, but now it would be more about family bonding and fun than structured therapy.

From the meeting, she had to rush to the opening of her after-school program. She arrived just in time, breathless but glowing, still riding the high that had lifted her for weeks. Lately, her feet refused to walk, they danced every step. Her friends teased that her smile had gone beyond "mega-watt" to "radioactive"—a health hazard if you stood too close.

Shawn hadn't made it to the ribbon-cutting ceremony. Mild disappointment prickled her, but she tried to understand—his clinic usually ran late. She'd tried to text him, but her phone had finally given up. No amount of charging or rebooting would wake its three-quarter-lit screen.

Wait. She still had the extra phone—the one Shawn had given Mami and Abuela. She was on her way to grab it from her car when Betty intercepted her.

"Oh, God. What's that woman doing here?" Betty muttered.

Fe followed her gaze to the blonde in scrubs weaving through the small crowd. The woman looked vaguely familiar.

"Who's that?" Fe asked.

"It's Shawn's ex-girlfriend, Gina," Betty whispered, her tone dripping with gossip.

Fe stiffened. As Gina drew closer, she recognized the face she'd seen around the hospital.

"I'm so glad I found you, you poor little thing." Gina wrapped her in a sudden hug.

Startled and uneasy, Fe pulled free. "I'm sorry. I don't mean to be rude, but I'm in a hurry."

"You don't know it yet, do you?" Gina pressed a hand to her chest in a show of sympathy. "You don't know that Shawn has a new woman. Some Emery he's been parading around the hospital."

Adrenaline jolted through Fe, but she steadied herself—something was off.

She squared her shoulders. "Miss, if you're trying to start a fight between Shawn and me, you're wasting your time." With a half-smile, she arched her brows. "The minute I leave here, I'll just ask him. We'll clear it up."

"You're in denial, like I once was." Gina tilted her head, eyes brimming with pity. "Back then, I spent long nights alone, telling myself he was devoted to his patients, that he had very little left to give a woman. Now I wonder if I was just naive—that all that time he was with her."

The mention of lonely nights unsettled Fe more than Gina's attempts to make her jealous.

She planted a hand on her hip and wagged a finger. "Honey, you have no idea who you're messing with. If there's one thing I'm confident about, it's my skills in bed. There's no way Shawn has energy left for other women after I'm done with him."

Gina blinked, clearly stunned.

Betty flushed, cleared her throat, and made a quick exit, mumbling something about Aidan.

Gina's expression wavered, like she was trying on different masks. Then, she gave a soft laugh. "You must be so proud to have caught him, darling. Fine, enjoy him while it lasts." She rested a hand on Fe's shoulder, leaned closer, and whispered, "He gives expensive gifts. Always go for the jewelry."

With a final wink, she sashayed off without looking back.

Fe stood frozen, trembling with rage. "What nerve!" She turned to Betty who returned with Aidan on her hip, sweat shining on her forehead. "Can you believe that?"

Betty's voice slipped back into gossip mode. "I'm sorry, I didn't want to say anything." She kept her eyes on Aidan, who traced the letters on her football jersey. "But … actually, it's true. Shawn brought that Emery to the house on Friday. She was hugging him, hanging from his neck in a way that didn't look … friends-appropriate."

A volcanic surge rose in Fe, but she forced herself to calm down.

"It's fine. I'll just talk to Shawn over dinner. He should be picking me up any minute."

"Any minute?" Betty checked the time on her phone. "Dr. McDevitt will never get out this early. He's in the hospital from five in the morning, sometimes until ten at night."

Apprehension tightened Fe's chest. Shawn had promised those workaholic days were over.

She tilted her head. "Well, he's been making it to Aidan's sessions at seven for months."

Betty mirrored her tilt. "And goes straight back to the hospital afterward. Just yesterday, I had to watch Aidan while he rounded late."

Dread crashed through Fe, heavier than any jealousy Emery's name could stir.

No. It couldn't be. Shawn had sworn she and the children would always come first.

She was still reeling when a limousine pulled into the driveway.

The window slid down and a uniformed driver called, "Ms. Hernandez?"

She nodded.

He stepped out and opened the back door. "Dr. McDevitt sent me. I'm your driver for tonight."

Fe hesitated before climbing in. She had been looking forward to riding with Shawn, chatting about their day. A driver was not the same.

As the car rolled away, she pressed her palms to her lap.

I'm worrying for nothing. He promised me he wouldn't let work drag him away.

She sighed.

Then why hadn't he shown up at the opening ceremony?

• • •

(Two hours earlier)

To say Shawn was ecstatic would've been an understatement.

At the office, nothing could rattle him. Insurance rejections, prima donna patients, office drama—he was immune to it all. His rounds moved faster than ever, and each patient received something extra: a dose of joyful energy.

He'd rearranged his schedule to leave early so he could finish rounds and still make Fe's ribbon-cutting ceremony. Tonight, he'd planned something spectacular—so dazzling it might be hard to top on proposal day. He'd even toyed with proposing now, after spending some time browsing rings, but decided against it. Too soon. He wouldn't risk scaring her.

He finished his last patient with time to spare. As he reached the hospital lobby, Lee Stewarts approached him, brow knotted.

"McDevitt." The name came out cold, without greeting.

Shawn's cheer deepened—Fe's lawyer had just reported Liam. *Your smugness won't last long.*

"Stewarts." He inclined his head.

"I understand you were consulted for a lung biopsy on Perez in the CVICU. My son declined the case at Riverview last week, and I strongly recommend you decline too. That patient isn't stable."

His words sounded clinical, but his eyes burned with something darker.

Shawn frowned. "We should be fine. I've done bronchoscopies on patients sicker than he is."

Stewarts' intense gaze seemed to send a message. "If my son passes on anything, there's a reason. You could save yourself a lot of pain and legal trouble by following his lead and saying, 'No, thank you.'"

The man's stare drilled into him. Shawn blinked, his pulse quickening. Were they really talking about Perez—or about Fe?

"If you'll excuse me, Lee."

He started to move past, but Stewarts stepped in his way.

"You seem to think I have something against you. But believe it or not, I care for you," Stewarts said. "I'd like to spare you some pain."

Yeah, right.

"Do you?" Shawn asked, lifting his brows as he edged back.

Stewarts gave a solemn nod. "Here in town, we all followed your pain after your wife's disappearance and death. I truly hope you find happiness again with a good woman." He paused. "I just hope you don't suffer my son's bad luck. His ex-wife was the most unforgiving woman alive, unwilling to understand the demands of his career."

Unbelievable. The man had changed tactics and had the nerve to drag Fe through the mud while pretending not to know about their relationship.

A long silence stretched, broken only by the hospital speakers calling a code blue.

"If you'll excuse me, Lee. I'm in a hurry."

He tried again to leave, but Stewarts caught his elbow. "Some women are impossible to please. No matter how hard we try, they're never happy with us." His voice dropped, carrying a weight that pressed against Shawn. "I hope you learn to steer clear of them."

He straightened his coat and strode off without another word.

For a beat, Shawn froze, then heat surged through him. He wanted to punch Stewarts—at the least, give him a piece of his mind.

He was about to chase after him when his phone buzzed with a FaceTime request. Emery.

He shoved down his anger and picked up. "Please give me some good news."

In answer, she lifted her hand in front of the camera, showing off a huge diamond engagement ring.

"Yes!" Shawn pumped a fist. "Congratulations, cousin! When's the wedding?"

"ASAP!" She snapped her fingers three times. "Those babies are *not* going to make themselves!"

Still holding the phone, he pushed through the hospital doors, grinning at the screen. "I guess I'm in trouble now! With Ken as your fiancé and lawyer, you'll be playing hardball negotiating your contract!"

Emery's smile slipped. Shawn had a premonition a storm was coming.

"Actually, cousin …"

Shite.

Emery never called him cousin unless she'd done something bad that affected him.

"Ken and I … well." Her eyes darted away, then returned to the screen. "Ken offered to relocate to Miami for me."

Shawn stopped in his tracks. The dreams he'd built—Emery joining his practice, cutting his hours—shattered in an instant.

Emery scrunched her face, apologetic. "I'm so sorry, buddy. I know how excited you were about me moving there and becoming your partner, but, hey, isn't it great that Ken is so selfless he's willing to relocate for me?"

Shawn didn't answer. The bastard Ken Carter was the furthest thing from selfless he'd ever known. The guy was a skunk, and Shawn hated himself for ever rooting for him just because he'd hoped for a partner.

But he wasn't going to spoil Emery's happiness. "I wish you both the best. Talk soon."

He ended the call and pressed a hand to his forehead, drained. He'd hoped to share the good news with Fe today. But it wasn't in the cards yet.

He was nearing the parking lot when his phone rang again.

"Yes?" he answered, distracted.

"Dr. McDevitt."

It was Steve, the ICU nurse in charge. His tone said something serious had happened.

"Yes?"

Steve's voice sounded tight. "We need your help with a code blue in the ICU. We can't get the patient intubated."

Shawn sighed. "I'm sorry, Steve, I'm not covering the unit this week. Where's Dr. Jones?"

A pause stretched, heavy with dread.

"Dr. Jones *is* the patient," Steve muttered. "Massive heart attack."

CHAPTER 38

THE CHATTY OLD LIMO DRIVER KEPT FE ENTERTAINED ON THE way to one of the fanciest restaurants in town. Relief washed over her when she learned the company had instructions to pick up Shawn and her together—he must've planned to be at the opening ceremony, and something had come up.

Inside, the maître d' led her to a table for two in a private alcove overlooking the marina. A string quartet played, while hundreds of roses and orange blossoms—her favorite—perfumed the room. The scene could've been pulled from a fairy tale.

But Fe couldn't enjoy it. A knot of apprehension tightened inside her.

He doesn't get it. This isn't what I wanted. All I needed was time with him.

On the table sat a box wrapped in golden paper, marked *Open Me.* Inside lay a red dress and a jewelry box with matching earrings and necklace. She could only pray they weren't real diamonds.

Gina's words echoed, sharpening her unease. *He gives expensive to all his women.*

Shawn hadn't chosen these himself—he'd been too busy to shop. Betty or his secretary must've done it.

She scolded herself for not being grateful and started toward the restroom to change, but stopped. She liked the turquoise dress she'd worn to the ceremony.

When she returned to the table, Shawn still hadn't arrived. She wished she had her phone to check on him.

A waiter brought fine champagne. She sat listening to the strings and breathing in the scent of the flowers, patiently waiting for her beloved to arrive.

• • •

Shawn had never seen so much go wrong in a single night.

Dr. Jones turned out to have the most unusual anatomy he'd ever encountered—maybe he was a vampire rather than human after all. Finding central venous access had been a nightmare, and Shawn had to stay with the cardiologist to help place a temporary pacemaker. In the midst of it, other patients crashed in the unit, and he couldn't leave until everyone was stable.

He'd called Fe a dozen times, leaving three apologetic messages. The second he could sign out to the eICU, he sprinted to his car, scrubs still stained with blood.

As the engine roared to life, the dash clock made him curse. Not only had he missed the opening, but he was two hours late for their dinner.

Driving out of the garage, he checked his phone. No reply from Fe. Just three missed calls from an unknown number. He called back.

"Riverview Bistro, how may I help you?"

The restaurant.

"This is Dr. McDevitt. I had a reservation at six but was delayed by an emergency. Is my girlfriend still there?"

Murmurs hummed in the background, then the voice returned. "She left half an hour ago."

Dread clenched his chest. At the next intersection, he yanked the wheel into a U-turn and tore toward Fe's house.

• • •

The moment Shawn set foot in Fe's house, he knew it: he was in the deepest trouble of his life.

Fe's swollen eyes and smudged makeup showed she'd been crying. Even her hair—her pride—was undone.

But what hollowed him out was the absence of her smile—the one that usually lit every room.

"I'm so sorry!" he blurted. "There was no one else to cover the unit—"

She lifted a hand, slicing the air. "You stood me up. You left me at the restaurant for hours. Alone. Like an idiot. Waiting."

"Fe, it was an emergency—"

"You broke your promise." Sadness rolled off her in waves; her voice carried a pain that pierced straight through him. "You said this dinner would be symbolic of our life together. And if that's true, I don't want that life. I've been there before, and I'm not going back."

He stood frozen, words trapped behind the tightness in his chest.

She paced away, pressing her temples. "I didn't need your fancy limo, or roses, or diamonds. I used to have all that, do you understand?" Her voice rose. "I swore I'd never accept it again from a man who couldn't give me what really matters—his time. His presence."

Tears slid down her cheeks, shredding him. But the worst part was the dawning realization that she wasn't talking to him. She was talking to the man before him, the one who'd broken her.

"I called you," he said in a weak voice. "Haven't you checked your messages?"

"That's irrelevant. You promised to be there." Her uncharacteristic calm worried him more than her anger. "A part of me knew you're addicted to work, and that in every addiction, relapses happen. But for the love of God, this was our *first* date. You couldn't make it work for *one* day?"

She covered her face and sobbed quietly. That alone would've flattened him. But then, she whispered, "I had faith in you, and you let me down."

Guilt and shame crashed over him like an avalanche.

He'd missed the mark again. He had failed.

"*This* is the story of my life," he muttered. Nothing I ever do is good enough."

All hope drained from him. He raked a hand through his hair, the other still gripping the gift he'd bought her online—the third one.

Little by little, his despair hardened into fury. "But I've had it. I'm sick of apologizing to you for being who I am and doing what I do." He paced the living room. "Yes, maybe there's something wrong with me and with all doctors. Why else would anyone choose a life of sacrifice and self-abuse? But, Jaysus!" He flung a hand in the air. "Can you look at what I do that's right and cut me some slack?"

Shutting his eyes, he shook his head. "But I'm done! Are you listening?" he shouted. "I refuse to take abuse from the world, from you, or anyone else. And that means no more beating myself up."

He marched to the door, then stopped at the threshold.

His anger deflating, he turned around to face her. "Instead of lashing out at me for being a workaholic, you could've felt compassion." His voice softened. "Maybe I lack something you have—the ability to say no, to stand up for myself, to stop and rest when work is drowning me. Instead of judging me for choosing this life … maybe you should see me like one of your kids with special needs."

She startled at his words.

"Instead of anger, maybe what I needed was patience," he added. "Maybe you could've taught me, the way you taught Aidan. Lured me, baited me with something I cared for." He let out a ragged sigh. "Maybe that anchor could've been your love."

He set the gift box on the table and walked away.

As he slid behind the wheel, he knew yelling had been a mistake. One he'd regret for the rest of his life.

CHAPTER 39

GABRIELA'S HOME PT SESSION HAD JUST ENDED, AND SENSING Fe's blues, Abuela offered to put the girl to bed.

The past week had been a nightmare. Angry about the child support case, the Stewarts had left veiled, threatening voicemails from different numbers so Fe couldn't block them. Rainbows had gone suspiciously quiet, and Fe feared the scandal over suing Liam would make the doctors wary of "taking sides" by recommending her.

And, of course, she ached for Shawn. His wounded expression before he walked out still haunted her.

As she carried the hamper to the laundry room, the sight of the new washing machine tightened her chest—another of Shawn's secret gifts for Abuela. Every two steps, something reminded her of him. Mami's blood pressure meds with his name as prescriber, Mami and Abuela's cell phone, only Gabriela used, Diego's microscope—Shawn's Christmas present. Every sunrise reminded her of the pictures he used to text.

Behind her, Allison whispered, "See, girls? I told you. This is serious."

Hope gasped. "It's true! Fe, the fashion diva, is wearing *sweatpants!*"

"And no makeup!" added Joy.

"And her hair!" Hope shuddered. "Is that a hint of brown roots?"

"But that's not the scariest part," Allison said. "Earlier, we talked for ten minutes, and she didn't wave her hands once."

Hope pressed a hand to her chest. "Someone call nine-one-one."

Fe shot them the stink eye. "Girls, you do know I can hear you, right?"

With a paper bag in hand, Joy took a cautious step forward. "Hi, sweetie. I brought chocolate ice cream."

Allison held up a box. "I brought seven self-help books."

Empty-handed, Hope smirked. "And I have the number of a hit man willing to beat up Shawn for cheap."

Fe poured laundry soap into the washer. No fabric softener left. "Don't bother, Hope. I already beat him up enough." She shut the lid, turned it on, and walked out. Her friends trailed after her.

Fe dropped herself into a chair on the back porch.

Darn it. The yard only reminded her of that night under the mango tree, holding Shawn as he grieved Aidan's diagnosis.

"How are you doing?" Joy asked, settling beside her.

Fe exhaled. "Well, after Shawn left that night, I cried for an hour straight. When I thought I was done, I opened the gift box he'd left—a tiara. The note said, *No need to wait for Halloween.* That set me off all over again. The next day, I went to get a new phone and retrieved the messages he'd left, apologizing for running late. I spent the night replaying them … and crying. And now I'm better." She hesitated. "I think."

"Are you still angry at him?" Allison asked.

"No. I'm furious at *myself.*" She covered her face. "The way I overreacted, the way I raised my voice—" She swallowed hard, then straightened. "It's all my fault. I should've listened to myself. I knew I wasn't ready for another serious relationship with a doctor. And I knew he couldn't give me what I needed."

Joy fidgeted. "You should call him."

"What for?" Fe threw her hands up. "He warned me once that he doesn't forgive rejection. And he's the only person on earth more stubborn than me." Burning pain surged in her chest. "These were supposed to be the days of brand-new, before reality hit. If we clashed this soon, imagine a year from now—or five, when the kids would've bonded even more. Better for things to blow up now."

Joy clasped her hand. "Sweetie, it hurts seeing you like this. You've always been the one telling us not to give up, inspiring us with your faith in people."

"I'm just seeing reality again." Fe gave a small shrug. "Why did I ever think I had a shot at a fairy-tale story? There's too much on my plate." She swallowed. "And on Shawn's. Thinking we could make this work was delusional."

At her friends' silence, she forced a smile. "But I'll be fine. You know me. Give me a few days and I'll be back to normal. I'll be bargain shopping, doing hair, and running from Chihuahuas." She turned to Allison. "Hey, you'll finally get someone on your side. Joy and Hope will be pro-relationship, and you and I will defend the theory that all men in the world suck. Won't that be fun?"

Despite her strained cheerfulness, her voice cracked, and tears stung her eyes again. As if sensing the bluff, Joy and Hope rose from their seats and wrapped her in a symmetrical hug.

From her chair, Allison mumbled, "I would join the hug, but I prefer to send you my love via Wi-Fi and Bluetooth."

Joy shot her a sharp look.

With a theatrical sigh, Allison got up and joined the embrace.

• • •

The house had never felt colder, quieter, and darker. Only now did Shawn realize how much he'd grown used to the background buzz, soothing like white noise. Abuela's melodramatic telenovelas in the kitchen, Fe working with Aidan, the machine-gun chatter in Spanish. Little footsteps running around. Without Diego and Gabriela to chase him, Aidan just sat in a corner of the living room, spinning his toy car's wheels.

But the worst part was the absence of her laughter.

Damn, that hurt. Every corner of the house carried a memory of Fe. The yard where he'd pulled her into the pool, the staircase where they sat on Halloween when she tried to quit, the upstairs deck where they'd flirted and bonded.

And of course, his bedroom.

"Don't you lock your door, man? Are you tired of living?" Richard's voice from the living room barely surprised him.

Maybe, unconsciously, I am.

"What's up, man?" He offered a half-hearted fist bump.

Richard dropped onto the couch across from him. "New update. Ramón Blandino's in town. Security cameras caught him buying cigarettes at a nearby pharmacy."

Shawn perked up a little. "Nearby? How close?"

"Right across the street from your clinic."

The words hit like ice water. Shawn reached for the hand sanitizer in his pocket. "What does that mean? Is he still stalking me?"

"We have to assume so. Any new letters?"

Shawn rubbed his hands, thinking. "No. Now that you mention it, they seem to always show up when I'm happy, then vanish when I'm miserable."

Richard frowned. "Why are you miserable?"

"I don't feel like talking about it." Shawn flopped back in his chair, suddenly drained.

Richard scanned him from head to toe. His voice came flat, more statement than question. "You had a fight with Fe."

Damn Richard and his FBI eyes.

Shawn stayed silent.

With a sigh, Richard rolled his eyes. "Okay, let's get you drunk."

"What?" Shawn blinked.

Richard dialed a number. "You know me, I don't do pep talks. I'm not touchy-feely—except with my woman. So let's call that bodybuilder friend of yours and go get you drunk."

CHAPTER 40

J AY AND RICHARD'S ATTEMPT TO CHEER SHAWN UP AT A SPORTS bar didn't do much. Both were off alcohol—Jay training for a triathlon, Richard on some spiritual fast. Drinking alone wasn't fun. Jay had shoved some self-help book by Allison Connors at him, but Shawn couldn't bring himself to care.

He still felt miserable the next morning on rounds. The minute Dr. Jones came off duty, the hospital conjured two locum tenens physicians—as if Stewarts had them in his back pocket, withholding them just to drive Shawn away.

To Shawn's surprise, Emery showed up to continue her hospital tour. He'd assumed it was cancelled after she turned down his job offer. To cap off the day, his father came with her.

Seamus's eyes shone suspiciously as he caressed the ICU counters. Shawn cringed, picturing the billions of germs clinging to the nurse's station. But his father seemed lost in nostalgia, aching for the times before his forced retirement.

"So, things with the cute speech therapist didn't work out?" Emery asked as they entered the telemetry unit.

Shawn shrugged. "No big deal. I'll live."

But what a lousy life.

"It sucks. She was really nice." Emery fiddled with her tan suede jacket's fringe. "And I loved her fashion style. I was already hoping she'd take me shopping the next time I came to town."

Shawn eyed her warily. "You only saw her once. How do you know her fashion style?"

"I spied on her Instagram and Facebook. Look." She swiped her phone and handed it over.

The image hit him like a punch to the gut. Someone had tagged Fe at her business opening—the ceremony he'd missed. She looked radiant in a turquoise dress, beaming. Her eyes sparkled with all the joy and optimism he loved in her—the same light he'd stripped away hours later, in their fight.

Unable to stand, he lowered into the workstation chair and covered his mouth with one hand.

"Are you okay?" Emery asked, worried. "You look like you're about to cry."

He returned the phone. "I screwed up so bad."

She slid into the chair beside him. "Can't you just call her? Make it up to her?"

With a groan, he shook his head. "She asked me for *one* thing, and I failed her. And then I yelled at her like *I'd* been offended. I'm the biggest idiot alive. An eejit. A gobshit. A gombeen."

Silence stretched. Emery pressed a hand to her chest, her full lips trembling. "Those are the most beautiful, real words I've ever heard you say!" She hugged him tight.

When she let go, her almond-shaped eyes brimmed with motherly concern. "Don't worry, buddy. I'll help you get her back."

He shot her a warning look. "Uh … Emery, please. Stay out of this. I don't need help."

"Yes, you do, Shawny." She patted his face. "I know exactly how to get this woman to talk to you." She kissed him on the cheek and dashed off, leaving him baffled.

"Where is she going?" Seamus asked as she jogged out of the nurse's station.

"I don't know," he muttered, "but I fear she's up to no good."

Before he could go after Emery, a nurse approached. "Dr. McDevitt, Dr. Jones would like to talk to you."

Shawn was discharging Jones today. It was a miracle the man had survived with nothing worse than a few coronary stents.

"Mark is still here?" Seamus' face lit up. "I have to say hello!"

Not even his father's bromance with his rival rattled Shawn today. He dragged his feet to the room, Seamus trailing behind, and found Jones sitting on the bed, already dressed and waiting for transport. The ghostly figure had shrunk even more over the past week.

Seamus and Dr. Jones greeted each other. Then Jones turned to Shawn. "I haven't had a chance to properly thank you."

Shawn shrugged. "I was just doing my job."

"I owe you my life," Jones said. "I know I haven't been easy to deal with lately, but I want you to know that despite my attacks, I deeply respect you as a colleague."

Another time, Shawn might have been touched—and secretly pleased his father had heard that. But today, he felt nothing. "You have my respect too."

He bowed his head and started to leave, but Jones's next words stopped him.

"Would you consider taking over my practice?"

Shawn froze. Slowly, he pivoted to face him, refusing to believe what he'd heard.

"I've been dreading retirement for years," Jones went on. "But my body's yelling that it's time to slow down. I plan to return to work tomorrow, but if you joined my practice, I could start cutting down, letting you take the new patients, and phase out over the next few years."

A few months ago, the offer would've been Shawn's dream come true—an instant boost in income and prestige. Riding on Jones' reputation, he'd never struggle for patients again. His practice would be busier than ever.

But it would also mean even less time for Aidan.

If I don't have Fe anymore, what's the point in having free time?

"I'll have to think about it and get back to you," he said finally.

Jones nodded, and Shawn stepped out.

Following him down the hallways, his father exclaimed, "Are you out of your mind? Of course, you have to take his offer! Do you have any idea how much money you'd make?" He threw a hand up. "But think beyond the money! Clinical trials, your name associated with publications, medical students and residents shadowing you! You'd no longer be just a community physician." Ecstatic, Seamus opened his arms wide. "You'd finally be *somebody*!"

Shawn stopped in his tracks. "*Be somebody?*"

A surge of molten anger flooded through him. Everything around him turned red. He pivoted to face his father, shuddering with each breath. "Believe it or not, I *am* somebody."

He stepped closer, and Seamus took a step back. "Do you have any freaking idea how many lives I've saved in my career? No, you don't. Because *I* don't know it either. I lost count a long time ago."

For every step Shawn took forward, his father retreated one. "But do you know what I never forgot? The patients I lost. Anyone I treated who had any complication. No. Those I run through my mind again and again, never forgiving myself for the mistakes. And do you know why that is? Because that was what I learned *from you*."

His chest heaved, his hands trembling at his sides. A vein pulsed in his temple, and heat prickled up his neck like fire ants. "Do you know what else I learned from you?" His voice rose. "To beat myself up. To never believe anything I did was good enough. To kill my life's joy, trying to prove myself to the world—even if that meant neglecting everyone I cared for. Just like *you* did with us."

Backed against the service elevator wall, Seamus muttered, "Son, what are you talking about?"

Shawn clenched his fists to clamp down the pain. "And I ruined it! I pushed away the only woman who might've saved me from becoming *you*." He stopped, a new understanding settling in. "And the worst part is that every word I yelled at her is a word I should've said to *you* years ago."

To his surprise, his father showed no anger, only a weary affection.

"My son. You never needed to prove anything to me. I would've been proud of you no matter what you chose to do."

Shawn felt too raw to take comfort. "I could've done other things with my life, but not anymore. I can't quit now because, as Fe says, *I'm the best damn doctor in the whole freaking galaxy.*" He shut his eyes and drew a long breath. "And that's precisely why I don't have anything to prove to anyone." He turned and walked away.

He strode back to the telemetry floor, went straight to Dr. Jones' room, and announced, "I thought about it. Thank you, but the answer is no."

Before Jones could reply, Shawn stormed out and took the fire stairs down to the CVICU, where the thoracic team was rounding.

He marched straight to Stewarts and grabbed the lapel of his white coat. Startled, Stewarts ducked, as if bracing for a punch.

Shawn ripped off his badge and shoved it into Stewarts' pocket. "I won't stop being a doctor, but I'm done working for you. Find someone else to run your ICU." He leaned closer. "And listen carefully, you and your family stay away from Fe, or I'll make you regret the day you were born." His voice stayed low and controlled; the silence that followed made the threat land harder than any shout.

He let go of Stewarts' lapel and walked away.

CHAPTER 41

F E COULDN'T SUSTAIN THE MESSY-HAIR STRIKE FOR LONG. COUSIN
Glennys nearly had a coronary at the sight of her dark roots
and frizzy curls, then launched a full-scale intervention with
dye, keratin, and a flat iron to cheer her up. But Fe still tied her hair in
a plain ponytail and refused to wear makeup to work that morning.

Marla showed up unannounced to congratulate her on the new
after-school camp, raving about Fe's role as Rainbows' new business
leader. Any other time, Fe would've been beaming with pride.

While Marla caught up with the other therapists, mumbles outside Fe's office drew her attention. She recognized the whimpering at
once. Before she could move, her door burst open.

"I'm sorry for showing up without calling," Betty stepped in, carrying Aidan. "He's been inconsolable, and I don't know what else to do.
His new therapists can't help me either." She wiped her sweaty forehead
with her sleeve. "I figured you and the boss had a fight or something,
so I was afraid that if I called ahead, you'd refuse to see me."

Gathering herself, Fe focused on the boy. This wasn't a tantrum.
Aidan wasn't yelling, kicking, or screaming. Just crying softly, his little shoulders trembling. The despair on his face seemed out of place
for his young years.

"What's going on, my boy?" Fe asked, taking him from Betty's
arms.

When Aidan saw her, his sobs deepened. He clung to her, burying his face in her shoulder.

"He's been down since you stopped coming over," Betty said,

fidgeting. "But it's worse since this morning. He won't eat. He doesn't want to play. His temperature's fine, no tags or labels bothering him. I'm out of ideas."

Fe drew him back gently to see his face. "What's the matter, honey? Are you sad?"

"Sad," Aidan said.

That answer was probably just his echolalia, making him repeat the last words he heard.

She tried again, her voice tender. "Are you hungry?"

He didn't answer.

Fe stroked his back in slow, calming circles, leaning close to keep eye contact. "Are you tired?"

He kept sobbing.

"Are you sad?"

"Sad," he repeated.

Fe raised her eyebrows. "Do you miss Daddy?"

He stared at her in silence.

"Do you miss Grandma?"

Aidan didn't answer—his chin tucked against his little chest, lower lip quivering.

"Do you miss Diego?"

"Dego," he answered. "Dego. Bela."

It was the closest thing to a conversation she'd had with the little boy.

"Who's Bela? Abuela? Gabriela?"

He burst into tears again.

Still carrying him, Fe walked to the PT room where Gabriela was in her session while Grandma watched. The instant Aidan saw them, he pushed out of Fe's arms and ran to Abuela. The old lady cried out with joy and smothered him in kisses, murmuring in Spanish how much she'd missed him.

As soon as Abuela loosened her grip, Aidan ran to Gabriela's wheelchair and stood in front of her, jumping up and down. "Bela! Bela!"

The girl beamed wider than Fe had ever seen and wrapped her weak little arms around the boy, giving him a clumsy kiss on the head.

Fe's eyes filled with tears.

"You made such a great family," Betty mumbled, wiping her fogged glasses with her football jersey. "Are you sure there's no way to fix things?"

Fe swallowed past the knot in her throat. She wished she could run to Shawn and mend things, but knowing how stubborn he was, she feared she didn't stand a chance.

"Let them spend some time together. Maybe that will cheer him up."

Betty nodded and Fe stepped out.

When Fe returned to her office, two men were waiting inside. For the first time ever, the sight of Lee and Liam Stewarts didn't rattle her—she'd run out of emotions.

As usual, Stewarts senior spoke first. "I'm flabbergasted, Faith. I can't believe you sank so low as to sue my son."

Liam stepped forward. "You can't threaten legal action against the father of your children—not without trying to talk it over first."

"You can't do this to our family—"

Fe raised a sharp hand to cut Lee off. "You two have no idea what that word even means."

She faced her ex and looked him square in the eye. In the past, she'd failed to *use her words*, open up about how much he'd hurt her, and Shawn had been the innocent bystander of that pain.

But now, she no longer felt the need to tell Liam anything.

Her voice stayed calm. "You know what, Liam? If you want to see your children, schedule it through the court app. Anything else you have to say, talk to my lawyer." She stepped closer, inches from his face. "But *never* again will I waste one more thought, one more tear, or one more fear on you."

She pivoted toward his father. "But you, Lee, you're going to hear me out now." She pointed a thumb toward Liam. "I get that he had resentments and a bruised ego after I left him. But *you* … I expected more from you."

Lee must've registered her resolve; he didn't interrupt.

"You were the only father I had after mine died. You used to be the voice of reason when Liam and I argued. I used to respect you. And *I know* you loved me. Under all your scorn about my lack of refinement, I'd grown on you. Why did you have to destroy those good memories by treating me like this?"

When he stayed silent, her voice rose. "I will never—*never*—again let either of you belittle me or intimidate me. You're nothing but bullies. And cowards."

No one moved. The words hung in the air, heavy against the hum of the AC vent.

Doubt flickered across Lee's eyes, but he recovered quickly. "Please! Your low class is showing." He scoffed and stepped away, lifting his hands. " Liam should've never married you. I tried to warn him about your other-side-of-the-track manners, your complete ignorance about personal boundaries, your loud, nosy family."

Inexplicable peace settled in Fe's heart. "Some time ago, those words would've hurt me, but now I know better. The same things you hated in me, someone else once found lovable. The problem was never me—*it was you.*"

Shawn's loving words returned to her mind. Not even the pain of losing him dulled the calm that filled her. "Some things in life are worth excruciating pain, and guess what?" She smirked. "*I* am one of those things." She picked up the phone and dialed an extension.

"Security? This is Fe. Please send someone to my office to kick out a couple of intruders."

• • •

Another time, watching security escort her ex and his father out the door would've delighted Fe. She would've also celebrated another win in initiating a restraining order against Liam. Today, however, it all felt bittersweet.

"Are you okay, Fe?" Marla asked in her hoarse voice, patting her shoulder.

Fe nodded. "Everything happens for a reason."

She may no longer deserve Shawn's forgiveness, but she'd found the silver lining in her loss: the courage to confront her greatest bullies.

Her office phone rang from an unknown number. It couldn't be her ex since security had him occupied at the moment.

She picked up. "Hello?"

"Hello, Fe. This is a friend."

The voice sounded deliberately rough, as if the caller were affecting a lower, raspy tone.

"Who's this?"

"You need to check Shawn's Facebook page. It's urgent!"

The line went dead.

Fe stared at the receiver. Could that have been Shawn's ex, trying again to upset her?

Curiosity won. She grabbed her cell and opened Facebook.

The famous Emery had tagged Shawn in a dozen pictures. Her newest post read, "The new man in my life. Meet Shawn McDevitt, my other half."

With trembling fingers, Fe opened Emery's page and scrolled down. A previous post said, "Shawn McDevitt, the answer is yes." Right before that, she'd changed her relationship status to "engaged."

The ground under Fe's feet seemed to cave in as if an earthquake had hit. Thunder rolled around her. All the sadness she'd been nursing vanished, shoved aside by heat and rage.

She must have screamed out loud, because Marla jumped to her side. "What's wrong, Faith?"

Fe couldn't stop shaking. "I might commit murder today!" she blurted, then screamed again.

But even in the panic, a tiny voice of reason whispered.

This doesn't make sense.

I know Shawn loves me.

Emery must be trying to discourage me so she can snatch him!

She drew in a long, steadying breath. "But before I commit murder, I have an errand to run. I'm going to fall on my knees in front of Shawn and beg him to forgive me for being such an idiot." Then she bolted out.

She rushed back to the PT room but found only Grandma and Gabriela.

"Abuela! Where's Aidan? *Dónde está Aidan?*" she asked, desperate.

"*Se fue,*" Abuela said, pointing at the door.

Fe hesitated for only a split second. "*Venga conmigo, doña.* Come with me."

Pushing Gabriela's chair, she strode through the hallway to the building exit. Abuela followed at a slower pace—still remarkably brisk for her age.

Betty was still in the parking lot, fastening Aidan into his car seat.

"Wait!" Fe called out, breaking into a run, Abuela trailing behind.

Aidan wiggled, excited, at the sight of Gabriela.

"Do you know where Shawn is?" Fe asked Betty.

"Not long ago, he texted he was heading to his office to finish paperwork."

Seeing Gabriela's extra car seat still in Shawn's van sparked an idea. "Betty, can I borrow Aidan and the van? I need to convince Shawn that we can still be a family."

Joy and relief lit up Betty's face. Grinning, she held out the keys. "Go get him, babe!"

CHAPTER 42

At his office, Shawn sifted through the pile of labs and reports in his mailbox. He had much to plan for his proposal to Fe.

He wanted it to be spectacular, and as daring as their first stolen kiss. He even considered surprising her with a trip to Paris—kidnapping her maybe—to prove he could be spontaneous. But airport security and international travel complicated things. Maybe he'd blindfold her and take her to his cabin in the North Carolina Mountains. There, he'd lock them both in, fall to his knees, and swear to not let her go until she agreed to marry him.

He had a new weapon to prove his commitment not to let work take over their life: Emery. Her change of heart about his job offer had been a welcome surprise—though she'd chosen a strange way to accept, with that odd Facebook post.

He was about to leave when the door opened and Gina stepped in.

"I'm sorry, Gina," he said, reaching for his keys. "I'm on my way out."

Her reddish eyes showed she'd been crying. "Would you explain that Facebook post?"

Shawn's jaw tightened. She must've seen Emery's announcement. "Sorry, I don't have time for this. I'm in a hurry." He started for the door, but she caught his arm.

"Have you been using me again?"

The smell of alcohol on her breath hit him.

Shite. Which personality is she showing today?

Carefully, deliberately, he pried her fingers off his arm. "Gina, I never used you."

"Yes, you did." She burst into tears. "You used me to get over the humiliation of your wife leaving you. You used me to get back on your feet after she died. You used me for sex and company for a year. And now you gave me hope we could get back together, just to use me as an informant."

Before he could reply, she threw her arms around his neck, sobbing.

"And I knew it, but I'm such an idiot I was willing to take you back the moment you asked me."

He weighed how to free himself without harming her. "Gina, I've felt terrible for months for having hurt you. You didn't deserve it. But I'm in love with someone else."

She shoved him away with such force that his back slammed into the wall.

Her eyes glassy, she got right in his face and shouted, "You piece of garbage! Don't give me that crap about Emery. If she's really your girlfriend, she needs to know you've been sleeping with your son's speech therapist."

Shawn stiffened.

Gina sobbed and ranted, "You thought I'd buy your 'she's a professional' story for a minute? I've seen the way you looked at her from the start. I saw you kiss her on Thanksgiving. I should've killed you the day I saw you hugging her in the pool."

"*You!*" The realization hit him like lightning. "You're my stalker."

At his words, her expression fell. Panic flickered in her eyes and, in a flash, she slid her hand into her purse and pulled out a gun.

Shawn knew nothing about handguns, but one look made it clear: that thing was *not* a toy.

"Gina, put that down." He backed away.

She stepped forward, closing the distance between them. "You used me. I was just your rebound."

"I never promised you anything. I never said we could get back together."

"You didn't deny it either!" she yelled.

There was no point in arguing; she'd gone past reason.

She pressed the muzzle to his chest. His pulse thundered, the office shrinking to her finger on the trigger.

"I should've let Ramón kill you," she said. "I shouldn't have stopped him the day he threatened you in the hospital hallway. But, stupid me, had to talk him into the other plan." Rage and regret tangled in her voice. "Then he turned out to be a wimp who didn't even have the balls to finish Tara."

Shawn's blood froze in his veins. "Oh God. *You* did it! You killed her?"

Her face twisted between pain and pleading. "I did it for you. To free you from her so you could marry me." Rage flared again. "And then you dumped me."

The elevator ding broke the moment and startled Gina. Seizing her distraction, Shawn grabbed her arm, trying to wrench the gun away.

She surprised him with raw strength as they grappled for seconds. Then, someone knocked on the door. He didn't have time to shout.

Gina kneed him in the groin. Grunting in pain, he doubled over and collapsed to the floor.

She leveled the barrel at his temple and hissed, "Don't say a word."

• • •

Fe decided not to call Shawn before heading to his office. If he sent her to voicemail, she wouldn't be able to handle it. But as she pulled into the parking lot, terror seized her.

What was she doing? Her hot Latin blood had hijacked her logic again. What if his pride was still hurt? What if he did care for Emery?

After some debate, she decided not to bring the kids inside, so she didn't have to risk him rejecting her in front of them.

The parking lot sat empty except for Shawn's car and a white pickup truck. She didn't want to leave Abuela with Aidan and Gabriela for too long. Not knowing any English, the old woman wouldn't be able to explain to security why they were there after hours.

Remembering Shawn's extra phone in her purse, Fe checked that the battery wasn't drained and handed it to Abuela.

"*Si alguien viene, llámeme.*"

She tried to show her how to use it, but Abuela eyed the phone with suspicion, so she gave it to Gabriela instead. "Here, honey. Call me for Abuela if she needs help."

Leaving the van running with the AC on, she slung her purse over her shoulder and stepped out.

As she walked toward the building, she ordered her heart to settle. She wouldn't try to talk Shawn into anything—not yet. She'd read his face first, see if there was any hope left. If there was, she'd make an appointment to talk later.

Her palms were slick by the time she entered the building. She crossed the empty lobby and took the elevator to his office on the second floor. The ride seemed endless.

In front of his office, she braced herself and drew a long breath. With a trembling hand, she knocked. Only then did the sounds reach her.

Muffled voices arguing, a grunt and a heavy *thump,* as if something—or someone—had hit the floor.

She pushed the door open, and her heart plummeted.

Shawn lay on the floor.

Gina aimed a gun at him.

Without thinking, Fe lunged and tackled the woman to the floor. Never before had she fought with such passion. Every bit of unruly Latin fire and un-refinement she'd tried to erase from her life surged back with a vengeance. She hit Gina with everything she had—kicked, scratched, yanked her hair. Nothing else mattered but fighting for the man she loved.

"Leave him alone!" she yelled, straddling Gina and slapping her again and again.

Recovering from the shock, Gina twisted her body and launched Fe off with her legs. Fe crashed onto her back, pain shooting through her spine and skull as she hit the floor.

Before she could get up, Gina snatched the gun and aimed it at Fe's forehead.

"Stop, or I'll put a bullet through your brain."

Fe froze. Her heart hammering, she scrambled to her feet and edged back from the gun.

Keeping the gun trained on Fe, Gina fished her phone from her purse with her free hand and dialed.

"Ramón? Come upstairs. Things got complicated."

She slipped the phone into her scrubs' pocket and started toward Fe.

Shawn staggered to his feet and stepped in front of Fe, shielding her with his body. "No! You came for me," he said. "Leave Fe out of this!"

"No! If you're going to shoot him, you'll have to kill me too!" Fe tried to move in front of him, but he spread his arms, blocking her.

The gun trembled in Gina's grip. She pointed it back and forth between them.

The door burst open, and a man stepped in.

"You're just in time, Ramón. I need help," Gina said.

So, this was the famous Ramón Blandino. For all she'd heard about him, Fe had expected a menacing looking giant. But the man was shorter and chubbier than she imagined, barely resembling the pictures she'd shown Aidan.

Jittery and fidgeting, he held a gun in one hand and scratched his armpit with the other. Fe had definitely seen him before.

"Damn it, Hill. I didn't want a complication like this!"

She recognized the voice instantly.

In her mind, she added a beard and stripped away his clean clothes and neat haircut.

It was José, the homeless guy.

He shuffled toward Shawn, mumbling, "I can't catch a break! One crazy month off my meds, and now I'm gonna spend the rest of my life cleaning up the mess."

CHAPTER 43

FOR SHAWN, IT FELT SURREAL TO FACE THE MAN WHO'D terrorized him for months with his threatening letters—the man who'd convinced Tara to run away and cost him a year without Aidan.

And then to realize he'd been near him all along. That José the panhandler—the snarky, funny guy who'd waved during bike rides and given him love advice—was none other than Ramón Blandino.

As he stepped toward Shawn, an almost sheepish look flickered across his face. "Man, I can hardly remember why I wanted to screw you so badly; I actually started to like you lately. But I'm not going to jail over this."

"You idiot, stop talking!" Gina yelled. "You're going to have to kill him—you know *I* can't."

Shawn's gaze fixed on the gun and what he assumed was a silencer on its tip. Fear clawed at him as Blandino leveled the barrel at his chest.

"Trust me, man. It's not personal anymore."

The door burst open. Terror tightened Shawn's throat as Abuela filled the threshold. *No, please. Not her too.*

But Abuela showed no fear. She charged in, ranting in Spanish and wagging a finger at the man. "*Mire! Buen ratrero! No le da veigüenza? E que'uté no tuvo una madre que le enseñara decencia?*"

Her scolding landed like a slap. Shawn didn't need a translation; the archetypal angry mother had Blandino shrinking back, embarrassed and off balance.

Seizing the moment, Shawn grabbed the nearest weapon—the

gallon bottle of hand sanitizer on his desk—and slammed it onto Blandino's knuckles. The man grunted and cursed, clutching his hand as the gun clattered to the floor. When he bent to grab it, Shawn snatched his stethoscope and looped it around his neck. Gasping, Blandino clawed at the tubing instead of reaching for the gun.

"Let him go or I'll shoot you!" Gina shrieked.

Amid the chaos, Fe wrenched off a stiletto, grabbed Gina's wrist to pin the hand that held the gun, and hit her on the head with the heel again and again.

Shawn flinched at the sight of that absurdly tall, skinny heel coming down on Gina—even if she deserved it.

Surprisingly strong, Blandino jammed an elbow into Shawn's chest, knocking the wind out of him, then flipped him facedown and slammed him into the floor.

• • •

When Abuela burst in, Fe's first thought was for Aidan and Gabriela—two defenseless special needs kids left alone in the car, so close to this danger.

Then terror hit her: Abuela had risked her life by coming inside.

Now, as Blandino slammed Shawn to the floor, Fe stopped hitting Gina and seized the gun she'd dropped. She had no idea how to use it. She pointed at the ground and pulled the trigger—nothing. Was it locked? Unloaded?

Blandino was already recovering his own gun. Still ranting at him, Abuela had crouched beside Shawn.

Desperate, Fe pointed the useless weapon at Blandino and reached for her purse, hoping to call for help. "Freeze, or I'll shoot you, José!"

If her hands would only stop trembling, maybe her bluff would sound more convincing.

The man smirked. "Sorry to disappoint you, miss. But Gina's gun isn't loaded. I'm not *that* crazy. I wouldn't trust that wacko with a working one."

Damn it!

She set the gun down.

A distant siren wailed. It was probably an ambulance heading to the nearby hospital, but she took the chance. "The police are on their way; I called them," she lied. "They'll be here any minute. If I were you, I'd run while you still can."

He hesitated, glancing from Shawn and Abuela on the floor back to Fe. "I still have time to get rid of witnesses."

To her horror, he turned toward Shawn and raised the gun.

Frantic, Fe dug through her purse for something—anything—she could use to defend her man. Her fingers closed around a can of hairspray. She aimed and sprayed Blandino's face.

The man screamed. "My eyes!"

Fe pulled out the heaviest thing she could find—her flat iron—and swung it at his head again and again. Ducking and flailing to shield himself, Blandino stumbled backward, tripped over Shawn, and hit the floor. His gun skittered away.

Gina, still dazed from Fe's earlier blows, struggled to rise, rubbing her head.

Afraid even to touch the fallen gun, Fe kicked it away and dropped to Shawn's side.

"Help me before his vision clears! I don't know how to use a gun!"

Abuela's worried expression warned her even before she reached him.

He made no effort to get up. His face had blanched; his breathing was shallow. His fingers trembled against the front of his shirt.

"My chest hurts," he croaked.

The world fell away. Every trace of fear she'd felt until then shrank beside the terror of losing him.

Had Blandino shot him in the struggle? Was he hurt worse than she realized?

"We have to call an ambulance!" she yelled.

As if on cue, four armed policemen stormed into the office.

Fe's mind, still foggy, couldn't fathom what was happening. How could they have arrived when she'd been lying about calling them?

"Don't shoot! I surrender!" Blandino yelled the second his burning eyes caught sight of the police. Gina shrieked and kicked, but soon lay face down, her arms wrenched behind her back.

Abuela, far more composed than Fe, explained everything in *Cibaeño* to a Latino officer, as they handcuffed Gina and Blandino and led them away.

Shawn kept clutching his chest.

"He's hurt!" Fe shouted. "Please, someone call an ambulance!"

"The ambulance was right behind us," said one of the officers, kneeling beside them and unbuttoning Shawn's shirt.

Fe stood frozen as he examined him and confirmed there was no bleeding. She wanted to hug Shawn, kiss him, beg him to forgive her, but had to step aside when the paramedics arrived.

"I don't see any wounds or major contusions," one of them said. "But we can't rule out a heart attack after such a scare. We have to take him to the hospital."

"This is *not* cardiac chest pain!" Shawn protested, always the doctor in charge. "I know the symptoms!"

Everything blurred as they started IV lines and oxygen. Then, they lifted Shawn onto a stretcher and rolled him away.

As Fe followed, Shawn reached for her hand. "Don't worry, I'm not having a heart attack, just a few bruised ribs," he said, trying to reassure her. "I'll be fine. And you and I have to talk—"

Before he could finish, the paramedics wheeled him off. He kept protesting all the way to the ambulance.

A policeman approached Fe. "Miss, we need to ask you a few questions."

Overwhelmed, she turned to him. "How … how did you even know to come here? Who called you?" She glanced at Abuela. Maybe she'd figured out how to use the phone after all. "*Usted llamó a la policía*, Abuela?"

The old lady shook her head and pointed toward the van. "*Yo no. Gabriela.*"

In disbelief, Fe walked to the van, where another officer stood with the kids. Gabriela still held Abuela's phone, a small, satisfied smile playing on her lips.

The policeman grinned at Fe. "The nine-one-one dispatcher wasn't sure this was a real call or a prank, but we couldn't take any chances. You've got quite a team here. Watch this."

He turned to the kids. "Tell us again, Gabriela. What happened?"

In her usual slurred speech, Gabriela mumbled, "Help. Bleese. Pleez."

Aidan translated. "Help, please, police."

"Mean leddee haz a gan," Gabriela added.

"Mean lady has a gun," Aidan said.

"Comme h-help m-ma m-mami."

"Come help my mommy," he translated.

The policeman chuckled. "That's how they talked to the dispatcher. She tracked the call and sent us in. And when we got here, it didn't take long to see what was happening through the window, especially with this little guy yelling so loud. These kids are the real heroes."

The horror of the last minutes vanished. For a moment, even her fear for Shawn's health grew smaller. Fe forgot the bruises, the soreness, everything but the two children before her.

Maybe her dreams for Gabriela or her hopes for Aidan hadn't been just lies she told herself. Beneath her daughter's fragile body and slurred words lay a brilliant mind. And under Aidan's "problem kid" label, stirred the potential for a brighter future than the pessimists could ever predict.

Fe hugged them tight and cried tears of relief and gratitude.

CHAPTER 44

THE MOMENT FE STEPPED INTO THE ICU, A TALL, BRAWNY man in blue scrubs intercepted her with a handshake. "You're Dr. McDevitt's girlfriend, aren't you? Thank God, you're here!"

It took her a second to place him—Steve, the nurse who'd drawn Gabriela's blood the day she was sick.

Before she could answer, he pleaded, "Please! Take him away! He's driving us all crazy! He's the most impossible patient in this unit's history!"

Shawn's unmistakable voice carried down the hallway. Fe followed it to one of the glass-walled ICU rooms. He sat in bed, scowling at a young nurse who looked one step away from tears.

"It's not that I doubt you already disinfected your hands," he said, "but humor me and do it again—right here, in front of me. I'd rather not pick up a rabid MRSA infection from the guy next door."

He turned to a young man with a phlebotomy tray. "And you, vampire wannabe, I'm not a pincushion. Someone drew my blood barely an hour ago. If you need more, go find those samples and add your order to them. You're not getting another drop from me. Understood?"

The two staff members retreated, shooting wary glances over their shoulders. As they left, two other men came into focus.

This was probably the first time Fe had ever seen Dr. Jones smile. He seemed to take pleasure in seeing Shawn confined to a hospital bed.

"Now, pal, take it easy," Jones said. "Those rage fits send your blood pressure through the roof. And you're not leaving until your vitals stabilize."

Shawn grunted. "It's *not* funny! You know damn well I was never sick enough to end up in the ICU. I've just got a bruised ribcage. Stop this nonsense about ruling out a cardiac event and let me go!"

The other man in the room was Richard. His eyes sparkled with amusement as he tried—and failed—not to laugh.

"It's so satisfying that our roles are finally reversed," he said. "I'm the one standing up, and you're the one in the ICU bed."

Shawn's gaze found Fe's, and for a split second, his face almost lit up. Then he turned to the two men and shot them a killer look. "Out. Both of you."

The visitors snickered on their way out. At the sliding glass door, Richard paused beside Fe. "Someone's cranky and high-maintenance again," he whispered. "You'll have to do something about that, sister." With a final wink, he pulled the privacy curtain shut behind him and walked away.

Fe and Shawn stayed quiet for a while, studying one another. Distress flooded her at the sight of the monitors and IV tubing. The pale blue-green hospital gown he wore over his regular pants made his eyes seem lighter than usual and his skin even paler.

She'd had so much to tell him yesterday when she went to his office. But after the terror they'd lived through, all she wanted now was to make sure he was alive and unharmed. Everything else could wait.

She took a cautious step forward. "Hi."

"Hi." His eyes latched on to her with unnerving intensity. Was that a hint of a smile on his lips?

Gathering courage, she approached the bed. "I … I just wanted to make sure you were doing okay. I'm glad to see—"

She never finished. As soon as she was within reach, he tugged her arm, making her lose her balance and fall onto his lap in the narrow bed.

He silenced her gasp—and any other words—with an ardent kiss.

The feeling of his arms, his mouth, shattered her last thread of control. Fe burst into tears, kissing him back.

She had been so scared. She could have lost him. She would never have survived seeing him die.

Relief postponed the guilt for a few seconds, but then it clicked.

She pushed away from him. "Wait! Emery!"

To her surprise, Shawn burst into laughter, choking, bending over, slapping the bed like she'd missed the funniest joke in the world. Still chuckling, he hit the nurse call button. "Steve? Can you send our new attending in, please?"

Fe was still trying to understand when the privacy curtains pulled open and Emery appeared.

She looked radiant in tailored mint-green scrubs that hugged her figure and made her eyes pop. Besides Shawn, she might've been the only other person alive who looked that good in scrubs.

Shawn grinned. "Fe, this is Dr. Emery Love. Pulmonary and ICU specialist. She's my new business partner, and kind of my cousin, though not by DNA."

Fe rose from the bed, more confused by the second.

Clapping and cheering, Emery stepped forward and hugged her. "I'm so sorry if my post scared you, darling! But when I realized you weren't getting how crazy Shawny is about you, I had to do something drastic!"

"I don't understand." Fe blinked. "Emery, you said he was *your other half.*"

"We'll be working together as one physician—for scheduling purposes," Shawn explained. "Instead of covering the ICU every other week, we'll rotate every *four* weeks while Dr. Jones keeps his same rotation. So even without permanent hires, I might not need to quit after all. Emery's also taking half my patient load, and we'll cover each other's vacations."

Fe's mind stalled, slower than ever to catch up.

"I don't know anyone in town," Emery said. "I'd love to get coffee or go shopping sometime."

"Sure!" Fe answered automatically, then smiled. "Actually, I have a group of sister-friends who'll be happy to adopt you. Being a hugger, and with that last name, you'll fit right in."

"Can't wait to meet them!" Emery shimmied with excitement. "Now, I'll be good and leave you two alone so you can …" she cleared her throat, "catch up." She winked at Shawn and scurried out.

Fe turned to Shawn, debating whether she should be jealous. "That woman is gorgeous. And scarily exotic. And what's that thing about her not sharing your DNA?" She frowned. "Are you *sure* that she's only your business partner?"

He chuckled and pulled her to sit on the edge of the narrow bed. "The main reason why Emery's relocating from Miami is that she's newly engaged to a man who lives in town. And this job is ideal for her because she's planning to start a family soon and wants less hectic hours. Just like me. See? We're a match made in heaven. Maybe my luck is changing."

Fe wanted to cry out from pure joy. "Is this even possible? Are you really planning to cut your work hours and … spend more time at home?"

Smiling, he brushed a lock of hair off her face. "Emery is well warned. I'll be covering for her during her honeymoon and later when she's ready for maternity leave. That means that she has to pay me in advance by taking most of the workload while I spend some time with my new girlfriend." He paused. "You and I are going to Paris together."

Fe gasped, then giggled. "My goodness! Wait, this is too much, too soon! Shouldn't we start slow and just go somewhere closer first?"

"We'll go wherever you want later," he said. "But for months I've had a list of things I want to do with you, and Paris is on it." He leaned forward, his breath warm against her ear. "And get some rest while I'm still in the hospital; it's a long list."

She was about to ask what else was on it, but then he was kissing her again, and nothing else mattered.

She melted into his lips as his hands traced her body, and every shattered piece of her found its place again. For the first time, she could kiss Shawn with no fear, no guilt, and no doubt.

EPILOGUE

S HAWN WOKE GENTLY. A DIVINE PAIR OF HANDS RUBBED HIS BACK, drawing a low moan from his half-asleep body.

He never got over it—this miracle of rousing to her touch. Every morning, when his wife stirred him from sleep, he whispered a prayer of gratitude for his impossible luck. Falling off his bike, his son's autism scare, even the nightmare of life with Tara—they'd all been blessings in disguise. Each trial a paving stone leading to the bliss he lived now.

"Merry Christmas," Fe murmured in his ear, then kissed his neck.

"How did I ever function without this?" He sighed.

"Don't ask me!" Her lips trailed a path of love-bites across his shoulder. "You'll need an extra charge today, before the stampede arrives. They'll be here any minute."

He caught her left hand, kissed it, and stared at their matching wedding bands. Sometimes he had to, just to believe she was really his. No more running away.

A rumble of footsteps thundered up the stairs, followed by the hum of the elevator rising.

"Brace yourself," Fe said, laughing. "The stampede is here!"

The door burst open. Diego, Aidan, and cousins Luisito and Maggie stormed in, everyone talking at once.

Aidan leaped onto the bed. "Santa was here!" he yelled, clutching Shawn's face inches away from his own. "Santa was here! Come down and see the presents! Santa was here!"

At the same time, Diego babbled to Fe about the giant packages under the tree. Luisito—visiting from New York—and Maggie, home from Boston for the winter break, hovered near the doorway until Fe beckoned them closer. Soon all four piled onto the bed, voices tumbling over one another.

Then came the soft whir of the home elevator stopping. Shawn turned toward Gabriela, beaming as she backed her electric wheelchair out and maneuvered into the room with growing confidence. She had come such a long way.

Gabriela steered the chair up to the bed and held out her arms, a proud smile lighting her face. Shawn gathered her in, grinning at the effort it took. She was gaining weight—putting on muscle.

As soon as he settled her on the bed, Aidan grabbed his face again.

"Santa was here!" he repeated. "Come down and see the presents, Daddy! Santa was here!"

"Okay, okay!" Fe chuckled, holding Aidan by the shoulders to calm him. Then she turned to Diego. "Why don't you guys separate the presents by name? We'll be down in a minute."

For being so little, the kids did sound like a stampede of horses as they bolted down the stairs.

"Wait, Diego!" Fe called after them. "Don't forget your sister!"

Diego darted back into the room, the other three kids right behind him. He dragged Gabriela off the bed and into her wheelchair, then rushed her toward the elevator. Aidan's never-ending chant faded as they all raced back down. "Santa was here! Santa was here!"

Fe turned to Shawn. "Do you remember a year ago how worried we were that Aidan wasn't talking?"

With a huff, he mumbled, "Yes! And now I'd do anything to get him to shut up for at least five minutes!"

Laughing, Fe smacked him with a pillow, and he cracked up too. Of course, he was kidding. He couldn't be more grateful for the boy's progress. Aidan's speech was still behind other boys his age—almost five—but he was catching up fast. He was thriving in his special-education pre-K, and at this rate, he might enter a regular kindergarten next year with only minimal support.

Still in her Christmas pajamas, matching his, Fe headed for the kitchen to make coffee while he freshened up—God bless her.

As Shawn came down the stairs, he counted heads. "Fe, we have extra kids. How come I'm counting seven? Wait—" He pointed at a boy jumping on the couch. "Who's that?"

"That's Lispboy-Terrorist, one of my cases. His mom dropped off a holiday basket last night, and he refused to go home. They don't celebrate Christmas, so I told her he could stay for a sleepover." She handed him a cup of espresso.

Shawn took a long sip, then nodded toward a redhead kid in the family room, devouring Santa's cookies. "And that one?"

Fe squinted over her own mug. "I think that's our neighbor's grandson. He's visiting for winter break."

"I'm pretty sure Mr. Branson's grandkid is a girl."

"Oh!" Fe blinked. "In that case, I have no idea who that kid is. But he's been here for dinner the last three nights." She gave him an apologetic smile. "I'm turning into my grandma, aren't I?"

Shawn gazed at her with unabashed adoration. "I can't imagine anything better." He kissed her forehead.

Then, lowering his voice, he murmured, "But what about the presents?"

"Oh, don't worry." She waved him off with her free hand. "Fe, the bargain-shopping-queen, always keeps extras—just in case."

Laughing, he set both mugs on the counter and tugged her a few steps into the kitchen pantry—their secret hideaway. Closing the door behind them, he drew her close for a coffee-flavored kiss that felt like heaven. He still couldn't believe she was real.

"I'm counting the days to the kids' New Year's Eve sleepover at your mother's," he whispered between kisses. "It's been way too long since we had time to ourselves."

"Come on! It hasn't been *that* long." Giggling, she squirmed in his arms in the narrow dark space. "How about the marathon we had the other night? There's *no way* you're that desperate."

He chuckled against her neck, his hands sliding to the backside that had haunted him since the day they met.

"After all this time … you still don't know me?"

A crash outside shattered the stolen moment. Fe didn't even flinch.

"Someone found his Power Wheels. Let me make sure he knows it's not for indoors."

They stepped out of the pantry, and Shawn grinned as he watched her walk away.

His phone buzzed in his pajama pocket. He pulled it out, still smiling.

It was Jay.

"Hey, Jay, Merry—"

"Why is Allison Connors at your house?" Jay cut him off. "How do you know her?"

The abrupt, anxious question threw Shawn off. He faltered. "Uh … she's a friend of Fe's. We invited her over for Christmas breakfast, since she had no other plans. But I don't think she's here yet."

"Yes, she is. Her car's in your driveway—a gray Mercedes with the bumper sticker that says *Men Suck,* and the plate *N0-80YZ.*"

"How do you even know that's her car?" Shawn frowned. "Jay … are you stalking Allison?"

A long silence fell on the other end.

"Of course not!"

Jay hung up.

Shawn stared at his phone, his smile fading. He rubbed his neck, trying to make sense of the call, then headed for Gabriela's room, looking for Fe.

"Hey, honey. Is Allison—"

The words died on his lips.

Allison sat on the floor between Maggie and Gabriela's wheelchair.

A grin transformed her face as she waved a doll, speaking in a high-pitched voice.

The moment she noticed Shawn, she stiffened, and the glee drained from her expression. A flicker of embarrassment crossed her face.

"I haven't seen anything," he blurted, backing out and shutting the door behind him.

Maybe there was more to Allison than the cold, severe woman they all thought they knew.

Before the presents, Diego had to finish a call with his dad and grandpa. They'd moved to Boca Raton—close enough for an occasional visit, but, thankfully, far enough to never run into them.

Once the call ended, Fe gathered everyone in the family room and had them sit cross-legged around the Christmas tree. Shawn sat beside her as the kids took turns unwrapping gifts.

He couldn't wait to see what Fe had gotten him this year. For his birthday last month, she'd blown his mind with a kids' bike trailer—but that hadn't been the real present. Behind his back, she'd been working with Aidan to get him used to riding in it. Now Shawn didn't have to choose between a bike ride or time with his son; they both loved going together.

And, of course, Fe had outdone herself again. Her first gift this morning was a pair of walkie-talkie headsets, so he could talk to Aidan while they rode, describing everything he saw. That way, the fun ride could double as speech therapy, just like they practiced at the grocery store with the shopping cart.

That woman was amazing.

Fifteen minutes into the gift opening, Shawn's phone rang. The ICU.

He answered, impatient. "Hello? This must be a mistake, I'm not on call."

"Dr. McDevitt?" Steve went straight to the point. "Dr. Jones had another heart attack, we need you to cover the unit."

Shawn palmed his face and mouthed an Irish curse. "Give me a minute."

He lowered the phone and met Fe's eyes, where disappointment softened into understanding. He rose from the floor and signaled her to follow him, over the kids' protests about pausing the gift opening.

Once they reached the kitchen, he exhaled. "Damn it. Why did this have to happen the one week Emery is out skiing? I promised you we'd have a peaceful Christmas this year."

She rubbed his arm. "It's not your fault. I understand. I'll take the kids to Mom's."

It still amazed him how far she'd come in trusting him. Yet he hesitated. "But I didn't want to miss that visit. I'm finally starting to understand Abuela."

Fe tilted her head, thinking. "*Or...* I could take the kids to *your* parents' first. That way, we check the family box, and *you* have an excuse not to come."

Elated, he cupped her face and kissed her. "I so married the right woman! You're the best!"

He returned to his phone. "Okay, I'll help out, but I have some conditions. Number one, you'd better cut a deal with the eICU, because I need to be done by five. I'm not missing Christmas dinner with my family. And number two—" he paused, glancing at Fe, "I'm in the middle of something important right now that can't be rushed. The earliest I can start rounds is an hour and a half from now. You'll need to get help from the hospitalists until then. That's my final offer, take it or leave it."

After a mumbled agreement on the other end, he hung up.

"Okay, we have some time. Who's opening the next present?"

Misty-eyed, Fe laced her fingers through his and tugged him back into the kitchen pantry. Once inside, she threw her arms around his neck. "Thank you. This means so much to me." She kissed him. "Did you know you're the best damn husband in the whole freaking galaxy?"

With a smirk, he wrapped his arms around her. "Yes, but I still love hearing you say it." He kissed her back—slow and deep.

Knocking and banging rattled the pantry door, followed by Diego's voice. "I know you're hiding in there! Stop kissing! I want to open my presents!"

"No sitting for presents!" Aidan shrieked, his voice muffled through the door. "I want to ride my car!"

"That's not polite!" Gabriela scolded.

Sighing, Shawn looked heavenward.

Fe stroked his back. "See, honey? We shouldn't have been in such a hurry. Once they finally learn to talk, all they do is contradict everything we say."

Ignoring the protests outside, Shawn kissed her again and let his mouth linger on hers.

Yes, he thought, for the thousandth time. *I'm the luckiest man in the world.*

Exclusive Gift and Bonus Scenes!

(Please don't forget to return here afterward, for a message from the author and to leave a book review)

Have you read *Just for Joy* already?
If not, you can get it for free here:
pichardo-johansson-md.com/just-for-joy-free-book

Join my newsletter to have access to exclusive bonus scenes from *Faith is Fearless*:

My Friend Allison: Why does Allison hate men so much? What did Richard mean when he hinted he knew her secrets? And what's the secret behind her obsession with Botox? Fe hints us into Allison's story.

My Friend Jay: Is Jay officially crazy? Why was he wearing a Roman soldier costume that day? What did Shawn mean when he said Jay stalks women?

www.pichardo-johansson-md.com/fif-bonus-scenes
You'll also gain access to:

-Opportunities to read future books for free.
-Sneak peeks of upcoming releases.
-Notifications about special sales and offers.

NOTE FROM THE AUTHOR

You made it to the end—gold star for you! Thank you for spending time with my characters. If you enjoyed this book, please leave a review, it helps other readers decide whether to take a chance on a new author (and it's the literary equivalent of tipping your server).

I write the kind of love stories I couldn't find anywhere else: entertaining *and* soul nourishing, a little spicy, and centered on real love, not just infatuation. My goal is to make you smile, think, and sigh, with scenes that are sensual yet classy. My books live between *Wholesome* and *Whoa There*, and between *Inspirational* and *Irreverently Funny*.

My stories are meant to leave you with an aftertaste of joy, hope, and a reminder of the lesson I learned as an oncologist and cancer survivor: *Life is too short to live without passion—follow your heart over your brain.*

If you'd like more, I'd love to send you behind-the-scenes extras and sneak peeks. Just visit my website www.pichardo-johansson-md.com/author-home or sign up for my newsletter here www.pichardo-johansson-md.com/fif-bonus-scenes.

And if you ever want to say hi, email me at pichardojohanssonmd@gmail.com—I do my best to reply to every message.

Love,
Diely

OTHER BOOKS IN THIS SERIES

Check my website http://www.pichardo-johansson-md.com/books/
for more information and other series.
Love,
Diely

ABOUT THE AUTHOR

Dr. Pichardo-Johansson is a retired physician, life coach, and #1 Amazon bestselling author. She's a happy wife to her soulmate and a mother of four children, including one with special needs.

After fifteen years practicing oncology—and after becoming a cancer survivor herself—she decided she no longer wanted to make a living fighting death. Instead, she now teaches people to fully embrace and enjoy life.

As a fiction author, she specializes in romance that is "a connection of minds and souls, more than only bodies." Her mystery twist? "How to murder someone and ensure a negative autopsy." (Don't worry, she only does that on paper.)

As a nonfiction author and life coach, she helps professional women who are highly sensitive or empathic find authentic joy and live their fullest, healthiest lives. Her mottos are: Life is too short to live without joy, and Aliveness is a quantitative variable.

She lives in Melbourne Beach, Florida, with her soulmate-husband, David, a reformed eternal bachelor turned happy stepfather. He is her inspiration for writing and the main reason she deeply believes in romantic love.

For more about her work as both an author and a Love, Purpose, and Wellness coach, visit: www.pichardo-johansson-md.com